RAVEN
BOOK THREE

Abra Ebner

Crimson Oak Publishing

Pullman, Wa 99163
Visit our website at www.CrimsonOakPublishing.com

Ebner, Abra, 1984 -
Raven: A novel / by Abra Ebner
Edited by Christina Corlett

www.FeatherBookSeries.com

Summary: Love spans and eternity, at least for Edgar and Estella. As She
fights to figure out her past, she finds something much more. There is a whole
world of history about her and her complicated special life. Estella comes
into her own in her first great adventure, in the life she was born to live, and
die for.

printed in U.S.A

1 2 3 4 5 6 7 8 9 10

For my Fans,

Thank you for all the support,
encouragement,
and of course, love...

A Dream Within A Dream

Edgar A. Poe

Take this kiss upon the brow!
And, in parting from you now,
Thus much let me avow-
You are not wrong, who deem
That my days have been a dream;
Yet if hope has flown away
In a night, or in a day,
In a vision, or in none,
Is it therefore the less gone?
All that we see or seem
Is but a dream within a dream.

I stand amid the roar
Of a surf-tormented shore,
And I hold within my hand
Grains of the golden sand-
How few! yet how they creep
Through my fingers to the deep,
While I weep- while I weep!
O God! can I not grasp
Them with a tighter clasp?
O God! can I not save
One from the pitiless wave?
Is all that we see or seem
But a dream within a dream?

Some say that the gods leave our world from time to time, giving us weeks, years, decades, millenniums to rule on our own, only returning when things are at their worst. Could we handle this power on our own and thrive? Or would we simple destroy it, polluting this planet beyond what is reversible, depleting it of all its resources. If the gods are leaving us, then will they return? Do we deserve to be saved once more? Or will this be the last time...

RETURN

Edgar

"You cannot do that to her and you know it." Sam's voice crashed through the trees of the forest.

"I can. I have to see her." The anger inside me was so profound that I wanted to rip Sam to pieces, and I could. I slammed my fist into my palm, angry that I could even think of such things.

Sam looked at me with a skeptical face. "I doubt you could actually go through with it. You could never kill me."

"Stay out of my head, Sam. I've warned you," I growled, pacing from one tree to the next. "And I don't care, Sam. I need to know that she's alright."

Sam shook his head. "She needs to grow, Edgar. You know what she is as well as I do. You can't cage her like a wild animal."

I clenched my fists at my sides. What did Sam know anyway? He had no idea how it felt to be me, to feel the hatred and anger of the whole world weighing on my soul everyday. Elle was the only thing that could calm me, the only thing that could make my mind clear.

"Coming to find you was enough of a burden for her. She needs another month to recover. She needs to find the strength she needs if she is to do as is prophesized. Then—" He laughed. "Then you can come back and tell her what she needs to know. If you know what I mean." He glared at me.

Sam's words struck far too close to home, causing my anxiety to mount. I stopped pacing, halting abruptly as dirt gathered under my heels. "I know what she needs, but that's not my concern."

"How is it not your concern?"

It was a stupid thing to say. Of course it was my concern. Everything in her life was my concern. There was an indescribable selfish feeling inside me, though. It wanted to take over.

Sam continued to glare. "If you won't tell her about it, then don't come back at all." He crossed his arms against his chest, making a stand against me.

I shook my head. "What is this, Sam? *Are you in love with her?*" It was the first thing I could think to say. I had left her with him without thinking it through, and I knew he had the mind to.

Sam threw both his hands in the air and laughed in a mocking tone. "Hardly. She's all yours, *cowboy.*"

His statement only made me feel mildly better. I was looking for a fight, but he was playing it smart. He knew just what to say to keep my emotions at bay, just enough courtesy to justify peace. But, peace was the last thing I wanted.

"Look, Edgar. She needs a little more time. I knew you were coming back. I came to the forest to stop you because I don't want you to barge in on the process that's going on. Right now she still needs to be away from you, so that she can feed on the power independence gives her. But soon enough, she's going to need you. I realize how weak you are right now, but you have to wait." He laughed under his breath. "And by the way, you look like hell."

I narrowed my eyes at him, still hoping that he would give me a reason to slash his throat.

"This is one of those times where you need to be a civilized gentleman, though I know you lack the ability. If you rush to see her now, it is likely you will end up becoming overwhelmed and kill her." Sam took one step toward me and I felt my will to stop myself begin to falter. "I'm thinking in her best interest. Apparently you're not."

That was it. That was the accusation I was looking for. I lunged at him, but before I even got close, he managed to spring up and into a nearby tree.

A deep laugh rumbled from his throat. "I told you, Edgar. You are *weak*."

I shook my head, feeling the whole world whirl around me like an angry cloud.

"Her friends are getting married soon. That will be a good time for you to show up, if not a little sappy. It will give you a month to regain some strength, and pull yourself together." Sam lowered himself from the tree with one hand. "Besides, you have a problem that needs to be addressed."

I took a deep breath, looking at him with hatred in my eyes. "And what is that?" I asked through clenched teeth.

Sam crossed his arms smugly against his chest. "You left that holograph of yours behind, down at the college, and its beginning to cause problems. I've found it lurking in the woods out here, looking to find Elle and take the soul for his own. It thinks it can live!"

I let out an annoyed sigh. "Piece of junk."

"Well, you created it," Sam retorted.

"Shut up, Sam. It's not a big deal." My jaw was fixed. What was that thing thinking? A murderous rage rose in my chest. The desire to kill was so sweet that it made my bones ache.

I tried to calm the feeling, remembering that I had declared never to take a life unless it was a righteous cause. *But this was,* I thought. I laughed to myself, remembering the day I had vowed to uphold the code, laughed as I saw Matthew beside me, making the same vow.

I sighed and let the anger roll off my chest. Killing this ghost would help me. Murder was always the quickest way to regain my strength and quench the thirst that burrowed in my heart.

Sam rolled his eyes, and I shot my gaze to meet his.

His face sank into a frown, his penetrating mind unable to ignore my angry thoughts.

"I'll warn you one more time, Sam. Stay out of my head." I lifted one brow, eyeing him.

Sam smiled and turned away from me, muttering something under his breath as he walked back toward the meadow.

"Where are you going?" I snapped, following after him with my feet pounding the earth, threatening to crack it open.

Sam's wings unfurled from his back as he leapt into the trees in time to avoid my angry swing. My arm sliced through empty air, knocking me off balance as I fell to the ground with a resounding thud.

"I'm going home, Edgar. If you know what's good for you, you'll get your act together before attempting to see her. I'll be watching you." Sam hovered over my head before landing. He placed both feet on my wrists, trapping me against the ground, taking advantage of my weakened state. "After all, she is mine to keep, and I will do whatever it takes to do so. If I so much as sniff one ounce of danger from you, I will not hesitate to sacrifice all I have. I will freely give away my life and my privileges here—*if there are any.* I will not hesitate to protect her."

I struggled to get free as he once again took to the air. "Edgar, heed my words. I will be back in a day, so I suggest you set up camp and get comfortable. There's not much more you can do." He smiled at me. "Oh, and... you're going to need to acclimate yourself to those." He pointed behind me, and I looked to where he had. Shocked, I grabbed at my shoulders, seeing I had wings.

Sam's laughter echoed through the trees. "You should have known, Edgar. Though you still retain all your previous abilities, you *did* die saving her. You're an angel now, and a raven."

I snarled as I righted myself, sitting in a puddle of mud. I watched Sam disappear between the trees before exhaling. As much as I didn't want to hear it, Sam was right. I had saved her but had also forgotten what that sacrifice meant. I still felt the raven inside me, but now this? What more did I need to endure to prove myself? Was this another way to protect her?

Elle was something special, something different. I had been warned of the consequences of being her mate, but what could I do? Leave her alone? Leave her empty? I had done that for far too long–I was done. I had always thought that I was put here to protect her. Never did I expect that one day she would come to save me. Never. I thought it was my job to remind her of who she was, to bring her back, but now I was no longer certain.

Why had she forgotten everything about our life before, and everything she knew about herself? Why, if she was so important to us all, had she forgotten what she was destined for? I was beginning to think that this whole thing was what Fate had planned. Perhaps she wanted to see what Elle would do when placed in these painful situations, tricking her into falling in love with the human race in the hopes of making her feel sorry for them. It was no secret that Fate always hated the rule the gods had over us. Fate wanted her to want to save us, and destroy them.

She was the ruling goddess of all things, a myth in most parts of the world, but a true being. They say Fate is more gorgeous than any creature you can imagine, and more powerful. She knows what will happen in the future because it is her that creates it. No one can sway Fate her from the path she decides, because no one can *find* her. Fate finds you. From time to time she will gift us with an idea of what will happen, or a prophecy, but it is rare.

I believe now that Fate wanted her to have enough anger in her heart so that she would grow strong. Still, the essence of the plan Sam and I had made, before Elle had forgotten it all, was finally unfolding. Whatever Fate's reasons, we were still going to take back what was rightfully ours. We would save all those that had been tortured as we had, and torture those that deserve it–namely the corrupt gods.

I smiled as excitement filled my heart. Finally, it was time. Finally, the end of the reign of the gods was coming. But if this was going to work, then Sam was right. I needed to be smart. And right now, the smart thing to do was to wait.

RECHARGE

Edgar

I threw a log on the fire as I grumbled under my breath, hating every minute of this little camp-out. The fire crackled as the wet log worked to heat up, sending sparks into the air and landing dangerously close to my hand. I reached over my back and grabbed a feather from the wings that still protruded, yanking one out and bringing it to my face to inspect it.

I wasn't surprised that they were black, like a raven. And in fact, I was insulted by it, as though the gods were making it obvious that I had an evil heart. I drew in a deep breath, exhaling as the smell of smoke made me nauseous. The light from the fire cast a small circle around me, barely flickering enough to reach a nearby tree, but I didn't care. I wasn't afraid of anything.

I began to think back on what Sam had told me earlier,

about the hologram gone wrong. It wasn't the first time I had seen it happen, and it made me laugh as I thought back on my old friend Edgar Poe.

We had made a hologram of him once, as a sort of joke. We used it to thwart off a needy love affair gone bad. She was a fan of his work, fanatic really, and everyday she would wait for him outside his door, no matter what the weather. The hologram served as a sort of distraction, allowing him to escape when needed, leaving her with nothing but air. Soon though, the woman fell in love with it, and the hologram in return, fell in love with her. The stalker became the stalked, and eventually we had to kill it before a real murder ensued. The good thing is, she stopped after that.

I was happy that Edgar had found his happiness in heaven, and I looked forward to the day when I'd see him again. He was a true friend. I sighed, admitting to myself that Sam was a true friend as well, though at this moment, I wanted nothing more than to rip him limb from limb. He knew what was best. He always knew, and that's what bothered me most. I hated when people took a position above me, and though I tried to be strong enough to never allow that to happen, I was who I was, and at times I needed help.

I drew my watch from the lapel of my coat, opening the shiny silver cover and tilting the face of the watch toward the fire. It was nearing midnight, but it wasn't the time that had made me look at the watch–it was the engraving from Elle. I ran my thumb across the scratched letters, feeling the indentation ripple across the ridges of my finger. I was close enough to feel her warmth inside my soul, close enough to feel the emotion she held at any given moment–darting from happiness to tension in a heartbeat. She was anxious and afraid, wondering if I'd ever return. I wanted to hold her and tell her it was all right, but I knew there was also that part of me that held the desire to suck that very same life from her bones, ripping her heart apart like an animal.

I shuddered at the thought, feeling like a monster as I forced my wings back and away from me. I hid them in the shadows with shame, feeling as though I didn't deserve something so holy. I snapped the watch shut with one hand, still holding the feather in the other.

My body tingled with a strength I hadn't felt before. Though I was already strong, I wondered what becoming an angel had really done and what sort of power it had granted me. I could already fly, so getting wings seemed useless. I thought I was already strong, but perhaps stronger? I knew that Sam could read minds, but could I? I tried to think back to when I had seen Sam earlier, but could not recall hearing any thoughts. Then again, maybe he had the power to hide them from me as well.

Feeling bored, I tried to amuse myself with the memories of Matthew's death. I smiled, but it was short lived as the memories quickly turned morbid, knowing that my own death had followed. Finding there was nothing else left to distract me from the task at hand, I finally faced the facts and began to think of a plan.

Tomorrow I would set out and hunt down the hologram. Surely then things would begin to fall into place, and I would become more like myself again. I looked up at the trees as they swirled overhead in a gust of spring air, distracting me for a moment. Next, I would build myself a suitable camp, something with all the comforts of home.

A sneer grew across my face, thinking of how lucky I was to be a part of Elle's life and her grand existence. If it wasn't for the prophecies, I would have been killed and thrown away by the gods like a lump of trash–useless as Matthew was. Elle and I had worked hard to nurture the strength she needed to combat her fate, and luckily for me, her years spent alone and gone had granted me the time to hatch a plan for the future.

I tried again to tuck my wings into the bones of my back, succeeding as I felt each feather being sucked in and under my skin like an old Chinese fan, now resting along the length of my spine on either side. The corners of my mouth curled, finally content that I had achieved the feat, and relieved the wings were gone—*at least for now.* I cracked my neck, feeling as though something was out of alignment, but figuring I had a lot of time to practice.

I looked at a nearby tree, feeling it stare down on me with both fear and hope. The whole forest felt anxious, and it should. They knew what was coming. A smell of trepidation was secreting from their very shell, filling the air with a sour mist. Other than the sounds of the fire, I also noticed the stagnation. It was as though every animal also knew—also tried to hide, but there was nothing they could do, and nowhere they could run that would be safe.

The long journey was finally over, and we had arrived at the end. All we had worked for was now coming to pass. When I look back, I see that everything had its purpose—all those years I spent alone, all the time Elle spent in darkness and sleep. Elle had been groomed by a force even the god's could not understand, so there was no one we could look to but her. What was coming was unstoppable, inevitable and sealed. Only one could fix this, but only she could decide whether it was *worth* fixing.

Though Elle's fate was to be this chosen one, she still held the option to choose, and that's what the gods feared most. Her fate did not include an ending because it was undecided, but it made no matter to me. I found that not knowing the end was what I preferred. If I knew we would die, then why try—why hope? No matter what her decisions, I would stand by her, revel in the fact that she was my other half: the great one, *the one.*

I dropped my head into my hands, running my fingers through my hair and locking my hands behind my neck. The dirt below my feet seemed to teem with power, the whole world of Heaven in an uproar. It was times like this that I admired our race, the human race. For as smart as they claimed to be, they were still too involved with their lives to notice what was coming. I knew that they would be the last to sense the end, and I found it relieving. At least this way they wouldn't waste days with worry and fear, or at least not over this.

I felt my limbs tingle with a familiar emotion. Envy, the sweetest feeling, and one I seemed to wallow in like an endless abyss. Who was I kidding? Of course I wished that I were the one and not Elle, but it was never meant for me. That kind of responsibility could never be trusted to a heart like mine, corrupt and black, all but for one small piece that belonged to her. I struggled with this feeling all my life—knowing that I was less of a being—allowing Elle to prosper. It was this emotion that made holding myself back hard. Envy was powerful and bitter, a feeling that all the other ravens never had to deal with, but in this I knew I was stronger than them.

Like Sam had always said, I needed to rise to the task of being her soul mate, and be proud. Become the one thing in the world that could hold her up, and keep her going. I sat up straight on the log. Another gust of wind blew hard at my back, my wings extending as my arms erupted with goose bumps. There was a scent in the breeze that I recognized, even from this distance. I closed my eyes and breathed deep, my wings relaxing to the ground.

"Estella," I whispered. The corners of my mouth curled and I exhaled, blinking a few times.

It was getting late and I knew that tomorrow was going to be a big day. I slid from the log to the ground, propping my wings behind my head and allowing them to finally come of some use. I yawned, thinking that soon my love would come back to me; soon the fun would begin.

HOME AWAY FROM HOME
Edgar

The fire burst to life in a ball of flames. I laughed, never finding it got old to start a fire with such magical fury. A few fat drops of rain fell from the sky, filtering through the canopy from one maple leaf to the next, reminding me of how much I hated the outdoors. The ferns bowed toward the dirt, lower than usual, but it was to be expected. I looked up at the maples, an idea coming to mind as I remembered Elle's trees up the hill, where I took her on the snowmobile.

I put my hands up toward them, and for a moment, I saw them lean away from me in fear. *"Hush,"* I told them, smiling. "You know who I am. I will not harm you. I need your help."

I rolled my eyes, thinking to myself that it was a bit silly to talk to trees, but I needed them. I began to concentrate.

They tried to hesitate, but began to move as I continued to coax. Clenching my teeth and shutting my eyes, I tried harder—imagining what I wanted them to be. The image on my mind was presumptuous, but I had faith that they could do this, as a challenge perhaps?

I heard the crackling of the branches as they intertwined, leaves grazing my shoulders, but I refused to let it distract me from my imagination. I saw a table and chairs, bed frame and fire pit, drawing across my mind like a scroll pen on white paper. Soon the sound of crackling subsided, and I slowly opened my eyes.

Rain continued to fall on my face, dripping into my mouth as I licked my lips. I blinked away a few drops, my eyes falling on a small cabin that was rooted to the nearby trees, the leaves stretching to form a roof. I bowed to the trees in thanks before allowing my excitement to take over. I would finally be able to escape the rain.

"Ha!" My voice echoed through the forest, but my happiness was short lived as a figure emerged from behind a nearby tree, catching me off guard as I jumped, embarrassing myself.

My eyes snapped from that of my new residence to the figure, finding myself frozen. I took in the familiar outline of the figure, watching it's every move, feeling it as though it were my own. The figure stared back at me like a mirror, darkness filtering across its eyes—*my eyes.* A smile grew across my face then, laced with a hunger to kill.

"You." I laughed.

The figure smiled back with a vindictive glimmer in his eye. He nodded.

"Don't you remember you're no more than *air?* You cannot be me," I yelled across the clearing that had been made by the moving trees. I stepped toward the hologram as it took one step back, remembering how fragile it was compared to me.

I froze, but the figure inched back again. As he did this, I lunged, my large black wings filling his eyes with shock. My heart was racing with the thrill of the hunt, forgetting about the rain and the chill in the air. He twisted into a raven then, taking off toward the upper canopies of the forest as he left a trail of smoke behind him. He tried to use his small size against me, dodging through tight spaces as I struggled to keep up.

"I see you've learned a few tricks since you've been here. Been reading my books, have you?" I was close at his tail, nearly over him.

The raven looked up at me, his eyes beady but blank. He had no soul, but I could see he had evolved, left to his own devices for too long. He let out a cry and I used the moment to throw myself at him. His body dissipated like black smoke then, eluding me and making the anger inside my heart grow stronger. My laughter echoed off the soggy trees as I looked around, finding this little sport invigorating, and a test of my once dormant agility.

I grabbed onto a branch and swung myself around in the other direction, scanning the trees with my sharp sight, catching the glimpse of a man running a few yards ahead. I clenched my jaw, no longer noticing the way my heart pounded in my chest. I reached down and removed my shoes before jumping from the canopy, floating down until my bare feet met the wet forest floor, mud and needles squishing through my toes.

I whistled, calling to the hologram like a dog and loving every moment. I could feel his presence in my heart. He was just up ahead now. I knew where he was headed, thinking that the shelter of the school would stop me, but he was mistaken. His black hair was bobbing as he ran, my feet not too far behind his.

I readied myself, rubbing my hands together as I summoned the warmth of magic from deep inside my heart. The trees began to thin, and I leapt off the ground, allowing my wings to pick up the pace as I overcame him.

He looked up at me, feeling my fury as his image began to flicker like a television with poor reception. An electrical charge ignited in my now-warm hands, and I reached down to grab him, feeling not only his body, but also the feeling of fabric—of his clothing as the air solidified. Confidently, I commended myself for creating something so real, that it could mimic human emotion so well.

He looked up at me, and it was like looking in a mirror. It felt as though I was killing myself, but it was a thought that wasn't foreign to me. I tightened every limb around him as we fell to the ground like rocks, breath releasing from both our lungs.

I laughed. "You believe you can breathe now, too?" I kept a tight focus on the magic in my hands, not wanting it to fade or give him a chance to escape.

I saw fear in his eyes, a great play but not convincing. I tilted my head and smiled at him as my hands came to his throat. "You were so perfect." I looked him in the eye and grunted. "But unfortunately, you were *too* perfect."

The hologram made a move to speak, but I knew that if I heard his voice—my voice—it might throw my concentration. I was quick to destroy him, squeezing my hands as he began to deflate like a balloon. I balled the hologram up in my grasp, continuing to shrink him until he was no more than the size of a golf ball. With one last clasp of my hands, I felt him disintegrate into my palms, the magic returning to where it came from.

I took a deep breath and sat back, my body hot as sweat beaded across my skin. I felt intense warmth inside my heart, filtering a powerful blood to every limb. My power returned then, faster then it ever would around Elle. I laughed to myself between heavy breaths, feeling alive for the first time in a long while. It had been too long since I had taken a life, magic or not, and it felt good, like a drug. I felt my pupils dilate. The need to binge was strong, but I forced it back as always, reminding myself of my duty and my oath.

I tried to distract myself as I shut my eyes, thinking of the greater tasks ahead. An image of Estella came to my mind, smiling, finally coming into her own and learning so much. I felt the urge inside me subside, a cool feeling washing over me as each muscle began to release. You would think that thinking of her would make the feeling worse, but it never did. It was those notions that lead me to hope that we could have a normal life together.

Opening my eyes, I stood and brushed off my clothes, finding that now I needed a bath as well. I looked toward the sky as I filled my wings with air, pressing myself upward and back toward camp. I flew high over the forest, toying with the possibility that perhaps I'd see home in the meadow. The clouds overhead were growing dark and angry, the wind picking up as I squinted to see. The trees parted ever so slightly to my left, opening onto an expanse I had all but forgotten. I felt the desire for home tug at my heart, the desire to be with Elle so great it was hard to hide.

I blinked a few times, thinking I had seen something moving in the opening, not sure what it was. I brought one wet hand to my face to wipe the rain from my eyes, seeing now that there was something there, moving toward me in a frantic manner. I ducked down into the trees, the meadow disappearing and the faint smoke from my now dying fire rising from the trees. I landed on the forest floor, looking skyward as I heard a sharp cry cut through the wind and rain.

Remembering the noise, I smiled, letting out an excited hoot as I looked between the branches. "Henry!" I yelled, calling him to me. I heard another cry, followed by the sound of flapping coming from just over my shoulder. I quickly turned, just in time for him to land on my arm. He looked at me as he chattered, telling me how much he missed me. His claws dug into my shirt as he twisted about, unable to stand still. I ran my hand across his brow and down his back, rain trickling from his sleek feathers.

"Henry, old boy, how are you?" I turned and walked toward the small cabin, still suspended by the trees—their branches strained. Henry looked at the cabin, inspecting the strange structure and continuing to chatter. There were no windows, but it didn't matter. As I came close to the front, a door opened for me, the trees still working in my favor. I stepped in as they braided back together behind me, setting Henry on a branch that protruded from the wall.

I shut my eyes and focused on my wings as I once again felt them get sucked against my spine, and out of the way. Opening my eyes, I looked back on the space, finally feeling content with the idea of living in the woods. There was a small hole cut in the ceiling of the structure, where smoke from a fire pit, just below, could escape. In the corner, a few branches reached from the wall and down to the ground, creating a small table, or perhaps desk. Another branch reached from the earth, flattening out into a chair that did not necessarily look comfortable, but at least had its use. In the opposite corner, branches had created a frame in which vines had woven a hammock. I thought about how uncomfortable my back already was with the addition of the wings and cringed, figuring I'd grow used to it.

It was dark, so I walked over to the fire pit, placing my

hands above it as I conjured a fire out of nothing but air. The trees had done me enough service already, so to burn their own kind would be cruel. A blue light lit my face and Henry's, my stomach now growling from the hunt, but I knew I was unable to eat. It was a curse of the guardian angel that food lost its appeal, and our hunger was never satisfied. Henry let out a cry that pierced my ears, as though thinking exactly what I had, except for him, there was something he *could* do.

"Do you want to go hunting?" I asked. There was no reason why I should still deny myself the pleasure of the hunt, even if it couldn't be enjoyed.

Henry shifted his weight from one foot to the next, agreeing.

I nodded. "Well, then—let's go. Darkness is coming, and now is the best time." I walked toward him and put out my hand for him to climb on. "Like old times."

THE PURPOSE

Edgar

It had been nearly a month now, and I was growing bored of the same routine. A rabbit hung in the smoke from the fire, cooking as it filled the small cabin with a delightful smell. I was spoiling Henry, and torturing myself. Soon I figured I'd grow out of my hunger, and get used to the feeling. Henry stood on his perch, leaving only to hunt but always returning. Since he'd been back, I saw that something was different with him. There was a look of guilt in his eyes, and I wondered why that was.

To my surprise, there was a knock on the side of the cabin, and it echoed in my head. I had become so accustomed to the silence of the woods that my hearing had heightened, looking for anything to entertain it.

"How does this work?" I heard an annoyed, but familiar voice from outside.

I shook my head.

Sam snorted. "Hey, I know you're in there, and I heard that."

I let out a contented laugh. "Well, you're right, I am in here. And you're an idiot."

There was a sharp pound against the wall as the branches tightened, refusing to allow such abuse, and rebelling against letting him in. The pounding stopped.

"Fine. Have it your way." Sam was talking to the trees now, and trying to convince them. After one last moment of resistance, they gave and the door formed, revealing my visitor.

"Hello, Sam." I sat at my desk in the corner, my watch in hand.

"Sweet little set up you have here." Sam waltzed in as the branches poked at him—still offended by what he'd done.

"Thanks." I rolled my eyes and turned away from him, looking back to the book that lay open on my desk. After I killed the hologram, I had gone down to the college to gather a few of my things to help pass the time.

Sam poked the rabbit, making it swing and spread smoke into the air.

"Could you please," I began.

Sam laughed. "What are you doing with this? Wishful thinking?"

I shot him a cold stare. Sam continued to poke at the rabbit, making Henry anxious as he began rocking from one foot to the next on his perch. "Sam—"

"Yeah, yeah. I heard you the first time." Sam stepped back, sauntering over to the desk area and looking around for a chair. Finding none, he looked toward the ceiling. *"Please?"* He said it as though the word pained him, but the branches listened, and a chair formed. He plopped down, the chair pinching him in one last attempt to pick a fight, though it did little to affect Sam.

"So what brings you to my humble part of the woods?" I looked up at him under my eyebrows, acting as though his visit was an inconvenience, and hoping he couldn't read that inside, I was actually excited to have the company.

Sam chuckled to himself, revealing he'd known. He looked at Henry. "So that's where you went." Henry looked away, ashamed.

I laughed. "I knew he was hiding something. It was the fact that he had become your pet in my absence." I paused, looking at Henry and tilting my head. "Good to know you're a fair-weather pet, Henry."

Henry let out a cry in his defense.

Sam waved him away. *"Anyway,* so I'm back."

I nodded. "I can see that."

Sam smiled and sat up straight, lacing his fingers in front of him. "How are things?"

I shook my head, my eyes fixed on the page in front of me. "How does it look?"

"Okay, let's cut through the formalities." Sam gave up and got to the point. "Have you controlled yourself?"

I looked up at him. "You're the one that can read minds.

I'm sure you already know the answer."

Sam nodded. "So you have. Good. And the hologram, that was brilliant. Well played." He commended me.

I pursed my lips, knowing I'd slaughtered better.

"So, I can expect you back soon, then?" Sam tried to be nonchalant.

My attention perked. "Oh, so I can come back now?" I tried to seem annoyed.

Sam nodded.

I looked him in the eyes, feeling as his thoughts massaged mine, looking for answers. "Why can't I read your mind?"

Sam let out an arrogant sigh that angered me. "Because that was *my* power. Yours is something else."

"Strength?" I added.

Sam nodded, leaning back and testing the power of the branch.

I watched him, seeing he was trying to act tough, because he knew that now, I could beat him. His little act of strength when I had first come back was the last chance he'd have to flex his power over me, but now it was gone.

Sam rolled his eyes, admitting his weakness as he heard my thoughts. "There is much to do when you come back, much to plan for," he tried to change the subject. "It's on our doorstep."

"So you've noticed it too?" I leaned back as Sam had.

Sam licked his lips. "Yes, I've noticed the change. Elle's seeing it too, but she hasn't yet asked me about it. I don't want to be the one to deliver her the news, either. I figured that was *your* job."

A half smile lit across my face. "Too chicken?" I asked.

Sam defended himself. "I'm not *too chicken*. This just isn't my war."

"It was once," I chimed.

Sam's expression became bitter.

I lifted one hand in apology. "I was joking, Sam. Didn't you get that?"

"Well, this is no joking matter. Things are dying, and the end has begun—thanks to your kind," he stabbed.

It was annoying that he no longer saw himself as a human, though he once was. "It's not their fault. They didn't know. The humans are so manipulated by the gods, that they've never been trusted to take care of things on their own. If the gods know what's good for them, they'll let Elle fulfill her prophecy, and they'll get out of our world. The humans could use to manage this world alone for a couple thousand years."

"You mean shut off the bridge between Heaven and Earth?" Sam looked shocked.

"Yes, I mean a separation. That is, if we survive this thing. That's up to Elle." I looked down at my hands.

"Why does she get to choose? And what is this power controlling our fate?"

I laughed. "*Fate* is controlling fate. You know that."

Sam didn't believe in Fate as a being because he'd never seen her first hand. "I thought the gods controlled everything about this world."

"Clearly, they don't. Fate does." It was like beating a dead horse. "The humans are the ones that have polluted it to the point that the delicate balance of nature is deteriorating. The gods didn't have control of that, she did. And besides, who do you think gave the gods the world to begin with? Clearly it was given to them with the understanding that they would care for it, not allow their creations to kill it. This is their punishment. I think Fate wants this world back." I shook my head. I was amazed that I had finally found clarity and reason for all that had happened, and it felt good to know. The gods were losing their world because they could no longer control it. Things had gotten out of hand.

"So, only Elle can save it?" Sam reiterated.

"Yes. She is the last, after all."

Sam's face grew jealous. "What about Margriete?"

I shrugged. "What about her? She's dead, remember?"

Sam looked at me with a shocked expression. "*What?* What tree have you been living under?"

I narrowed my eyes, looking at the house that surrounded me. "Very funny."

His face remained serious. "Oh true, you *were* under a tree." He paused to laugh. "She isn't dead, Edgar. You remember that white cat, don't you?"

I thought back, remembering Elle's ridiculous claims that there was a cat in the meadow. "Yeah, so? Did you finally take it the pound?"

Sam let out a low growl. "No. *Of course not!* Though at

first that's exactly what I wanted to do." He shrugged.

I was silent for a moment as I tried to remember the cat. "That was real?" I saw that he wasn't joking.

Sam's face was smug. "Perhaps you should learn to trust people. That cat was Margriete. She was locked in that form by the gods as punishment for all that had happened with Matthew. They did it to spite her, and she could only be released if someone cared enough to recognize it was her and say her name." He laughed. "Clearly, that *wasn't* you."

A feeling of guilt filled my black heart.

"But Elle did see it. You should be ashamed. Margriete was part of the group that came to try to save you. Perhaps you should thank her." Sam looked down his nose at me.

I looked at him closely, seeing there was something more behind all this. "You have a thing for Margriete, don't you?"

I sharp breath blew from between his tight lips. "Whatever." He looked away.

Laughter filled the room as I found myself unable to prevent it. In all my time knowing Sam, I had only seen him love one girl—that pathetic *Jill*. It was at least nice to see him branching out, but then what of Margriete? In love with a guardian angel? Come on. I never thought I'd see her stoop to that level.

Sam's eyes burned a hole though mine. "*Shut up*."

"I wasn't speaking." I choked between laughs.

"You know what I mean." He pounded the table, but it did little to threaten me.

"I'm sorry, it's just—" I began to laugh again. "It's just so *pathetic*."

"Anyway." Sam continued to stare.

I calmed myself. "*Anyway.* I doubt Margriete would hold the power like Elle does."

Sam nodded. "No, you're right. Margriete has lost a lot of the healing power she once had. She's lost the raven inside her."

I chuckled. "Yeah—*for a cat.*" I couldn't help myself.

Sam glared.

I stopped, losing the humor in the situation. "So, Elle is it? Matthew killed everyone else?"

Sam nodded, still to angry to speak.

"That's too bad. I was hoping there would be someone to help her." My face fell, thinking now that she really was *The One*.

Sam blinked a few times. "You know you can't help her, right? So don't think that. You know as well as I that when it comes time, you can't be there."

I cringed as he said it. I wanted nothing more than to be there by her side as she fought against the universe, fought to calm the coming destruction, but I couldn't. The prophecy stated that all those close to her must leave, and recede to where they were born to grant her the strength—myself included. Without me, her powers were stronger, and her heart true.

"I know." I finally answered.

That's why preparing her will be an important task. She

needs to see the prophecy for herself.

My eyes grew angry as they shot to his. "No. I won't allow that."

"But why? *She has to see it.*"

I felt my heart grow restless and dark. "She cannot see it. She cannot know her own future because it will effect her decisions.

Sam nodded. "Exactly, that's why she needs to see it. We need her to know how important this all is. She needs to know that she is the only one that can save this world, inside and out. The universe trusts her to know what the right decision is, and if she decides that this world is not worth it, then that is what will be. For whatever reason, she lived a divine life in their eyes. She is the chosen judge of us all."

"The gods fear her?" I asked, wondering what it was like when they saw them.

"Of course they *fear* her. They were so shaken with anxiety just knowing she had the dagger, thinking that if they got that back, she would never be able to control them—but they did not understand the power of the prophecy. I think they thought that they could change it, but their powers are useless when it comes to the universe and fate. The knife held little power to Elle. No matter what weapon, or magical spell, she will inevitably lead them. She has the divine right and blessing."

I will not show her the prophecy." I stood by my decision, though I knew it was the wrong one. I was stubborn, and if

Fate wanted to play, then I was at least going to put up a fight.

Sam shook his head. "Whatever you say, Edgar. You are as naive as the gods. What is meant to happen, will. You can't change fate." He was echoing me now.

I stood, walking away from him, tired of hearing his voice. "*Leave.*" My brows were sewn together.

I heard Sam stand. "Fine, but I'll see you soon."

I did not acknowledge his statement, but I knew he already had his answer as I felt him inside my mind.

The branches were more than happy to let him leave. The door opened up, and he walked out, not another word said. As the branches folded up behind him, I felt my whole body relax. I took a few calming breaths, thinking about home and allowing some essence of excitement to return.

The sun began to shine through the hole in the ceiling, falling on my back. Its warmth reminded me of the beauty in the world. This place was worth fighting for, and I knew Elle would see that, prophecy or not. She knew what she had to do, because it was ingrained in her very existence, and in her *heart.*

HERE COMES THE GROOM
Edgar

I paced across the floor of the cabin, nervous, though I didn't understand why. For the first time in what felt like decades, Elle was finally independent again. She did not need me like she did before, and I was afraid she would no longer crave the energy of my touch and would finally see me for the horrible man I was.

I straightened my jacket, freshly cleaned in the nearby river and then dried in the sun, making it smell like the lilac it once had—before all the campfires and hunting. My hands were rough, and my eyes tired. What would she think of my wings? Would they repulse her? Would she no longer feel the same because I had moved away from the human I once was, now something ethereal?

I walked toward the wall as the branches opened up for me. I squeezed my wings to my spine, as though it would make a difference, hiding them more effectively then I had before. Outside, the sun still filtered through the trees, giving the Earth one last burst of energy and life. I looked back at the cabin and then the trees.

"Thank you. You can let go now." It was as though the trees that had formed my cabin let out a tremendous sigh of relief, and the crackling of branches began. I watched as the shape of the cabin dissipated, and the trees reached back toward the sky and the sun. They shook their branches one last time before falling silent, the magic inside them retreating back into the roots.

Where the cabin had been, there was now a bare spot, but it was quickly covered by some anxious vines, all looking for a spot to take root and wait out what was to come. Looking around, I noticed that there were no bugs. I missed their busy presence flying about the woods. They had always reminded me of the life that was now beginning to fade. The rays of sun were nothing but void light, lacking the nourishment they need to survive. I breathed in one last time, already smelling the tinge of death in the air. I nodded to myself, turning and heading toward home.

As I reached the clearing of the meadow, I hung back, seeing the crowd of people through the trees. *What were they doing?* I looked toward where the invisible house was and saw Sam standing there in a suit, a white cat at his heels. Confused and mildly put-off, I scanned the rest of the crowd. A girl in a white dress caught my immediate attention. At first I did not recognize her, but as my memory caught up to me I remembered.

"*Sarah?*" I murmured out loud. She seemed to turn and look in my general direction, as though she had heard me say her name. I ducked behind a nearby huckleberry bush, afraid to let everyone see me.

The anger in me grew. *Why had Sam done this to me? Why couldn't he have told me to come back any other day?* It was then that I remembered that he had in fact mentioned a wedding, but the word itself was so sentimental to my own history, that I must have drowned it out, remembering my own wedding instead. I looked back to where Sam had been, seeing him now looking over his shoulder at the spot where I was standing, a delighted smirk on his face.

"*I hate you, Sam,*" I muttered. He knew I hated weddings, or crowds for that matter.

I saw him shrug, though he was so far away, it could have been a laugh as well.

It was then that she appeared out of nowhere, and my anger faded almost immediately. While the guests were turned, looking at Sarah, Elle had exited the house. My heart stopped, remembering her youth and beauty. It calmed my fleeting emotions. I forgot all about the wedding, and the crowd, now only seeing her.

"*Estella,*" I whispered, and I saw her stop dead in her tracks, looking around. She was powerful again, able to hear every sound as she once had. She continued forward, shrugging it off and blaming it on her creative mind.

Everyone began to group together, taking their seats

as I began to feel nervous. I was likely more nervous than the groom himself, my palms wanting to sweat though they were cold as death. I swallowed hard, conjuring a spirit I had nearly forgotten—that of the raven. As my body struggled to change, I began to wonder how the angel wings would play into this, but as I finally got in the air, I still felt them tucked to my spine like a spare pair.

I flew in circles upward, erupting from the canopy and flying overhead. No one's attention faltered from the bride, and as Elle came into view, I saw her eyes were closed, dreaming. There was an unmistakable smile on her face, and I knew now that she could feel me.

She still loved me.

As carefully as I could, I circled in behind her, fluttering down onto the seat beside her.

She drew in a sharp breath, and it made my body shudder. I tucked my wings behind me, feeling my heart race in a way it hadn't since that day she appeared in my class, like a ghost. I watched her exhale slowly, wanting to look, but her mind trying to convince her to give up, telling her I was gone.

I gently snapped my beak, trying to gain her attention. Unable to ignore the noise, she looked at me. I gazed upon her face, my raven eyes wide, drinking in her every feature. Her face did not change, surprise thwarted by the animal before her. I saw her draw her hand up and grasp at something around her neck. A slow smile grew across her face then, and she looked away, as though she still could not believe what she saw.

Shock now laced in with the smile and my heart pumped even harder. Feeling it was time, I changed back into my human form, silent like the wind.

Her hair blew in wisps around her face, her hand never leaving what she held around her neck. I smiled, breathing slowly as I saw Sam look at me and then her, enjoying every moment of this little reunion. I leaned in toward her neck, wanting so badly to kiss her skin, to feel the cool softness against my lips.

I drew close to her ear. *"Thank you."*

I let my breath graze her face, and I saw the hairs on her neck stand on end. She turned to face me then, and I felt a fire erupt in my soul. I brought my hands to her face, no longer able to suppress the desire to touch her. Her skin was warm against my frozen palm. I pulled her toward me and pressed my lips to hers, feeling the peace I always did in her presence—the darkness dissipating long enough to allow me asylum in her heart.

She brought her hands to my arms, and grasped onto them. Her touch was gentle and slow, but full of a power I had all but forgotten. It was hard to deny that she was truly *The One*. She knew how to calm all the fury in the world, to tame whatever creature came across her path. As I pulled back, she refused to look away.

"Edgar, *you're back*," she whispered, a tear forming in her eye.

"I'm back," I replied. The calm feeling in my heart began

to twist as her touch remained, and the familiar darkness and desire to kill replaced what little peace there was left. I pulled my arms away from her, and she let go, the release just as sweet as our first touch. Disappointment grew in my heart. Every time I touched her, I wished I could hold on longer, remain in that calm place with her forever, but it always turned.

She smiled. "Its okay, Edgar. I don't need it."

The words stung, feeding the doubts I had in the forest. It was true she did not need me like before, and I hoped the feeling was still strong enough to grant me purpose as her other half. I looked down into my lap, but she brought one hand to my chin and tilted my face upward.

"But that doesn't mean I don't *want it*." It was as though she knew exactly what I was thinking.

I smiled. "I love you."

She let a tear finally fall. "I love you, too."

CATCHING UP

Edgar

The crowd began to stand and filter toward the bride and groom. I watched as some eyed me, likely wondering where I came from, and who I was. Sarah glanced at me and gave me a wink. Scott did the same. I winced, remembering them as students, uncomfortable with this change in our relationship.

Elle laughed. "Edgar, *don't glare.*"

I looked at her, her blue eyes so bright they were hard to watch. "Sorry, it's just…"

She cut me off, rolling her eyes. "I know, *sickening*, but they're happy."

I laughed. "Glad I'm not the only one that thinks that."

She gave me a playful slap on the arm. "You don't have to act fake with me, Edgar. *Ever.*" She continued to stare, still in awe that I was back.

I kept my hands in my pockets, wanting so badly to hold her, but knowing my strength was still unpredictable.

"Where were you?" she asked.

I eyed Sam. "I'm not sure."

She looked disappointed by my reply.

"Here, follow me." I drew her away from the crowd and deeper into the field. "Things are going to be different," I whispered.

She frowned, perplexed. "What do you mean?"

I didn't know how to say it, how to admit to her that I was different, that things were not necessarily *well*. Her eyes were still caught up in the beauty of things. I didn't want to ruin it for her. Not yet.

I saw her look back toward the crowd then, a small smile on her face. Seeing that no one was looking, she lunged toward me, grabbing me around my waist and pushing me through the vortex and into the house. She landed on top of me, and we slid across the black granite of the entry, my head hitting the base of the stairs with a thud.

"*Ouch.*" I brought my hand to my head, bending my knees as she straddled my stomach. She looked down at me and I let my hands fall to my sides, afraid to touch her. She pulled her long, blonde hair away from her face, breathing hard and laughing.

"Sorry—I just saw an opportunity." She climbed off and stood, seeing my discomfort and the deep black of my eyes.

I took a minute to regroup as deathly images crossed my

mind, images of Elle I never wanted to see. I stood, placing my hand on the stairs for assistance, my feet slipping. Now standing, I straightened my jacket and looked at her. She continued to breathe hard, her face alive. I swallowed, controlling my anger but not my desires. I stepped toward her and grabbed her around the waist, pulling her against my chest and kissing her with fury. She grabbed at my back, allowing me to control the situation and control myself. I ran my hand through her hair, grasping it hard as I felt the wings on my back release and spread.

She yelped and jumped back, her cheeks reddened and her face confused. "*Edgar—*"

I was breathing deeply as my chest rose and fell, my mind whirling as the whole room seemed to spin. I was controlling the fury, and it felt good—addicting even. I walked toward her but she took another step back, distancing herself.

"Edgar, *what is this?*" There was fear in her eyes.

I clenched my fists and pressed back my desires.

"You have *wings*," she continued, staring at them with what seemed like fascination, but also uncertainty.

I nodded as I stepped toward her, my teeth clenched in resistance of my desire to hold her and never let go. She stopped backing away from me, allowing me to come closer. I could smell her apprehension, but she was braver now than before. She ran her shaking hand along the length of one wing, walking behind me and drawing the same hand down the other.

"Angel wings. Like Sam's," she stated.

I swallowed. "Yes, like Sam's."

"So then," she paused. "You're a *guardian angel?*"

I nodded again. "Yes. I died for you." I felt a sense of pride saying it.

I watched her face, afraid of her reaction, afraid it would change the way she saw me. A smile grew across her cheeks. "Will you be *my* angel?" The way she said it sounded seductive, and it was hard to hold back.

I swallowed again, my throat now dry. "Sam is your angel." I felt relief—she did not hate me.

She continued to smile, pressing her body against my chest. "That doesn't matter," she whispered in my ear, tracing her lips along my cheek.

She found my current state *attractive?*

I tried to hold my hands away from her, but as she continued to tease, I lost my control. I pressed my hands against her back, grasping the fabric of her dress as she looked at me, no longer afraid of what I could do to her. Her breath fell across my face as she searched my eyes, loving the danger.

I drew in one shaky breath and she smirked. "What's wrong, too much?"

I wasn't used to her like this. "No." I stammered.

She brought her hand up behind my neck, pulling me in to kiss her.

I had control. I could handle this. She knew what to say to make this a challenge, something I thrived on. Her body was stronger now, her bones able to handle my strength.

I was no longer afraid I would kill her. I lifted her off the ground, and she wrapped her legs around me, her warmth something I craved. Her lips were intertwined with mine, her breathing the only sound that mattered. This is what I had always wanted, but it was too soon.

I had to stop.

"Elle—"

Her lips froze, my hands guiding her away from me. She tilted her head, her eyes filled with disappointment.

"I know, Edgar."

COMING CLEAN
Estella

"I see you found it." Edgar played with the chain around my neck, making it tickle my skin.

I took it from his hands, looking at it as it glowed white and burning hot against the skin on my hand. "It was black all this time." I had forgotten about the ring in the excitement, for the first time noticing it had changed.

He rolled toward me, our bodies separated by a safe pile of pillows. He traced his hand up my chest to the chain, twisting it until he found the clasp and released it from my neck. I felt relieved to have it off me, the power of it letting go of my soul. I watched Edgar let the ring slide from the chain, filling the room with a delightful tingling sound of metal.

He held it in his hand, flipping it over and over. "Where did you find it?"

I smiled, and looked toward his desk, the black sheets tangled around my arms as I tried to point. "In there."

He looked mildly angry. "I tried to keep you out of here." He looked up at all the paintings with a glimmer of shame in his eyes.

I didn't want him to feel ashamed of who he was. "I love them. I love this room."

He looked at me in surprise. "You do?" He sat up, and I admired his strong bare chest, his wings now retracted. We were lounging in his room, trying all we could to resist what we both wanted. I knew he still felt weak, but I felt in control. We were so close, but still, he would not allow me into the deepest regions of his heart.

"Yes, I slept here while you were gone. It's you, the Edgar I always wanted to know." I touched his face. "This is beautiful, a true sense of your soul, the opposite of mine, but still a part that is essential to my existence."

He looked amazed.

I reached toward him, and took the ring from his hand. "Here." I grabbed his finger and slid it on, a flash of the past returning to me.

He laughed. "Thanks."

I held his hand as his eyes filtered to black, just as they had been all night. I was no longer afraid of it. He would not kill me. I knew he couldn't. There was something inside me that felt more confident now. I would no longer be afraid.

"Don't hide from me, Edgar." I slid my body next to his, our skin touching as his eyes now filled with anger, something I found seductive. "I am in love with the darkness inside you. I want to embrace that."

He leaned in and kissed my neck, his grasp strong. I put my hand on his chest and pushed him away. "I want to be the wife—" I paused, looking deep in his eyes. "The wife I was *supposed* to be. I want us to be together, completely."

He took my hand and kissed it, his teeth grazing my skin, my touch driving him mad. I smiled. This image of him in my head was the man I'd always wanted, not the man tortured by anger and holding back his desires. At times I wanted to escape my beautiful life, embrace danger and feel the dark side.

"Edgar, we are here together. This is *our* life, as one life." I laughed.

He touched my chin. "Though it's an endless life, Elle, I have learned that it does not mean it isn't fleeting. I can still lose you. I just got you back. I'm not ready to risk that."

I grinned. "I want to spend every second with you."

He chuckled. "*Every second?*"

I gave him a playful slap on the arm. "Edgar, you know what I mean."

His smile was striking. "I won't allow us to part ever again, Elle. I'm sorry we ever did."

"We won't." His eyes were pitch black. I leaned away from him, allowing him space.

"I won't allow us to separate as we have so many times,

and I promise to be true to you, to be the other half I am supposed to be," he declared.

I took his words to heart, believing the look on his face. "What was it like?" I changed the subject.

He shrugged, knowing exactly what I was talking about. "Much like what I assume you felt when you disappeared, though I was dead and you were just asleep."

"Why weren't you in Heaven, then, like everyone else?"

His lips pressed together. "I suppose I was, but perhaps caged. Did you see me while you were there?"

I nodded. "Yes. They had you at the white castle."

"Yes, I must have hovered there under some spell. Drugged, so to speak. Anyway, in Fate's eyes, I must have died at some point, otherwise I wouldn't be an angel. Perhaps the gods managed to bring me back from the dead? Struck a bargain of some sort?"

"Yes," I agreed, affirming what I already knew, but I had hoped there was more.

I thought about that day at the castle, and the little girl that had led me there—*my mother*. I began to wonder how this all worked, who was in charge, and why. I looked toward the window where the curtain was cracked, reveling a rainy sky.

"Looks like the bad weather has returned." I frowned.

Edgar's face changed, and I tried to understand why. "Seems so."

I read into his reply. "Do you know why?"

He shrugged. "I'm not sure." His voice was flat, his eyes staring into mine as though he wanted me to say something, but there was nothing.

There was a knock on the door then.

I wrapped the sheets around me and sat up, not wanting to be seen in my camisole and underwear. "Yes?"

I heard someone begin to turn the handle. "Hey, Elle. It's Margriete."

Edgar's face changed back to happiness. "Margriete! Come in!"

I looked at Edgar with an angry face. "*Edgar!*" I hissed.

He looked at me, remembering we were practically naked, but it was too late.

"Hey, guys!" She came bounding in, halting as she saw us. "*Whoa* there, put on some clothes." She shielded her eyes and turned away from us.

"It's not what you think," I said with resentment.

Edgar jumped from the bed and I grabbed one of his shirts from the floor, putting it on while Edgar grabbed a fresh shirt, letting the hem fall over his still-intact jeans.

"Are you decent now?" She peeked over her shoulder, content that I had a shirt, "Don't you know that's dangerous? You shouldn't get that close." She barked, referencing what we had done. *"Young idiots playing with fire is what that is."*

I laughed, thinking of something that would shut her up. "I know what you and Sam do, so…"

Her jaw dropped. "I do no such thing!" she denied, but the smirk on her face said it all.

Edgar's expression showed disgust. "So it *is* true? Margriete and Sam really are a thing? That's *repulsing*."

I laughed.

Margriete hissed. "No worse than you. I hear you're an angel now, too—" She paused for a moment. "*Pillow talk*," she added, just to piss him off.

Edgar pretended to gag.

"So, Edgar." Margriete stared at him. "Long time no see." She put one hand on her hip, giving him a sassy face.

I watched the both of them, neither one flinching as though stuck in some sort of face off. Margriete hadn't seen Edgar in decades, since she had run away, and I wasn't exactly sure how they would interact. Considering the circumstances, and Matthew's death, I wasn't sure if it would be a delightful reunion or a dreadful fight. Though she had been with me down in Heaven, the Edgar we had seen there wasn't *real*.

They continued to stare, inhaling and exhaling in even breaths. The tension was unbearable, and I found myself covered in a cold sweat. It was then that I saw a smile begin to form on Margriete's lips, and I rolled my eyes, a breath of relief releasing from my lungs.

"Oh, Edgar!" She ran toward him and jumped, wrapping her legs around his waist and giving him a big dramatic kiss on the cheek.

Edgar struggled to hold her, his eyes changing to black, sensing the creature she was.

Margriete leaned back, sliding her legs from around

him and back to the floor, looking at his eyes. "Oh, *Edgar*. No need to be so overdramatic. Cool it." She gave him a playful smack on the shoulder, which I doubt made the situation any easier for him.

His skin was glistening with sweat. "Thanks Margriete." He paused and cleared his throat, walking toward his desk where he shuffled through some papers to distract himself. "I didn't expect you to be so bubbly." Edgar turned and looked at me. "Was she always like this? I can't remember."

I glared at him. "Yes, darling. She was."

Margriete grabbed my arm. "Hey, come have some coffee with me."

I looked at Edgar over my shoulder, but he was still busy going through the papers on the desk.

"Oh, come on. He's busy anyway," she pleaded.

I nodded, and she grabbed my hand, pulling me through the stacks of books and papers to the door, where we made our way down the stairs toward the kitchen.

"So, tell me—" She leaned in close, staring at me from under her brows with a smirk on her face. "How far did you guys get?"

I snorted. "Not a story for little girls like you." I crossed my arms and stuck my nose in the air, taking a stool at the copper bar in the kitchen. I looked down at my reflection as I always did, seeing it seemed to change everyday, depending on my mood.

Sam had his back to me as he stood by the fire, humming to himself. Margriete skipped behind him, running her fingertips down his back with a smile.

"Wasn't that a wonderful wedding?" She grabbed two mugs from the cabinet, her voice loud as though she were hinting at something.

Sam stopped humming and stood up straight. "No."

Margriete pouted. "Why not?" She frowned.

"Because weddings are dumb. If you love someone you love someone, there's no need to declare it to the world."

Sam had a point, but I sided with Margriete.

She shook her head. "You're so *new age.*"

Sam laughed. "No. I'm just not one that believes it has to be sealed with a ring. And for what? So the gods can laugh at us? I think marriage seems pointless when you're immortal." Sam looked at me. "No offense, Elle." He then looked back at Margriete. "The god's are practically our friends. I don't need them teasing me."

Margriete snorted. "You have a skewed sense of friendship. Last time I checked, we were enemies." She grabbed the coffee from the coffee maker and filled the two mugs, adding sugar and milk to mine before handing it to me. She rolled her eyes, her back to Sam.

"I saw that." He was still facing the fire, stirring something that smelled familiar, and cheesy.

"Let's go into the other room." Margriete hissed over her shoulder, grabbing my hand and ripping me from the stool, dragging me down the hall to the library.

"Hey, *don't go!* I made this for *you*—" Sam's voice trailed off as we left him behind.

I wriggled from her grasp and escaped to the couch. Rubbing my arm, I sat, leaning into the soft leather and tucking my legs under me.

"That man is impossible," she whispered.

"I can still hear you!" Sam yelled.

Margriete burst into a fit of laughter, shaking her head. "If he wasn't so cute, I wouldn't be with him." She turned her head to speak over her shoulder. *"That's for sure!"* she yelled back.

I took a deep breath and blinked, thinking I was far too happy to deal with their playful bickering. I prayed that Edgar and I never got like that, hoping we had better ways to handle indifference. I repositioned my back against the side cushion, wiggling my feet as I sat on them, trying to warm them up. I brought the coffee to my nose and breathed deep, shutting my eyes.

Margriete sunk into the chair opposite me. "Dreary day, isn't it? Seems weird for summer."

I opened my eyes and looked out the window. "Yeah, seems strange." I looked over the grasses of the field to the forest, noticing the way the trees seemed yellowed, the grasses sad. I looked at the sky, covered by thick layers of clouds, making it feel like night.

"I get this weird feeling, you know—" She tried to think of the right thing to say. "I mean, *do you feel that?*"

I shrugged. "Feels like a rainy day to me. Though I will admit it's been happening a lot more than normal."

Margriete's face pursed, as though trying to concentrate

on the feeling that was right on the tip of her tongue. "No. No, it's like I hear something. Like a buzzing noise. Sort of like putting a bunch of bees in a thick jar and closing the lid."

I half-heartedly tried to listen more closely. "So, like a beehive?"

She looked at me with a face that seemed like she was giving up. "Never mind."

I shrugged. "Sorry."

Margriete changed the subject. "So what did Edgar tell you about what happened?"

I took a sip of coffee. "He says he doesn't remember. He thinks he was somewhere between sleep and death. But I think it's apparent that, somewhere along the way, he did die, but like he said, I think they made a bargain with someone to bring him back. It just seems odd that they'd go through all that trouble just to get that stupid dagger."

"He doesn't remember anything?" She let out a sharp disgusted breath. "Well, that tells us nothing."

"What were you thinking he'd say?"

Margriete thought for a moment. "Well, I figured he'd tell you why it was he got to come back. What the real reason was, because like you said, it seems a little weak that they'd go through all that trouble just to get a dagger. I mean, no offense or anything, but I really didn't think they'd let him go. It's not like them to act like that—merciful."

I nodded, trying to follow. "Yeah. I mean, like they said, anyone killed by the dagger dies, even them."

"Exactly. He should be dead. End of story."

"Well—" I sat up a little. "I mean, they kept him because I had the dagger, and they brought him back so that I'd give it to them."

Margriete shook her head in a sharp, annoyed manner. "It just seems like an awfully generous trade to me. Maybe that's what they want you to believe. As far as I've known, they've never let anyone out of Heaven like that. In a way, they admitted defeat by doing so."

"Well, Edgar is a guardian angel, and they let them out." I kept trying to thwart her speculations, believing it was what it seemed: a simple trade. The last thing I wanted was to believe something else was coming. I was prepared to relax and enjoy life for once.

"Yeah, *yeah*. But who does he protect? Certainly he's not *your* angel. You have Sam, and I have no angel at all, nor do I want one." She laughed to herself in a thankful manner. "Guardian angels only leave Heaven when they have a soul to protect, and he has none."

"I think you're reading into this too much." I took another sip of coffee.

"No, I think the god's are buttering you up for something. They're gonna come back and ask for more. That's what beings like them do. Just watch."

"What makes you think they aren't content with what they've got already?"

Margriete glared at me. "Come on, girl! They're never content. And besides, you didn't sign anything."

I tilted my head. "Should I have signed something?"

"Did they have something for you to sign?"

"No."

Margriete sat up suddenly. "Then, *yes!* You should have signed something, anything, a napkin for goodness sakes. You needed to draw out a contract stating *'this is it, don't ask me for more'*."

I began to get frustrated. "Well, you were there. Why didn't you tell me this?" I barked, feeling I was being attacked.

Margriete sat back, finally tasting her coffee. "I had other things to worry about."

I could tell she felt mildly guilty, but at the same time, what was I to do? I had been inundated by many emotions that day, and now she tells me I should have signed a contract, too? That I should have sat there longer, and drawn something up like a bunch of lawyers at a divorce hearing? I don't think so.

"So, pretty much you're telling me I'm screwed?" I began to feel foolish, as though I should have known.

"Well, maybe. Maybe not. You just better hope they don't need you for something, because if they do, then yes, *you're screwed.*"

Her words held little comfort as I remembered the way the gods had treated me, as though I was someone they needed alive, but why? What was in store for me that I did not yet know about?

Edgar walked down the stairs then, and all I could think

about was my future and my imminent loss. "Edgar? Should I have signed something?"

His pace down the stairs slowed, pressing his brows together. "Signed something? For what?"

"When I traded you for the dagger. Should I have signed something saying they need to leave me alone, and that they can't come back and ask for more?" I searched his face as he made it to the bottom of the stairs, the sound of his feet echoing through the empty hallway.

"Maybe." He looked as though I'd caught him off guard.

"Well, they won't want me for anything that you can think of, right? I mean, I'm nothing special. It's not like I can move mountains like you can."

I heard Sam walk from the kitchen, probably intrigued by the conversation. "Yeah, Edgar. I mean, she has nothing to worry about, *right?*" He echoed me.

Edgar looked from my face to Sam's, and then back to me, shrugging. "No, I think you're safe."

Sam stared at him, but I couldn't quite understand the expression. What was he referencing? Was there something he knew? My heart leapt in my chest.

Edgar walked toward the kitchen then, Sam following.

"Do you think he's lying to me?" I whispered. I sat up, looking at Margriete with a steady stare.

She looked even more lost than me. "No." Her face twisted. "At least there better not be. Sam and I don't keep secrets." Her expression was one of displeasure.

I ignored her. "I mean, we just talked about how we wouldn't lie anymore."

Margriete lifted her brows. "Of all the people in the world I could never understand, Edgar was always on the top of the list, so don't ask me. I'm likely the last to know what he's thinking. When I think he's mad, it always turns out that he was really happy."

I sank back into the couch cushion, looking outside and wondering if I should trust him or not, wondering if his promises were fake. After all, he certainly didn't have a sterling record, so to what degree should I be so quick to trust him? Love was not the best reason. Loyalty had to be proven.

"He's your husband, you should trust him," Margriete finally concluded.

I looked back toward her. "Yeah... I guess you're right."

REPRIMAND
Edgar

"What are you doing? Why didn't you tell her?" Sam whispered behind me, following me into the kitchen.

"What? She caught me off guard. What was I supposed to do? Announce it to the entire group? *Oh, hey Elle, the world is dying and only you can save it.* Yeah, Sam. That would have gone over real well." I refused to turn around and look at Sam, instead grabbing a book and sitting on the lounger in the sitting room across from the kitchen. I was avoiding the subject at all costs.

Sam pounded his fist on the copper counter. "*Damn it,* Edgar! She needs to know. This isn't one of those things you just stumble upon and suddenly find the strength to handle. This is something she needs to prepare for."

I dropped the book into my lap, angry as I glared into his golden eyes, his hair a brighter red than usual. "I'll get to it. Just give me some time to think."

Sam whirled around on one foot and stormed toward the fire. "She doesn't have that time, Edgar," he snapped.

"Just do me a favor and stay out of this, Sam." My teeth were clenched, and I could feel the blood rushing to my face, my eyes turning a deep black.

Sam opened his mouth but quickly shut it, knowing full well what I could do to him. The ego grew inside me and my wings stretched out to my sides, flaunting the fact that I was stronger than he ever would be.

"Fluff your feathers all you want, old friend, but you know as well as I that this is not up to you, so stop pretending it is." Sam gave me one last long glare, and left the room, his footsteps fading into the hall. I heard the front door slam.

I winced, then pulled the book up to my face and continued to read. Though the book was anything but interesting, I didn't care. The last thing I needed was to think about what I knew, and what Elle still didn't. Avoidance would make it all go away, or so I hoped.

COMING TO AN UNDERSTANDING

Estella

My feet sank into the deep mud of the trail toward the college, the smell of damp sage filling the air. "Do you think this rain will ever stop?"

I looked back at Margriete as she trudged behind me. "I don't know."

This was meant to be a hike for exercise, but it had turned into much more than that. By now we were knee deep in mud, and it was more about survival at this point. Walking was an understatement as sweat beaded across our skin, my muscles weak and tired.

"What do you think Edgar is hiding?" I looked down at my feet, one boot suctioned to the forest floor.

"So you do think he's lying?" Margriete challenged.

I yanked on my ankle with one hand, managing to pull free and place my foot on more solid ground. "Well, I mean, I think he was acting weirder than usual. What else would it be but the fact that he is hiding something? You know what he's like."

Margriete laughed. "Weirder than usual? He's only been back for one week." She almost fell as her foot also released from the mud. "But I do know what you mean. He does have that mysterious side we all have to wonder about."

I rolled my eyes. "Okay, then. He's acting weird for anyone, regardless. I've never seen him like this."

"Like what? Withdrawn and alone? Of course not. *Never.*" Sarcasm laced her voice.

I snorted, admitting it was funny. Still though, he was different. Maybe only I could see it, but that was enough to convince me. Margriete let out a squeal, and I looked back just in time to see her land in the mud, her hands and arms covered in a thick layer all the way to her elbows.

"*Seriously,*" she whined.

I laughed. "Here, let me help." I made my way back toward her.

"I think I'm done." She was exhausted.

I laughed again. "Yeah, me too. Let's just get you up out of this mess, and then I'll fly us home."

She nodded. "Yeah, at this point, I think I'd be happier dangling by my tail in the air than sweating my way through this stuff. Why do we need exercise, anyway? We're plenty strong, and it's not like it matters if we're healthy. We're immortal, remember?"

I felt like a failure for thinking this little outing was a good idea. "It was meant to be more of a mental exercise. I need to get out of that house."

She nodded, lifting her brows. "Yeah, I can certainly relate to that."

I leaned down to grab her arm as a fern stretched toward me. I watched it as it tickled at my arm, sad and desperate.

"Margriete—look." I pointed.

She looked where I had. "What is it doing?"

I knelt down, touching it as it seemed to turn up toward me, though continued to sag. "I'm not sure. It's as though it's asking me for help."

Margriete narrowed her eyes. "Yes. Look."

She pointed to the rest of the ferns around us. I gasped.

"See? They're all leaning toward us, and they're pointing right at us," Margriete added.

"You're right. How long do you think it's been like that? I hadn't even noticed with all the mud." I looked up toward the trees, still noticing the way they seemed yellowed. "Look at that. Do you think it's because there hasn't been any sun? But I wouldn't think that would matter."

Margriete looked up. "Yeah, the bows are even leaning toward us. I don't think that's normal."

I looked back at Margriete. "Should I ask Edgar?"

She snorted. "What will he tell you? He's only going to say that you're crazy. Just like he did when you saw me, and look what that did."

I remembered the way I felt when he didn't believe me. "Yes, you're right. I'm not really in the mood to deal with that, either. Well, then who can we ask?"

"You could ask Sam." Her face went sour as soon as she said it. "Or maybe we'll just try the library, see if we can't find something in one of those books?"

I nodded, pulling her up off the ground with one hefty tug. "Yeah, that's a good idea," I agreed in a labored voice.

Margriete reached down and untied her boots, geared up to leave them behind. "Come on then. Let's go. I can't bear to watch them. It's breaking my heart." She prepared herself to transform into her changeling, shaking the energy from her hands.

"Yeah, me neither." I peered around at them one last time, almost frightened by their appearance. Looking away, I pulled my boots off as well, leaving them in six inches of mud. "Are you ready?" I stood on top of them, my socks soaking wet.

Margriete nodded as she changed, now balancing two paws on one boot and two on the other, afraid to get her pristine white fur dirty.

I laughed. "Alright." I jumped up in the air, taking flight as I circled once, swooping back down and snatching Margriete by the tail as she let out one discontented howl. Her squeals echoed off the trees, making the scene worse, as though it were the trees that were crying.

I tilted up and through the canopy of the forest, spreading

my wings as rain trickled down every feather, adding to our weight. Margriete spun below me, helplessly along for the ride, but growing accustomed to the abuse. Up ahead, the meadow came into view, and I saw Sam and Edgar outside, playing with a football in the yard. Both their wings were spread out as they threw the ball back and forth, up in the air and as far as they could. With their strength, the ball nearly flew from one end of the field to the other, an expanse of about two football fields. A throw like that would make any quarterback jealous, and even me.

I fanned air forward as I hovered down to the ground, placing Margriete on the grass before landing next to her. We quickly changed out of our changelings and made our way toward the house, walking between Edgar and Sam as the ball whizzed overhead.

"Hey, girls!" Sam yelled from the left and we both looked.

Margriete smiled and ran toward him, her stride growing more and more like a cat everyday. I looked to my right at Edgar, seeing he was smiling at me as well. He made his way toward me in silence, his black t-shirt soaked and his giant wings dripping.

I still was not used to the fact that he was an angel, and the wings seemed out of place. It felt weird to be with him, as though I was betraying my own kind, but despite all that, they were beautiful—a full-size rendition of his previous raven wings. Because these new wings were so grand, I rarely saw him use his changeling. Why would he? If I had that sort of thing, I would too. Much easier, though it had really ruined a lot of his clothes.

"Hey, there." Edgar reached me, putting one hand around my waist. He leaned in and kissed me on the forehead, sweeping my wet hair from my face with his other hand.

I leaned against his cool, wet body, hugging him, though I didn't want to. I was still angry that he seemed to be hiding something, and I didn't want him to catch on to the fact that I'd noticed, especially if there was no real reason behind his actions. I needed more time too feel him out, to see if his moods were simply a result of what had happened, and not because of something else.

"So how was the hike?" He looked at me with a sarcastic smile.

"It wasn't much of a hike." My thoughts were tied up by the way the ferns and trees were reacting. For a moment I thought to ask him, even though I had declined to earlier. I looked down at my feet, thinking that maybe I'd just mention it, and see what he does. "Saw something strange out there." I narrowed my eyes, noticing the grass in the field was also reaching for me, crawling along the ground as though tired.

"Strange? Like what. Was it a creature?" He put one hand on each shoulder and pulled me away from him, trying to look into my eyes, but I wouldn't allow him.

I was afraid that if he saw into my heart, he would know what I was trying to do, what I was trying to get out of him.

What if he was changed by the gods? What if they had bugged him with magic, somehow? "No, just—" I tried to think of a good excuse. "There was so much mud out there. I think the rain is taking a toll on the forest."

He nodded. "I'm sure it's nothing to worry about."

I shut my eyes, relieved that he didn't seem to know, relieved that he wasn't hiding anything from me. "Yeah, you're probably right. I'm just a worrier, that's all."

He pulled me back against his chest, rocking us back and forth.

"Hey, Elle!" Margriete yelled from across the field.

I pushed away from Edgar, and looked at her over my shoulder.

"Come on!" She waved me toward her with wide eyes, nodding as though holding back the real reason as to what we were doing.

I looked toward Sam, seeing him smile. He knew exactly what we were doing, but he was reacting in a way that suggested he wasn't going to stop us, either. He knew something. I felt betrayed, then, knowing that if he knew something, then Edgar probably did too. I saw Sam's eyes dart up over my head and then back at me, his smile fading.

I looked up at Edgar with sharp eyes. "What was that about?"

Edgar's face seemed solid, but it quickly faded as he answered me. "What was what?"

I shook my head, letting go of him in a way that was

meant to be cold, but he only laughed.

"Whatever," I said under my breath.

Sam threw the ball and Edgar caught it, releasing a sharp breath as it hit his chest with a force I was certain hurt, at least a little.

"See you at dinner!" I waved over my shoulder but didn't look back, too frustrated to be nice.

"Bye." He said it while releasing the ball, grunting.

I didn't bother to give another wave, and seem repetitive. I met up with Margriete, just as we reached the invisible porch. She stared at me, sensing my anger, but I didn't look at her, either. *"Pompous show-off,"* I said. Margriete giggled, and together we walked inside.

BOOKWORK

Estella

"Hey, Elle, look at this one!"

Margriete pulled a book from the shelf on the second level. I was searching through a few plant books on the lower floor that were located next to the books about glaciers.

I looked up at her, seeing she was waving a book over her head. "What is it?"

"Come up here! I think it's likely we'll find the answers in these books. These are all the *magic* books!" The look on her face was priceless, as though she had found something that was forbidden, her face like that of an excited child.

I dropped a book about botany and it hit the floor like dead weight. I leaned forward and stood with a grunt, making my way to the ladder. Once up, Margriete shoved the book toward me and I looked at it. I pressed my brows together, deep wrinkles forming on my forehead.

"What is it?" The book was all white, including the pages, and to the naked eye, you'd think it was nothing more than an unused journal, until I tilted it. "Oh, wow. Look at that. Did you see that?"

Margriete's mouth was gaping in an exaggerated smile, nodding her head with enthusiasm.

"Well, it's certainly a chore to read." The letters glimmered as it caught the light of the room.

She touched her finger to the page. "I think it's made for beings like us. Because we have reflective eyes, so we can read it." Her voice was laced with deep, dramatic undertones.

"You're right, Margriete. Look here." I had closed the book and was now reading the cover. "*A Book of Us,*" I read out loud, running my hand across a drawing of a raven.

"Yeah, that's what I was saying! I think it's about us, too!" She was shaking with excitement.

I laughed. "Wow, this could have come in handy last year, that's for sure."

"No kidding! So do you think it will have our answers?" She snatched it from my grasp, opening to one of the first pages and scanning what was there. She was whispering under her breath, listing things: "*Making of, first days, the cast away, survival, special powers, enchantments, wing maintenance, magic...*"

"Well?" I was growing impatient.

"Well—" She looked up, shutting the book. "Seems

like there are a lot of interesting things here, but nothing that could tell us what is happening. It seems it's mostly about us, as the title suggests." She shoved it toward me as though it were now no more than a stack of useless paper, the excitement now gone from her face as she dove back into the stack, looking for more.

My smile faded as well, but I kept the book anyway, figuring it had some use—particularly in the wing maintenance section. I sat back against the rail, taking a deep breath and slowly exhaling. "This is useless. I don't think we will find our answers here. Most of these books are centuries old! Surely they cannot *foresee* the future."

Margriete's face was just inches from the books, scanning every spine but finding nothing. "Gosh, where did you guy's find all these books! I mean everything is here, *Griffins, Unicorns, Guardian Angels*... Oh! Guardian Angels! *This is handy.*" She ripped it from the stack and placed it in front of her.

I repeated myself, this time louder. "We won't find anything here, Grietly. We need something like your journal, something that, at the very least, can tell us the present, something that says why the plants are doing that."

Margriete sat back, finally listening, her head resting on the bar of the railing. "Yeah, we need someone that can see into the future. Like a fortune teller."

I perked up. "Do you know anyone?"

She laughed. "Ha! *No.* No one can do that, well, unless you believe in myths."

"Believe in myths? Like what?" I touched her arm, intrigued by her comment.

She rolled her head to face me. "You know. Prophecies, Fate, and all that crazy stuff."

"Prophecies?" I began.

A door slammed upstairs and Margriete and I both jumped, looking toward the door of the library and dropping the conversation.

"What was *that?"* Margriete looked at me questioningly.

REPRIMAND
Edgar

Sam slammed the door to my room, closing us in darkness. "This is the last time I'm going to say it, Edgar. *Tell her!*"

I clenched my jaw, growing tired of his nagging. "In due time, Sam. So, calm down."

He lunged across the room, pointing his finger at me as his hair fluttered in some imaginary wind. "I will not calm down. I am sworn to protect her, and by you, of all people. And right now, your actions are getting in the way of that, so, I'm conflicted. I don't know how much longer I can stay silent before I will be forced to help her. I do not like lying to Margriete, but because of you, I have. For once, I'm getting a taste of how it must feel to be you and I don't know how you can stand it. *It's sick!*"

I shot to my feet, knocking my desk chair backwards and onto a stack of books. A vial of ink spilled across my desk, spreading like blood across the papers I had just been studying. I was angrier now than before. Those papers were hundreds of years old.

A growl grew in my chest like thunder. "You will do no such thing!" My voice was low. I had held my anger at bay for long enough, and my body could no longer handle it. I was a bomb, waiting to explode.

I shook my head. Sam had zero tact. The more he nagged, the less I wanted to divulge the truth to Estella. Besides, she was figuring it out on her own. So, why even bother?

Sam walked up to me, sticking his nose in my face. "Then you should have thought about that when you appointed me to watch her in your absence." If it could have, his face would have turned red with anger. "And you *should* bother. You're wasting her time!"

"You don't know where the prophecy is," I spat, grabbing his neck and threatening to snap it in half.

He laughed. "*Really?* Well, I can see that you don't, either."

I picked Sam up off the floor. "Stay out of my head, Sam."

Sam continued to laugh. "What are you going to do? Are you going to choke me? Before you try, ask yourself this, Edgar. Do we even breathe?"

I dropped him, finding my threat was indeed useless. "Sam, as the one that appointed you to watch Elle, I forbid you to tell her about the existence of the prophecy. No one even knows those really exist, and what does it tell you anyway? That some day you may find something? No matter what you do to follow it, it changes nothing!"

Sam sat on a stack of books, refusing to take my threats seriously. "I'm afraid you no longer have the power to forbid me from anything. It's Fate that binds me to Elle, not you. You may have been responsible for it in the first place, but not anymore. That loan has been sold to a higher power. I will do as I wish." His eyes were tiny slits. "And if she could read the prophecy, then it would help. It would explain to her what is happening better than we could. It can *show* her. Besides, the prophecy does not speak of the end, just the beginning—we have hope!" Sam finally sealed his lips as he stood and walked toward the door.

"Where are you going?" I bellowed. His exit seemed abrupt, and I wasn't yet able to get myself abreast of the situation.

Sam looked back at me, saying nothing as his hand grabbed the handle of the door, reading my jealousy.

"Don't you dare tell her, Sam." I tried to threaten him once more but he didn't even flinch. He opened the door then, and stepped out, leaving me distraught and alone.

I listened in anger as he descended the stairs, my body shaking. I felt as though my palms should be sweating but they weren't—they couldn't. I turned back to my desk and righted my chair. I sat, leaning my elbows on the wood with my head in my hands. I needed to tell her. I had to. The last thing I wanted was for her to find another reason to distrust me, and another reason to trust him instead.

Why had I made him her guardian, anyway? Why not someone else? Why not someone that couldn't read minds?

I dropped my hands from my face as the fallen ink bottle rolled, releasing more black ink across the pages. I tried to wipe it up but the more I tried the more it spread, just like the situation now. Why was it so hard to tell her? Was it the fact that I did not want to admit she was stronger than me? Was I that insecure, that selfish?

I visualized the prophecy in my head, glowing in the darkness of wherever it lay. I wanted to know where it was so that I could see it once more, but it had run from me long ago. I knew it was nearby because I could often hear its gentle hum, but for now, it was concealed.

Even if Sam did tell her about it, and she managed to find it, would she know what it was? How to use it? We had been born with it years and years ago, but when we were cast from Heaven, it had stayed with me, *not her*. I kept it safe, guarded it thinking that if she saw it, it would ruin our time together, as it still did.

I would tell her, I would, but not yet. I felt too far from the truth now, too far from myself. I was a mess, and it felt horrible.

LIES

Estella

"Sam, what was that?" Sam entered the library.

"Nothing. I just slammed the door by mistake. Sometimes I guess I don't know my own strength." He had a mocking look on his face.

"*Right.*" Margriete nodded, giving him a blank stare that suggested she didn't believe him but wasn't in the mood to know the facts, either.

"So, what are you guys up to?" Sam crossed his arms against his chest, looking up at us through the bars of the railing.

I pushed a few loose strands of hair from my face with a tired exhale. "We're looking for anything that can tell us why things out there—" I pointed out the large windows that looked out onto the meadow, "—are changing for the worse. I mean, it's summer and look at it. It's a mess out there." I grimaced as I saw the rain pool in the yard, the temperature never more than fifty.

Sam glanced out the window with little interest, pressing his lips together. "Yes, I know what you mean."

Margriete perked up. "So, it's not just us. You've noticed as well." She narrowed her eyes at him. "Why didn't you say anything?"

Sam's mouth curled and he let out one breathy laugh. "Why do I care what's happening out there? It's not my world."

I stood, gripping the railing in annoyance. "Yeah, but it is underneath all this. What happens here will affect that, too. It has to."

Sam tilted his head. "True."

"Tell us what's happening." I demanded, sensing he was hiding something. "You know. I can tell that you know."

Sam drew in a deep breath, clenching his jaw and letting the air escape from his cheeks as he thought.

"Why won't you just say it?" Margriete barked, growing annoyed. I had sensed a rift with them lately, and I didn't know exactly why.

Sam rolled his eyes. "It's not my place to say." He paused as his eyes grew wide with sarcasm.

Margriete tilted her head, giving him a warning glare that even scared me.

Sam's demeanor changed, as though Margriete had put him in some sort of trance. "But since he won't say it, I guess I will."

"Who won't say it?" I demanded. "Edgar? He knows about this?" I felt my heart sink—he was lying to me. My blood began to boil and the feeling of betrayal from my one true love grew stronger than the feeling of affection I'd previously had.

Sam shrugged as though shrugging off the blame, but I knew my accusations were right. Who else would it be?

I spoke through clenched teeth. "So what is it? What does it all mean? Tell me."

Sam swallowed as though afraid of me and I found myself shocked, wondering how that could be. "Listen, Elly. This isn't my beef, so don't blame the messenger, okay?"

"I won't." I seethed. I felt my body grow hot with anger and deception.

The smile returned to his face. "The Earth is dying. I give it a few months." He said it as though it were nothing, and at first I expected him to say he was kidding.

"No. Seriously, Sam. I don't need your excessive exaggerations." I put one hand on my hip in exasperation.

His smile faded, and he looked at me steadily, unflinching. "Elly, I'm not joking." His arms uncrossed as he threw them in the air, defending his comment.

Margriete gasped, bringing her hand to her mouth to silence it.

"What?" I sputtered in disbelief.

"The Earth is *dying*, Elle. *Everything*. The humans have finally done it. They've messed with the balance enough to send it spiraling into destruction." He was quick to lay blame.

"The humans have done nothing!" I was tired of his discrimination towards my kind. It was no one's fault but the gods. It was not I that wished to be created, to then spawn this entire race. The humans were an innocent breed, so self involved that they hardly knew what they had done. When I spoke again, I used his creation against him. "Besides, Sam. You always seem to forget that you were human once," I retorted.

He gave me a half smile. "Why does everyone keep reminding me of this? *Whatever.*"

I rolled my eyes at him.

"Well, is there anything we can do to stop it?" Margriete finally spoke.

Sam raised one eyebrow, looking up at us.

"There is, isn't there?" I put both hands on the rail, leaning toward him with hope. "Why else would you know unless there is? Why else would you act so relaxed about the whole thing?"

"*Touché.*" Sam pointed directly at me, winking one eye.

"What?" I demanded. "There is?" I hadn't really expected him to give it up so freely.

It was then that I heard heavy footsteps descending the stairs in the hall and we all froze. Sam turned and watched Edgar step with elegance and power, then turned back to me where he brought his finger to his lips, telling me to keep quiet on the subject—but why? What was Edgar hiding? Why was he doing this to me? Edgar placed one foot on the black granite of the entry, noticing us as we all stared at him with blank eyes.

He glared at Sam, and Sam shrugged. Edgar then looked at me. "What?" he asked, feeling the blame we all had put on him.

I steeled my spine, swallowing my hatred for him and hoping he couldn't read my mind as Sam could. I quickly tried to stash away every thought, just in case. "Nothing." I forced a smile, not knowing whether he was the enemy in this situation or an ally.

Edger looked us all in the eye, one by one, before slowly nodding and pointing toward the kitchen. "Just going to get Henry a snack." Henry popped his head around the corner where he stood on the floor, letting out a loud shriek, causing us all to cringe and cover our ears. Edgar looked at Henry. "What he said." He then turned on his heel, and marched into the kitchen.

We all exhaled simultaneously.

Do I need to fear him? I thought, hoping Sam was listening.

Sam shook his head.

Can he hear my thoughts like you can? He was looking back and forth at both Margriete and I.

"No—to both of you," he spoke. "You two are a lot alike, you know that?"

Margriete and I looked at each other and giggled, but it quickly faded as the mood fell somber.

So the world really is dying? I looked back at Sam.

He nodded. "But don't worry. In due time, you will get your answers. There are things we can do to stop it."

I pouted. "Like what?" My voice was loud, and both Sam and Margriete hushed me, both looking toward the kitchen through the small window in the wall of the library that looked into the sitting room adjacent.

"Right now isn't the time, okay?" Sam put one hand up to silence me, pressing the point.

I gave up, settling for the vague answers and looking out the window toward the field and trees, now seeing their sadness and their death. Margriete grabbed my arm and pulled my attention away from them, smiling.

"It doesn't seem there is anything we can do right now, Elly. Sam made it seem like the answers will come soon enough. There's no point in worrying about the things we can't control."

I exhaled. "I know, Margriete. But aren't you scared? We're dying—all of us."

Margriete gave me a sarcastic face. "Elle, really. You're overreacting."

"Why shouldn't I? We should *all* be overreacting!" I hissed.

Margriete nodded slowly. "I'll try to ask Sam more later on. Perhaps he'll tell me." She seemed doubtful of her statement.

"Are you and Sam alright?" I had to ask.

Margriete looked shocked by my question. "Yeah! Why?" Now she was the one overreacting.

I looked in the direction of the kitchen, dropping it. "Do you think I should ask Edgar?"

Margriete shrugged. "It's worth a try, but be careful. You know their temper." She seemed bitter when she said it, leaving me with bits and pieces about their relationship that I could put together on my own. "And besides, Sam didn't say anything in front of Edgar for a reason, so... I don't figure it's something to talk to him about. He might snap."

I laughed. "I can handle it, trust me."

"Shall we clean up all this?" She looked down at the piles of books.

"Yeah." I knelt down and began to gather them, placing them back onto the shelves. I blew off each cover, moving pile to pile. It was then that I picked up a red book and dusted it off, suddenly intrigued by the title: *Armageddon*.

"Did you pull this one?" I showed it to Margriete and she narrowed her eyes, putting a book on the shelf before giving me her full attention.

"Oh, I guess I did." She let out an uneasy laugh. "Sort of fitting, isn't it?"

"That's what I thought." I pulled it to my chest, feeling the tonnage of the subject in my hands. "I think I'll keep this one."

Margriete shook her head in disbelief as her hair fluttered around her. "Not a bad idea."

I stacked it with the iridescent book about our kind, and set it aside. After placing all the books back on the shelves,

Margriete and I both looked at each other as our stomachs growled in unison. We laughed for a moment and then slowly headed down the ladder to the kitchen to rummage for some food, the supplies getting lower every day.

We found the room empty, leaving me secretly disappointed. What had happened to Edgar and I? What had happened to the fairy tale love that seemed to bloom before? It was as though he no longer missed me as he had, the intoxicating touch we once shared, the electricity of our existence. I used to hover in that dream world forever, and a part of me still wished I was without our soul. I wished I could depend on him again, like before.

Margriete dropped a copper pan onto the granite floor, the sound reverberating in my ears, bringing me back to the present. I shook away my sadness, feeling more independent with every day I spent in this separation with Edgar.

I sighed, opening a cabinet. I began to push around empty boxes, hearing only bits of grain or crackers rattling inside. Today was eventful, despite the tension that had grown even thicker. Later I would confront Edgar—I had to. His ignorance and distance had infuriated me for the last time and I would not allow it to continue. What Matthew had done to Margriete was never far from my thoughts, leaving me hoping that Edgar was not headed for the same jealous doom.

I finally found a can toward the back of the cabinet, heavy with it's contents. "Here." I tossed it to Margriete.

She caught it behind her back with one hand, as though she'd expected me to throw it. I laughed.

She poured the contents into the copper pan and placed it by the fire. When it began to bubble around the edges she poured the soup into two bowls, too anxious to wait for a rolling boil. Besides, it was always too hot that way.

As Margriete and I chatted over the meal, I saw in her the best friend I had always wanted, and the family to love. Though Edgar was stuck somewhere I could not see, I knew I would have her at my side, like a sister. The coming task sat in the pit of my stomach like a ball of dough I could not yet digest. I was not ready to lose this again, and I sensed that what was coming was bound to be my fight—yet again. I had faced one challenge after the other in this world, and though I had never asked for it, it was my burden to bear.

VISITOR

Edgar

"What are you reading?" I walked through the door of Elle's room where she lay on her bed. Her feet where crossed at her ankles and a she had a book in hand, resting on her stomach. Seeing her like that made a small flicker in my heart ignite, my mind flashing back to when she used to gaze upon me with such adoration. She glanced away from the page and at me, her eyes full of disdain. I felt an invisible knife stab my heart.

I was acutely tuned into her movements as her lips parted and she spoke. "A book." She looked away from me and back to the page. I was no more than a fly on the wall to her—an annoyance. I began to wonder what Sam had told her, wondered if she knew just how much of a scum bag I really was.

"Well, I can see that," I replied, trying to laugh to lighten the mood, but I got no reaction. I locked my hands behind my back and sauntered across the room, feeling awkward and unwelcome. Reaching her bed, I bent down and tried to kiss her on her forehead, hoping that at least that would work. She shied away from me, not even bothering to give me as much as a polite decline.

I felt my bones fill with fury as I exhaled and stepped back. "Okay. What did I do?"

"Nothing." Her voice was sharp.

I tried to decipher her reply, cursing the female mind for being so full of loaded remarks. "Okay. So if I did nothing, why are you mad?"

She slammed the book shut and rolled her eyes, her body now rigid with anger. "Exactly, Edgar. You did *nothing*," she snapped. Her voice was low and contained.

I nodded, remembering that remark and noting that it literally meant, *'nothing.'*

Elle sat up, placing her bare feet on the floor. She stood on her toes, her nose just inches from mine. My lips quivered, longing to grab her and kiss away our aggressions, but I knew that now was not that sort of time. She pointed her finger between us, treating it like a fence. I looked down at the book in her other hand, recognizing the fiery red of the cover as my stomach sank. *Sam had told her.*

"You know about all this, don't you?" Her arm flailed as she slammed the book against my chest. Air heaved from my lungs. I took it in my hands, looking at the cover though there was no need. I already knew what it was.

"Elle, I—" I didn't know exactly what Sam had told her,

so I tried to remain vague. "What did Sam say?"

She blew up then, shaking with anger and grumbling like a mad woman. "It doesn't matter what *Sam* said, Edgar. You lied to me. Why didn't you want to tell me the world is *dying?*"

I took a deep breath, rolling the thoughts over in my mind as I looked up and out her dark windows. The rain streaked down the glass at a slant, the wind howling around the invisible peaks of the house. I struggled to find something to say as anxiety rippled through my bones. What was the right thing?

I finally parted my lips, trying to steady their shaking, to hide my sadness. "It wasn't time for you to know yet." I winced as I said it, knowing how arrogant that sounded and knowing she would have a remark.

"Wasn't time yet for me to know? Who are you to decide when I come to know of things? Especially something this big! Edgar, you cannot hope to keep me safe by leaving me in the dark like this!" I watched her lip tremble as mine was. "I fear what you are becoming, Edgar. I fear that you'll be just like *Matthew."*

My jaw clenched as the name filled the room. Just watching her innocent rosy lips form the syllables pained me. She did not deserve what he'd done to her, to us. I swallowed hard, trying to get rid of the bitter taste his name gave me.

In truth, I did see her side of it. I had all along. The reality of the matter was that there was no real explanation as to why I hadn't told her, other than my own selfish jealousy. Thinking it made me see the Matthew in myself. I felt like stabbing my own heart. The look on her face was one I had never wished to see when referring to me. I had always wanted her view of me to remain pristine, keep her madly in love with me. But then, what was I doing?

"I'm sorry, Elle." The word stuck in my throat, coming out in a hoarse whisper.

"You're *sorry!*" she screamed, pushing me in her anger.

I grunted, surprised to find myself flying through the air and landing on the floor a few feet away. I slid a few feet before coming to a stop, slamming against the wall. As I did, I thought about how startled I was to be in this position.

Elle gasped and brought her hand to her mouth, her expression horrified and her hand shaking.

I propped my hands under my body and sat up.

Elle took one step forward, her hand still over her mouth in surprise. "Edgar, I—" She let out one flabbergasted breath. "I'm so sorry. I... I never thought I could do that. I—"

A smile began to form on my face. Our argument had reached a breaking point. I saw her fear subside as she watched me. "Elle, it's okay. I deserved that."

She ran toward me and knelt down, her eyes checking over my whole body and straightening my coat. "Oh, Edgar, I'm so sorry—"

Her touch was almost unbearable as my body reacted in delight, attuned to the aggression of what had just occurred.

I grabbed her face and stared into her eyes. "Elle, I'm sorry. I know I've lied. I was jealous and selfish."

She ran her hand down my arms, adding to my desire. "How did I do that?" she whispered. "I thought you were stronger than me?" She straddled me now, her legs tight around mine.

She clearly no longer cared that I had lied to her, too distracted by the fact that for the first time, she had managed to overpower me. "Elle, it's just—"

There was a sudden crashing noise in the hall, and I exhaled, cursing whatever it was for stealing this moment from me. Elle's legs got tighter as the whole house shook, creaking as though the wind was tumbling it across the meadow.

"*What was that?*" Elle sunk to the floor beside me.

I further cursed myself. There was no hope for reconciling the moment.

Elle grabbed my arm as though I could protect her, though we both knew that it was likely her future had already made her stronger than me.

"I don't know." I sensed something in the air, something familiar. It was then that I heard the music begin to play, a light violin that was accompanied by a flute. I rolled my eyes and pushed myself off the floor, offering Elle my hand as she took it. I pulled her back to her feet and we both regained our composure.

We walked to the door, cautious. Elle hid behind my back, her head peeking around my shoulder. When we reached the door, I opened it and we both looked out. I scanned the space. Margriete and Sam were in the hallway downstairs, both as frozen in shock as we were. Elle looked to Sam and Margriete as they looked up at us, their eyes searching ours for answers, but there were none.

I whispered down to Sam. "What's going on?"

Sam blinked a few times, setting his mouth into a straight line and shrugging.

Opening the door another few inches, Elle and I both now saw that the bookshelf at the top of the stairs, where Edgar Poe's book once resided, had toppled over. Books were thrown across the landing and strewn down the stairs, decorating the room with words.

Sam stood on his toes to try and see what I had, his angle from below skewing his view. Margriete changed into a cat, running up the stairs, the pads of her feet keeping her steps quiet. She sniffed the books and then looked at Elle and me with wonder.

There was a crackling then, and our eyes shot to the wall where the shelf had previously been. Something began to grow there, like a plant, though not quite that organic. Our mouths fell open in amazement.

"Edgar, *look*!" Elle pointed from behind me and over my shoulder, also seeing what I had.

We both watched in amazement as the thing continued to grow and something that resembled brass popped from the wall, finishing the transformation as it all stopped. We stood in awe, Sam staring at me as he remained out of the loop. *There's a door,* I thought, keeping him informed. There was a door, a big red one, now filling the wall were the bookcase had previously been.

Elle's fingers dug into my skin. "What is it?" she whispered.

Smoke began to billow from the jamb in thick ringlets, filling the air with the scent of tobacco. The violin and flute that we had heard before began to play for a second time, still muffled by the intricately carved red door.

"Edgar, what is it?" Elle shook me gently, asking for a second time as though I had the answers.

I swallowed hard, knowing exactly what it was as the scent and sound was something I could never forget. "I don't know," I replied falsely, not wanting to face the facts. I was hoping that if I disregarded it, it would go away, and Elle and I could go back to what we were doing.

Feeling the need to take control, I took one step forward. Sam followed my lead and began to climb the stairs, meeting Margriete as she remained in her feline form.

"Stop," I hissed. I put my hand up and they halted. "Let Elle and I handle this."

I saw Sam smirk as he reached down, scooping Margriete into his hands. He was glad to see me snap out of my vegetative trance, so he didn't interject. Margriete gave him a curious but angered look of disapproval, her tail twisting back and forth and her claws extending into Sam's arms. Margriete did not like being told what to do about as much as Elle did, so I understood her anxiety.

I was so caught up in what Sam and Margriete were thinking that I hardly noticed as Elle pushed past me, taking the lead. Her face was fixed on the door, her arm behind her placed firmly against my chest, preventing me from getting ahead of her.

Without hesitation, she walked straight up to the door and grabbed the handle, inspecting its brilliance for a moment. Her other hand was resting against the wood, as though testing the temperature. She leaned in and placed her ear against it, her breathing shallow as she listened.

With a frustrated face, she pulled back, her hand still on the handle of the door. Steamy marks began to outline her grasp, her heart beat drumming in my head. She took one last deep breath before twisting the handle and pushing in, no longer faltering and ready to face whatever was on the other side.

I thought of her journey into Heaven then, wishing I was there to watch as she grew from a scared little eighteen-year-old girl into the strong woman I had always known, the strong woman I now saw.

My jaw clenched as smoke billowed from the door, washing over her in a wave of white and filling the hall with a noxious gas. Margriete sneezed in Sam's arms. Elle fanned her face. Her eyes were narrow as the smoke surely stung them, as it did mine. I looked to Sam one last time, seeing he was poised and anxious, on guard if we needed him. He nodded to me, allowing me to take control of the situation and be Elle's guardian for now.

Elle did not bother to look at me as she took a step forward and in, disappearing as the smoke engulfed her. I exhaled and followed her as I too stepped over the threshold, the smoke seeming to suck me in with open arms. I felt the thick smell of cigar fill my lungs, burning any taste bud I had left and making the air thick to breathe. Coughing the air out, I stopped breathing all together. I brought my hand to my mouth to cover it, batting away the smoke with my other. There was no need for me to breathe anyway, but it was a hard habit to break. The violin and flute continued to play, and as Elle halted before me, the smoke cleared and my eyes finally met those of our visitor.

"Hello!" His voice echoed off the walls of the small addition to our home, the smoke continuing to dissipate as though it were being sucked from the room.

I assessed the situation, seeing the grey stone walls spanned about fifteen feet all around. There was a pedestal on top which sat a red velvet throne chair, gilded in gold around the edges. I laughed to myself, recognizing and knowing how this particular visitor enjoyed a bit of drama. In my experience, he had always been the thespian, and as such, life in Heaven had reflected that. I was relived in knowing, no longer wondering what other possible threat it could be—this one could be contained.

I walked up beside Elle, turning to look at her. Her face was solemn and hard, my previous joy now fading.

Elle stood tall, her feet planted firmly on the ground. The god she had so despised was now sitting before us, invading our home. He leaned casually on the arm of the red velvet chair, three feet above us. He seemed cheerier than normal, but I suppose to intrude on us like this, he had to act like a pleasant guest. I watched him with a face that mimicked Elle's, trying my best to be supportive and gain back her trust. Smoked seeped from his mouth as he chuckled, blending with his long white beard, a smell that I was certain was impossible to wash out.

"I thought you promised to leave us alone?" Elle's voice was unlike anything I had heard before—a murderous rage coating every word in vengeance.

Chills racked my dead body as I looked at her with shock. She did not look back.

The god laughed louder now. "I did say that, didn't I? But, I did not say for how long." He looked amused by his reply as he narrowed his eyes. He chewed on the end of the cigar, leaving a film of glistening spit on the roughened tobacco leaves.

I could feel the anger emanate from Elle's body, filling my own heart with a hate I only felt in the darkest of times. She shifted her weight, like a lion does before a kill. I swallowed hard, memories of death rushing back to me as I took in the god's face.

When I had woken in Heaven, before I was sent home, this god was the first I had seen. He made me promise that I would condition Elle for his arrival and I feared now what he would do to me, knowing that I hadn't fulfilled his wishes. The old man looked at me then, as though he knew what I was thinking.

He raised one eyebrow as a half smile wrinkled his face. *"Hmmm."* His voice was deep as it echoed off the stone walls of the small space. I was afraid, something foreign to me.

I shifted my weight, feeling a cold tremble begin to form under my shirt. I did not fear much in this world, but after what they had done to me, I did fear them. As far as I knew, this old man was the leader. The god of god's, so to speak. Elle took a threatening step toward him then. Without thinking, I reached out and grabbed her arm. I tried to pull her back but she only looked at me with disdain, ripping her arm from my grasp as she slid with ease through my fingers.

"Oh, ha ha!" The god laughed, enjoying the tension between Elle and I.

She spun back to face the old man, in no apparent mood to entertain him. "I may not know you very well—" She marched up to the pedestal, her gaze even with his chest as she stood tall. As the thespian, he had chosen to sit in a raised position. It was just enough to create a sense of intimidation, but that didn't seem to faze Elle. "But I do know that you are a spineless excuse for a leader."

I winced, fearing her words and what they would do. I prayed that there wouldn't be a fight. I was not in the mood.

The old man laughed. "Please, my child. *Spineless?* Call me Nicholas instead."

"I do not care what your name is, nor do you deserve to

be addressed by one." Elle spat at his feet.

I cowered in fear. *"Elle, don't,"* I whispered under my breath.

She turned to me, hearing my words. "What?" Her eyes were raging. I found then, that for the first time, I was the weakest person in the room. *"He has no right to be here!"* she hissed.

I looked at Nicholas, and then back at Elle. "Well—"

Elle stormed back toward me. "Well, *what*, Edgar? Is this another secret of yours, a lie? I suppose this spineless cretin vacations here regularly, does he?"

"Well, no." I tried to defend myself, but I saw there was little I could say. For Elle, my excuses no longer held any clout.

Nicholas watched us with a delighted smile on his face, inspecting his nails as he leaned comfortably in his chair.

Elle gave me one last warning glare, looking to Nicholas instead. "Why are you here? Answer me now!" She stomped her foot.

Nicholas chuckled once before taking a deep breath, exhaling away the humor. "I see that Edgar has not told you! This is absolutely delightful. Bravo!" He began to clap, his gold rings clanking together.

Elle did not look surprised by his answer, and I felt heartbroken. I knew she had expected it. So much for reconciliation.

"Your Edgar here was given specific instructions to prepare you for my arrival." Nicholas rolled his eyes and lifted his chin, his cheeks now rosy. "But I suppose you can't trust anyone to carry out even the simplest of tasks these days." He yawned, allowing his hand to wave through the air.

His remark sent me into further guilt and turmoil.

"Since he has not filled you in on your intended task, or rather fate, then I will." Nicholas sat up, blotting out his cigar on the armrest of the chair, his brows poised. He cleared his throat and licked his lips. "There is a prophecy here for you." He waved his hands around in front of him, gesturing toward the house. "It is important you see it. There, you will find exactly what you need for this task."

Elle was concentrating hard. "A prophecy?" I saw the wonder in her face.

"Yes, dear." The god exhaled, now bored. "A *prophecy*." He was bitter, knowing that it came from Fate.

Elle looked down at the ground for a moment, then back to the god. "What task?" She was full of questions. "I promised you *nothing*. And if you can remember, I bargained that you would stay away from the surface of this world. Yet, here you are, as though those words meant nothing."

He laughed whole-heartedly. "My dear! Those words did mean nothing. How can you prove you even said them at all?" He tilted his head, glaring with one eye.

Elle growled at him, her teeth grinding as the sound edged in my ears. "Then why should I help you? Why, when you're nothing but a back stabber?"

He looked angry that she would defy him to such

degrees. "You will because you have no choice in the matter, dear child. You must do this task." The god's spine was stiff with anger.

She frowned. "Then I will ask once more, *what task?*" she yelled, causing the god to lean back and away from her.

After a pause, he laughed again, as though unsure just what to do: kill her or tell her. "*What task?* My child! You are to save us all! Only *you* can."

Elle's face sank, and I could hear her heart begin to race in the depths of our soul. "Me? Why me?" Her voice was breathy and scared. Her eyes darted about the room.

My nostrils flared. I wanted to comfort her, to tell her I was sorry. It was me that was meant to give her the news—not him. From my mouth it would have been better. At least then it wouldn't have seemed like a death sentence."

"You are the last pure child of Earth. The last that can give life," Nicolas answered with a smile, as though it wasn't true that his life and his world, was also in danger.

"What about you? You made us, so you should be the one to save us as well." She pointed her finger at him and I watched as her hand shook.

Nicholas's face grew solemn. "I could, but that would result in my death. I am not willing to die and allow all of you to live. *Ha!* Imagine, Nicholas the philanthropist saint! Not for me. I am far too shellfish for that. This is my world, after all. The creator should not be the one that dies. Besides, there is no guarantee that if I did try, that it would even work!"

Elle shook her head, her eyes beginning to water. "No—" I saw her stubbornness return. "No, I will not do this. I cannot do this."

"But you can." His voice dropped. "And you *will*." Nicholas stood on his pedestal now. "I will only warn you once, my child. If you do not do this now, then I will kill Edgar before this world does, and by doing so, you will be cursed to live an eternity as an empty soul. You will be doomed to roam the galaxies of this universe without a home, and with no one but yourself to comfort you."

Elle's fists were stiff at her sides, the blood running out of them as she squeezed as tight as she could. It was sadistic to think, but that simple gesture filled me with hope. She still loved me, despite my lies.

"You see, I can still bargain with you after all." Nicholas's smile returned to his face as she looked down his nose at her, his hands grasping the hem of his robes.

"But there is not enough time," Elle pleaded, her grip relaxing back to fear.

Nicholas tilted his head. "I suggest you get started then."

Elle said nothing, but was never given the chance even if she did. In a sudden pop, Nicholas had disappeared, leaving a swirling cloud of smoke behind him as the snuffed cigar fell to the ground. Elle broke down then, falling to her knees and putting her face in her hands.

"Elle, I—" I walked up behind her and tried to comfort

her by placing my hand at the base of her neck.

She spun away from me onto the floor. "You've done plenty of damage, Edgar. It's bad enough that all you are is a bargaining chip to be used against me. Let alone the fact that I am all alone because *you* refuse to help." Her voice became low. "So do me a favor, Edgar. Quit getting in my way." Her face held little emotion or color.

She stood then, storming past me as she flung the door open and exited into the hall. I followed, watching with a broken heart as she was met with open arms by Sam and Margriete. Their faces held anger as they looked at me, adding to the burn, the hatred for myself growing.

Why hadn't I done something? Why? Why did I let her fall to the mercy of this god?

I brought one hand to my dead chest, feeling only her heart beating, alone and scared.

CLEAR HEAD
Estella

Margriete and Sam released me from their hug. I looked Sam in the eyes, telling him with my thoughts where I was going. I had to get away. I needed some space to sort this all out. Sam nodded and gave me a sad smile. Without glancing at Edgar, I stormed down the stairs and to the front door, not bothering to find a coat—too angry to even care. I grabbed the handle as I lifted my gaze to look out the window at the stormy meadow beyond. The yellowing grasses swirled in the wind and rain, beckoning me toward them, whispering for help.

I watched the grasses get thrown about like helpless victims, my heart breaking, and my eyes filling with tears. With my hand still on the handle, I turned and looked over my shoulder, looking at Edgar, showing him what I felt. He had forced me into this situation, purposefully made it harder on me. That was not an act of love, but an act of jealousy. I scowled, angry that he didn't even bother to stand up to Nicholas, too weak to even resemble the strong man I had once known. I let a lone tear fall and then wiped my eyes to clear my vision. I saw Edgar blink a few times, hiding the fact he was hurt, but I did not care—it felt good to let him wallow.

With one last inhale, I turned back and twisted the handle, the door flying open on a gust of wind. I braced myself against the gusts as the chandelier in the hall filled the room with the sound of tinkling crystal. I quickly changed into a raven, using the loft in the windy air to my advantage. It would be a difficult ride from here to Seattle, but I had the strength of hatred fueling me, plus I needed the time to think.

As I took to the sky, I heard the door to the house slam behind me. I cut up and over the trees, following the same river that had brought me here two years ago. I watched as the blue grey water crashed below me, the rapids swollen with mud and debris. The dam of Lake Diablo loomed behind me, brimming with angered water and threatening to break. Adjusting the feathers on my wings like rudders, the wind carried me down the mountain. I blinked back the rain, streaming it to my feathers, now drenched and heavy. After a while of determined flight, the river finally spilled into the Puget Sound, the San Juan Islands speckling the enraged ocean below. I marveled at the color of the water, a deep turquoise as it churned like a whirlpool.

I tilted and followed the mouth of water south, keeping my eyes on the roughened shoreline. I flew over spent fields where tulips once thrived and rivers with swollen banks of mud that now engulfed the low-lying towns, leaving nothing but rooftops. Cows were gathered on hillsides that were surrounded by water, and as the country disappeared, I saw more and more cars littered across the roads, abandoned and gathered by the flash floods that had plagued the area.

I was shocked to see that it had gotten this bad—horrified by what had become of the place I had once called home. I had avoided it for so long, scared away by the memories and false existence I had lived here, lost and alone. I had avoided visiting my dear friends out of selfish fear, but I now ran to them, because I did not know where else to go and I did not know who else would even care.

Scott and Sarah had moved back to the city after the wedding, taking the money I had given them and investing in a small house on the hillsides of Seattle that was in one of the old neighborhoods. It was a place I was thankful they had invested in, high above the swelling waters and hopefully still safe from the wind.

Ahead, the port-side piers I had once visited every day came into view, but their docks were well under water, the roofs now peeking above the waves. I circled around the Space Needle, the blinking red light that once was so reliable now smothered out, the tip of it leaning as the whole structure began to sink into the sodden ground below. Long strips of black pavement were left cracked and barren, reminders of the structure that once existed here.

The city ahead was dark and abandoned. The once-busy streets were desolate as the air teemed with the sweet smell of wet cement. I circled back and over Lake Washington, the body of water that separated Seattle from the main land, connected only by two floating bridges that had blown away and sunk into the water.

Scott and Sarah had gotten a house that looked away from the Sound, on the protected side of the hill where the wind seemed calmer. They looked over Lake Washington, now resembling an ocean as the waves rose to twenty feet. I dove down, looking from house to house, trying to recall the color from the pictures they had sent me in the mail.

It was a small cream, Tudor-style home, with a round window over the door and a copper overhang. It was in need of remodeling, but it didn't matter to them. They had a home and that was enough. When they'd gotten it, I remember wondering how much had been in that envelope from my foster mother and how it was that Heidi had managed to afford it. I was the only child she had ever loved like a daughter, and perhaps in that love, she had found family.

As payback, I had sent her something in return, packaging up one of my many Van Eyck paintings and having it delivered. She was the one that had taught me to live, to breathe again. She was the only one that had faith in me when no one else did. I knew Heidi would have never accepted her money back, so the priceless painting was the perfect answer. I should have never abandoned her as I had—it was selfish of me, and cruel. If she had loved me like family, then why had I thrown that love away when I knew it was something to value? The answer was clear, though. I needed to find myself in order to love again, and I had.

I felt guilt fill my heart. Why hadn't I gone back? I wondered what she had thought of me and the painting. Had she wondered if I'd stolen it? Had she really worried about me like a mother would? I closed my eyes and shook my head, the rain splashing away and around me. When I opened them, there it was: the Tudor with the round window. It was facing the street directly below, right next to what looked like a park, or at least what used to be.

I dove down, leaving my guilt for Heidi behind and promising to see her in the end, when all was well. I aligned myself with the street and landed on the bare branches of a tree in their front yard. Looking to the windows, I saw a warm organic glow emanating from inside. I yearned to be near it, my wings trembling from the cold.

The tree below me slowly groaned and moved then, its bare branches curling toward me in desperation. With horror, I drew my attention away from the house and to the street. The neighboring trees had all been chopped down, leaving nothing but severed stumps. Following the sidewalk and down to the end of the street, I saw a pile of fire wood was stacked in the road.

What were they doing? I asked myself. They were speeding up the process. I looked back at the house, seeing the warm glow flicker once more. It was then that I realized they had no choice. Could I blame them? The humans needed warmth to survive, the trees sacrificed in their attempt to stay warm. I blinked hard, trying to justify it but finding it hurt something deep inside. I felt the same way I did about the trees as I did human flesh, and to me, it was still murder.

The tree under my feet branched out toward me, running a tip through my feathers with affection. A tear fell from my eye and over my beak, landing on the sodden wood where it sprouted a young green leaf. The tree acted surprised, the branch shaking with what I hoped was joy. I let out a happy cry, but as the whole tree began to shake, I started to worry. I pulled my wings from my sides to balance myself, the tree rocking and twisting from side to side. It was then that the whole tree popped with life in a sudden display of color and light. Sprouts shot up between my talons and I found myself dodging away from them, the tips exploding with flowers and leaves, like tiny fireworks.

How, why? My heart was racing, my wings tented on either side. *Was I stronger here?* This had never happened before, and never with such an abrupt reaction.

The front door to the Tudor swung open as the door slammed against the frame of the house. A figure wrapped in a plaid blanket ran out, halting as it saw me and then continuing forward. The wind howled around me as the figure stumbled up to the tree, their boots sliding on the dead wet leaves that coated the sidewalk.

"Elle!" I heard my voice between gusts of wind, the

figure's mouth moving. They drew closer, pulling the blanket from their head, revealing the thinned face of Sarah.

I let out one sharp *caw*, letting go of the tree and diving to land on the ground before her. I slipped out of my changeling, standing before her as rain streamed down my numb face.

"Elle!" she yelled again and ran to me, wrapping her arms around me like a vice.

"Sarah, how are you?" I pressed my hand against her back, feeling that she had definitely grown thin.

She pulled me away from her. "Oh, you know. Doing the best we can." She pointed over my shoulder and at the tree. "I saved it for you. I wouldn't let them take it." Her cheeks were rosy as she smiled.

I looked back at the tree, seeing now that it really was the only one left on the street. "Thank you, Sarah!" I was yelling over the wind.

She smiled, taking my arm and pulling me toward the house. "Come in. I'll make you some hot water."

I nodded. "Thank you."

I stepped up onto the porch as the door rapped against the siding, wind swirling freely into the house. As we crossed the threshold, the howling in my ears subsided, leaving them ringing. Scott stood to the left with blankets in hand as Sarah yanked the door shut with all her strength.

"Here." He shoved one toward me, wrapping it over my shoulders before also surrounding me in a hug.

"Oh, Scott." I pushed away, and looked him in the eyes.

The gentle features of his face had fallen to sadness and fear, his eyes like empty shells. His hair was oily and unwashed, his clothes hanging loosely on his body.

"Elle, what is this?" Scott asked, referencing the storm outside.

Sarah locked the dead bolt with a heavy clank. "What's happening?" She chimed in.

I sighed. "I'll explain, but first, how are you?" My main concern at this point was them. "You look—" I thought of the right thing to say, but found none. In the woods, food was still somewhat available, especially when Edgar and Sam didn't eat. In the city, however, panic had set in, and all attempts to remain productive, seemed to have failed.

"We're surviving. We've rationed a lot, and it seems we'll last about another few weeks. After that, though, I don't know what we'll do." I saw him try to smile, making light of the situation. "Heck of a way to go on a diet." He tried to laugh then, but I didn't find it funny. "How's Edgar?" He changed the subject.

"Edgar's fine." There was contempt in my voice and I was certain they had heard it.

"Are you hungry?" Sarah asked as she laid the wet blanket over the banister of the stairway in the hall.

"Oh—no. You keep that for yourselves. I'm quite all right." In truth I was hungry, but so were they. I would deal.

They led me to the left toward the source of the light and warmth I had seen outside. I saw the fire, trying to ignore what burned there. The fire back home was charmed with never ending logs that never burned out, much like the candles on the wall.

"Here, sit." Scott motioned me to a couch by the fire, the crackling wood causing the hairs on my arms to rise.

I sat and Sarah handed me a steaming mug of water. "I apologize if it tastes a bit off. It's from the lake. So we boil it here." She showed me a pot that was hanging over the fire. "Much like your place, right?" She smiled, seeing the upside of all this.

I laughed uneasily. "Yes, I suppose."

I slowly took in the room, seeing that it did indeed need some love and attention. Wallpaper was peeling from the walls and the wood framing was dented and old. Every painted surface was crackling apart, begging to be sanded. The fireplace was nice and made of a heavy stone, certainly something that had come in handy.

I stopped inspecting the space, knowing that now was hardly the time to even think of remodeling. The thought of it alone made the blackness in my soul flicker back to me as it once had. If I stayed in a positive mindset, I could do as Nicholas demanded. I needed to keep looking forward, not back.

They both watched me with anxious eyes, waiting for me to speak.

Sarah opened her mouth, but then shut it. She looked perplexed, if not a little nervous. She shifted in her seat, her back straight. She blinked a few times and then opened her mouth once more. "So, what's happening?" This was the third time now that they had asked, and I didn't blame them. They were frightened.

I took a sip of the water, holding it in my mouth as the musty flavor of it made me want to gag. I forced it down my throat with one loud gulp. "Yes—" My voice cracked in disgust. "Yes. It's dying."

"The Earth?" Sarah screeched. She cut right to the point.

I nodded.

"I knew it. Didn't I tell you? I was right." Sarah pointed at Scott. "And you thought it was some weird weather pattern that would pass."

Scott glanced at me, embarrassed. "Er, I—I didn't say that." I saw him try to discreetly glare at Sarah, but I caught it.

"It's dying, and there's nothing we can do to stop it." I paused. "Or rather, there's nothing *you* can do." I said the last bit under my breath.

Sarah perked up. "But you *can*. You can save us, right?"

I sank into the seat, holding the warm cup between my hands but refusing to take another sip. "I guess. It's just—"

"Just what? You have to stop this. Why even falter?" Scott looked frantic and scared.

"It's not that I'm faltering, Scott." I looked at Sarah. "It's just that I only just found out. I'm still letting the whole idea sink in."

"Well, who told you?" Sarah's face was white as a ghost.

"One of the gods I had told you about. He came to see me. Told me I had to save the world or he would kill Edgar before the Universe could." I looked down in my lap with shame.

"Again? Well, that's not very nice. I thought you said they were going to leave you alone?" Sarah continued to control the conversation.

"That's what I thought. And now Edgar is lying to me too! He kept this truth from me, or else I would have known sooner and it probably wouldn't have gotten so bad."

Sarah's face began to grow angry. "What an *arse!*"

I couldn't resist a chuckle.

"Why would he lie to you?" Sarah continued to look appalled.

I shrugged. "That's what I don't understand. I just don't see why he hid it from me, other than the fact that maybe he's jealous, but that's absurd! This is the end of the world we're talking about! I feel like telling him to get over himself, and grow up, but he's centuries old! I can't tell him to grow up."

Scott laughed uneasily. "*Men.*"

Sarah glared at him and Scott cowered.

"So, I'm left in the same predicament I started with, saving him to save *them*. But I don't want to save the gods." I wished there was a way to let their world die, but I didn't want that either. I loved Edgar A. Poe, and all the angels. I couldn't do that. Plus, that was Heaven, and it was beautiful.

Sarah thought for a moment. "Well, why don't you bribe them in return?"

Her response was so simple and yet profound at the same time. She was right. I had bribed them before, and in return, they did something no one had ever seen them do before. They had brought Edgar back from the dead, made one of our kind into an angel when we were never meant for that kind of duty.

"Sarah, you're right. But with what?" I began to think. I had already given them the dagger so I had nothing of true value left.

"Well, you said you wanted the gods dead, but what about *banished?*" Sarah looked at me with hopeful eyes.

I shook my head. "That's what I did last time, and it didn't work."

Sarah stood to her feet. "I know that, but that's because you never made them sign a contract." Her legal instincts were taking over.

I rolled my eyes, growing tired of that line.

"Make them sign something—something unbreakable." She jumped in the air. "A spell! Put a spell on it."

I laughed. As absurd as she was, she was right again. What if I promised them that the only way I would save this world was if they vowed to leave it forever? Even me, I would be glad to give up the surface to the human race. Banish all magic to the center of the Earth, to a place you can only dream of, literally.

"Yes, no more magic, no more—" Scott frowned.

"No more *angels*." Sarah finished his sentence, her tone sad.

I licked my lips. "But you could survive like that. You don't need us. I have you two to spread the word when I'm gone, to follow through with the new world."

Sarah nodded. "I would gladly take on that responsibility."

"The god's have ruled over the human race for long enough. It is your turn to take the reins." My voice was full of power and strength.

Scott looked frightened but strong. "I could. We could. All we needed was an eye-opener, and I believe this is it. It's a worldwide famine, a worldwide flood. Everything is knocked out of balance, and as much as we'd like to deny that, it was our fault. We know it's true. If we make it out of this, people will change."

Sarah nodded in agreement.

"Alright." I felt rejuvenated and alive. I hadn't felt this full of purpose since the day I entered the caves. "Then let's do this. Let's make a plan."

We talked for a few more hours and well into the night. The storm raged on outside, racking the house with all its might. Unable to sleep, we talked about the things they would do after I was gone, after I had used whatever power this prophecy had in store for me. They talked about rebuilding, and politics, knowing full well that it was one of the things that had gone wrong with the world.

As the light began to return outside, Sarah yawned and the conversation reached an ending point.

I yawned, too, finding it now contagious. "Well, I better get back. I need to find this prophecy that the old man told me about." I stood, leaving my now-cold mug on a nearby table, still full of lake water.

"Will we see you again?" Sarah grappled my arm.

"I'm sure you will," I reassured her. And I would. I could never bear leaving them without a goodbye.

Sarah smiled and Scott gave me a hug, leading me to the door. We stood there staring at each other for a moment, hearing a crowd of voices outside.

I pressed my brows together. "What's that?"

Sarah tilted her head, moving to the sidelight and pulling back the drape. She gasped, bringing her hand to her mouth as she let the drape fall back into place. Scott grabbed the handle of the door, and as we opened it, Scott and I gasped as well. The tree outside had nearly doubled in size now, surrounded by neighbors, all staring at it as though it were God himself.

"Look at it." Sarah's eyes were fixed, the tree reflecting in her pupils.

The tree was even more brilliant than it had been when I had given it life. Big pink flowers bloomed all over every branch, the leaves a vibrant green. Whatever power I had managed to gain over the past few months, was much more powerful than anything I had experienced before. What was I becoming? I looked down at my hands, remembering how I'd thrown Edgar across the room with little effort. I thought about what Nicholas had told me, about how I was the last, *The One*. Perhaps I had gathered the power of all my kind and all the souls killed off by Matthew. Their empty shells had been left to roam the earth, looking for a place to hide and live. That place had become me.

The wind still howled, though the tree stood still. "It's a sign. I have to do this." I reassured myself. My fists were clenched at my sides.

Scott patted me on my back. "You will, Elle." His gaze never left the tree.

I stepped out onto the porch, walking down the path. The crowd parted as I approached, wondering who I was and why this tree, in front of this house, had bloomed so beautifully.

The crowd whispered around me as I placed my hand on the trunk of the tree, its branches reaching toward me out of appreciation. The bark shook like a wet dog. *"I will be back for all of you."* I leaned close to the tree and whispered before releasing my hand and walking away down the street. The crowd watched me as I turned into a raven, spreading my wings as I turned and looked back at them. The crowd stared in silence, their hands at their sides in amazement. I allowed them to witness it out of hope. One of the last miracles they would see here, and a symbol of their last hope for freedom: the white raven.

ALONE

Edgar

I sat in the quiet of the library, my hands folded on my lap and my eyes staring forward. I hadn't felt this alone since Estella had been taken from me, since before I had ever met Edgar A. Poe. I wish I knew what to do, I wish I had someone that could see where I was coming from, and most importantly, where I needed to go.

I heard a dull ticking and my mind wandered to the sound, wondering where it was coming from. Taking a moment to leave my worries behind, I opened my ears, listening intently to the sound. *'Tick, Tick, Tick.'* I leaned down toward the chest we used as a coffee table that sat right in front of me. Putting my ear to the wood, I listened again. *'TICK, TICK, TICK.'*

Surprised, I brushed all the books off the lid of the chest and to the floor. They landed with a heavy crash. I fiddled with the old lock, unfastening the metal hook and placing my palms against the wood. As I lifted the lid, the ticking sound became clear, no longer muffled by the thick mahogany.

"There you are." I lifted a blanket, uncovering a collection of clocks that had been placed inside. When I had come home, I was not surprised to see them gone. Elle had always hated my obsession with time, and considering all the uproar since I'd been back, I hadn't bothered to look for them.

I looked to the wall where they used to hang, seeing the spot was now occupied by Elle's obsession: the painting. I stared into the faces of our happy group, remembering everything and how far all of this had come. Elle had known about the end then, kept it as our little secret. In that, she knew we would be safe.

I never wanted to believe in the prophecy, and I always doubted it could ever come true, especially when she had been taken from me. I thought that was the end of it. I thought I'd never see her again. I no longer trusted magic after that, but it seems that now, my faith has returned.

I have lived many lives, each one spanning a decade of time, each a reinvention of myself. This new life felt strange, though, the first where I have been forced to hand over the control and give it all to Elle, instead. It was a hard transition for me, but the last true test of my will.

I wiped my mind clear and turned back to the clocks. I carefully looked through the stack, remembering where I had gotten each and treating them with a care Elle hadn't. Toward the bottom of the pile, one clock caught my eye and I slid it from the stack. I brought it to the top before taking it in my hands and pulling it to my face. I sat back and admired it, watching as the second hand ticked in a counterclockwise direction. With a small smile on my face, I remembered Edgar Poe for a second time. He had made me this clock as a sort of joke, saying that it was the one clock that would defy time all together. "Put it next to all your other clocks," he had said.

I jumped then.

"Here you will stay in the same time forever!" A voice in the corner of the library finished my thoughts.

Shocked, I looked up but saw nothing. *"Edgar?"* Was I hearing things? *"Edgar?"* I repeated. I knew the voice well but could not believe what I'd heard. I cursed myself, blaming it on stress and loneliness.

An insane but light laughter filled the room then. "You know me too well, dear friend!"

For a second time I scanned the room, still seeing nothing. There was a crash from the railing above and my eyes shot to the source. I heard the voice again.

"Blast!"

My mouth hung open, my hands on the clock becoming numb. I tried to blink away his image a few times but it didn't budge. *"Edgar?* How did you—"

He brushed himself off as he stood, looking down on me from over the rail. "I was trying to make that a little more graceful, but—I failed."

I was frozen on the spot, still doubting this was really

true. "How are you here? You were, *dead.*"

The aged figure of Edgar threw his hands in the air like a crazy old coot. "Oh, everything is in an uproar. No one notices when an old retired man like me leaves Heaven anymore."

He threw his hands down, circling the upper platform and making his way to the ladder. He struggled as he turned himself around, walking backwards down each rung, having a difficult time finding his footing. Once on the ground, he took one triumphant breath and exhaled.

"There's nothing quite like the air of Earth, eh? Makes me wish I could breathe again!" He walked toward me with a little trot in his step, his wings dangling from his back. "Come on, then! Stand and give your old pal a *hug!*"

I was still stunned as he yanked me from the couch, the clock falling to the ground with a crash. The face cracked. He slammed me against his chest and I grunted. I suddenly found myself engulfed by the smell of burnt bacon and strawberry jam, tickling my nostrils and making my stomach growl with jealousy. "Edgar, I—" My voice was muffled by his wool coat.

"I heard you talking about me, and I figured twice in one day means you are all out of sorts! What's wrong, my little raven?" He shook me. "Why so *doom* and *gloom?*"

I pulled myself out of his grasp, not able to handle another whiff of bacon. "I uh—well." I looked outside. "It *is* sort of doom and gloom, so—"

"Meh!" Edgar bellowed, throwing his hands in the air

yet again.

I jumped, forgetting how eccentric and socially inept he really was.

He scratched his head, causing his pitch black hair to frizz further than it already had. "Don't mean to scare you there, old boy, but I frankly don't care about the weather! I figure I've lived much longer than I ever should have, what will come is just another beginning to me." He stood tall, hooking his fingers into the lapel of his jacket with pride.

I laughed, finally giving in and enjoying his positive outlook on the situation.

"So—" He looked around, rolling onto his toes and then back onto his heels. "Where is that marvelous creation you call *Elle?* Oh, and maybe that funny little boy, what was his name—" his face twisted. "Ah yes! *Scott.*"

I tilted my head in confusion. "Scott? When did you meet him?" I was mildly surprised.

A delighted smile grew across Edgar's face. "Oh, what a wonderful specimen he was! A real dreamer. Right there in my very house, dreaming about me, none the less!" He stood again on his toes and leaned forward in excitement, his eyes crazed.

I let out a sharp grunt. "Scott? A wonderful specimen? I think you may have the wrong kid."

"No, no. *Where is he?*" His eyes were wide and his teeth glimmering like a greedy dog.

"Well, I'm not sure." I had more important things to worry about than the whereabouts of some mere human.

"Oh." Edgar's face sank for a moment before perking back up. "And Elle?"

I rolled my eyes. "Don't get me started." I turned away from him, picking the broken pieces of clock off the floor.

Edgar's mouth curled into a half smile. "A lover's quarrel? How *delightful*. I must say, I do miss those."

I snorted. "I guess you could say it's a quarrel." I was beginning to grow annoyed. "She left."

Edgar turned his head, glaring at me with one eye. "You lied to her, didn't you? Oh! It's the oldest one in the book! Never lie to a woman, mind you."

He walked away toward the shelf, shuffling his feet along the floor and fidgeting with the books.

His energy was making me tense. "I suppose."

"Well," he barked, twisting back to face me. "You should apologize. The whole world is in an uproar over her. She is *The One* after all. Such a wonderful thing!" he sang. His eyes glazed over in thought.

"Why are you here again?" I was done playing games.

Edgar laughed. "Oh, well. I was sent here to collect you."

"*Collect me?* Why? But I haven't even finished—"

"Well, time does not wait for procrastinators." He shook his finger at me before turning to look at the bookshelf, running his hand along the spines. "Trust me, I know."

"Who says?" I demanded, letting my irritation come through in my tone of voice.

"One of the god's! That really bratty looking woman,

gorgeous, but boy she's a *real*—"

"Why her? What's her problem?" I was enraged, remembering the god, *Ariana*.

"My guess is she's jealous of Elle. Doesn't want her to succeed." Edgar shrugged. "She was awful spiteful about the whole situation, really. Dreadfully out of sorts, that one is."

I lifted my brows. "I know what you mean," I muttered under my breath. "Doesn't she know that by keeping me here, that's actually doing more harm to Elle's advancement? Wouldn't she want me to stay, then?"

Edgar turned to me, raising one brow. "Really? Why? Oh, this is a regular ol' mix-up, isn't it?" His black eyes glittered.

"It doesn't matter why." I thought hard. "What happens if I just don't go with you?"

Edgar shrugged. "She'll want to kill you? I mean, I don't know. I did my part, so…"

I knew why Ariana was jealous. It was because she liked me. When Elle was taken, Ariana had tried to take her place with little success. She was the one I tried to love but couldn't, and she never got over that. She could never let go.

I pursed my lips. "She's just trying to dig her claws in one last time. Ignore her." I blew it off.

Edgar jumped, throwing me off subject. "Oh, look! It is one of my books!" Apparently he had dropped the subject, too.

"Will you stay for a while?" I added, being polite, though I wasn't sure how much I could handle. I was now quickly regretting my earlier statements about missing him.

Edgar pulled the book from the shelf with delight, opening to a random page and reciting the words under his breath with a childish look on his face. When he wasn't talking he hummed, and when he wasn't humming, some other form of noise managed to escape his body.

"Edgar? Did you hear me?" I took one step toward him, trying to discreetly fan the flatulent air.

He waved me away. "Oh, *yes, yes.*"

He slammed the book shut and I jumped.

"Do you have any *cookies?*" His eyes got wide.

I pressed my brows together, wondering if he had indeed lost his mind after all this time. "Perhaps."

"That would be lovely. I'll take five, with a glass of cream, please." He began to sing now, trotting to a nearby chair to sit. "I'll just wait for Elle's return, then."

"Well, you may be waiting a while," I mumbled under my breath, walking toward the kitchen. Luckily, he hadn't heard me.

I exhaled as I walked into the warm room, heat radiating from the fire. I ran my hand along the copper counter as I made my way to the cabinet where Elle hid all her sugary snacks. The very place where I, too, used to hide my sweets that were now no longer something I could enjoy. I rummaged through the boxes, finding half eaten cookies in each. As I rummaged some more, I thought I heard a sound so I stopped, listening with my hand inside a bag of mint chocolate rounds. As I stood there, hearing nothing but my own breath, I then stopped breathing altogether, listening more intently as the feeling in my soul began to burn.

Elle was back.

I dropped the bag of cookies on the counter, abandoning the mess and rushing toward the front hall. I did not yet know what I would say, but I had to see her. Feeling this way was beginning to make my chest grow tight with emotion, and I hated it.

My eyes met Elle's and she froze. For a minute we just stood there, like two statues in the yard. I watched her breathe, measuring her emotions and wondering what she would say. She was soaking wet, the rain dripping from sodden strands of silky white hair. The water glistened on her skin, lighting her eyes. I was surprised by how much I already missed her face, my need for her reminding me of our inevitable love.

"Elle, I—"

She pursed her lips and turned then, running up the stairs and leaving a trail of wet footprints behind her. I watched as she stormed away, my eyes never leaving her. The door to her room slammed shut and I winced, my shoulders sinking as I finally looked to the floor.

"What was that? Was that, Elle?" Edgar shuffled from the library.

"Shut up, Edgar." I turned to him, fury burning in my eyes.

Edgar did not react the way I wanted him to as he jumped with delight. "Oh, *anger*. I love your anger."

I gave him a strange look, giving up on him. I shook my head and let my shoulders relax.

Edgar stopped smiling and stood tall, smoothing his coat in an attempt to collect himself, looking as though he had finally realized how crazy he seemed. "Do you want me to talk to her?"

I brought my hand to my forehead, smoothing my hair back. "Sure, wouldn't hurt, I guess." I let my hand fall limp at my side.

"Perfect!" Edgar sneered and I wondered what it meant.

"Just don't—" I tried to apply a few ground rules, but before I could say another word, Edgar was already halfway up the stairs, a strain of laughter trailing after him.

"He is so *weird*," I uttered, turning to resume my position on the sofa in the library where I could stare into space and wallow ever deeper into my misery.

PROPHECY

Estella

There was a knock on the door of my room and I was quick to assume who it was. "Go away, Edgar."

"Oh, alright," a voice replied, but it wasn't what I'd expected.

Trying to think and recognize the tone, I quickly stood from the blue velvet chair that faced my bed. "Wait!" I yelled.

"Oh—I. Uh—*yes?*" There was a shuffling outside in the hall.

"Edgar?" I asked, slowly walking toward the door and placing my hands against the wood, my ear just inches away.

"Yes! My dear. It is me!"

I screamed, launching backwards as the voice bellowed through the crack and into my ear like a trumpet. I fell to the ground as the door handle twisted, opening a crack. A head popped in then, and my shock turned to happiness.

"Oh, Edgar!"

"Elle, darling!" Edgar Poe swung the door wide open with his hands in the air, his fingers splayed.

I crawled up off the floor and jumped into his arms. "Oh, Edgar! What are you doing here?"

Edgar laughed as he spun me. "I'm here to help you, my dear."

I leaned away. "To help me? With what?"

Edgar laughed and clapped his hands together as he dropped me. "Oh, this is so delightful!" He took a deep breath and regrouped. "Well, I told Edgar, down there," he pointed at the floor, "that I was here to take him away, but really I am here to help you find your *prophecy*," he crooned.

"My prophecy? How did you—"

Edgar put his hand up to my mouth, silencing me, crushing lips against my teeth. "I was sent here by that old looking god, *Santa Claus*."

"You mean, Nicholas?" I snorted.

"Yes, yes. *Saint Nick!*"

"I hardly consider him a saint," I chortled.

Edgar continued, unfazed by my comment. "He told me I was to help you! Of course, I was delighted when—"

"Nicholas sent you?" I felt overwhelmed by the fact that now they were sending people to assist, whereas my Edgar wouldn't.

"Oh, isn't this fun!" He jumped again. "I love hunts. Perhaps that's why they picked me." He brought his finger to his chin in thought.

I put my arms on Edgar's shoulders, pressing his feet firmly to the ground. "Okay, calm down, deep breaths. Can't we just ask Edgar where it is? Doesn't he know?"

Edgar Poe shook his head. "Oh, well. He knows about it, but it hides itself. So, he doesn't know where that is. He just knows that it's here somewhere."

"In this house?" I asked. I was confused as to why I wouldn't have found it already.

"Yes, darling. Here!" He shook with excitement under my grasp.

"Well, why didn't I know that?" I felt deceived.

Edgar stuck out his bottom lip. "Well, I'm not really sure why no one ever seems to want to tell you anything. I feel sorry for you. So much unnecessary drama!"

I let one exalted laugh leave my lips. "Finally, someone notices."

"Of course, dear. I see everything. So! *Shall we?*" He motioned toward the door.

A smile crossed my face. This was so sudden, so unexpected. "Yes, Edgar. We shall!" I went along with his free nature and embraced the game he lived everyday. I took his arm. "Okay, let's go."

Sam came to the door then. "What in the world is going on in this house?" Sam was grabbing his head in agony.

Edgar looked at Sam. "Oh! The big guy is here *too!* Positively delightful!"

Margriete popped her head around the corner, as well.

"Ah!" Edgar sounded as though he was about to pop

with emotion. *"And you too!"*

"Edgar!" Margriete sang, pushing past Sam.

Sam rolled his eyes. "Really? This again?"

Margriete jumped into Edgar's arms, toppling me to the side as Sam caught me. "Edgar! How did you get here?"

He laughed. "I was sent on important business." He made it seem as though it was top secret, although, at this point it was anything but.

"They all know, Edgar. It's okay," I assured him.

Sam looked at me with a disgusted face. "He's supposed to help? How can he possibly help? It seems more likely that he'll foil it all instead."

I gave Sam a playful slap on the arm. "Oh, come on. He's innocent enough. Besides, he helped us last time. He's good with this stuff."

Sam grumbled. "They could have just asked *me* to help."

I snorted. "I doubt that."

Sam looked down his nose at me. *"Whatever."*

Edgar and Margriete were squealing at each other with excitement, like two school girls.

"Okay, *okay.* Break it up." Sam stepped between them. "Can we re-group and act normal about this? Please?"

Margriete smiled and put her arm around Sam's torso. "Alright, darling."

"Okay." I put my hands up, gathering the group's attention. "Let's start. Edgar—" he looked at me. "How do I find this thing?"

Edgar shrugged. "Beats me."

My hands fell as a snort of disgust escaped my lips. "I thought you were sent here to help?"

Edgar smiled. "I lied to the Santa man. I just wanted to visit! I never get to visit." He frowned.

"That's because you should be institutionalized and caged," Sam uttered.

Edgar heard him and frowned, sealing his lips.

"Can't we just get along, for once?" I glared at Sam, warning him.

"What?" he exclaimed.

I ignored him. "So, that's little help."

Sam spoke up again, clearing his throat in an obnoxious manner. "You are naturally drawn to it." He glanced at Edgar as though to say, *'I know better than you.'*

I thought for a moment. "So, you're saying it's likely something I already feel?"

"Yeah," Sam barked.

I pressed my lips together, looking around my room in thought. "Well, there are an awful lot of things I'm drawn to."

Edgar yelped before speaking. "Well, why don't we all just split up and start looking?"

I nodded. "I think that's just about the best thing we can do at the moment. So, let's split."

Margriete and Sam walked across the hall toward Edgar's room as Edgar Poe ran over to my journals, yanking them from the shelves and throwing them to the ground.

"Edgar!" I yelled.

He looked at me as though wondering what he'd done wrong.

"Be careful with those!" I pointed my finger at the journals that were now splayed across the floor.

He cowered. "Sorry." His eyes fell and he knelt to the ground to pick up the journals. "I was sort of hoping to find one of those *delightful* books where when you pull it, a secret door opens."

I grumbled. "That's not going to happen with *those* books, okay?" I thought back to the day I had thrown the whole shelf on the floor in frustration. No secret room.

Growing annoyed, I found myself overwhelmed with the need to get away. I turned and walked from the room with a brisk pace, making it out the doors as I grasped at my chest. I walked to the railing that overlooked the hall, grabbing it for support as I felt myself begin to hyperventilate. For the first time since the beginning of this, the anxiety was finally catching back up to me. A familiar dark feeling crept inside me like a shadowy reminder of what I once was. I put my hand to my chest. All this was supposed to be wonderful. I was supposed to feel happy. But why, instead, was everything such a mess?

Thunder crashed outside, rumbling the house and making the chandelier in the hall shake. I looked up at it, the sound heightened in my stressed state. I was tired of running, tired of fighting. I just wanted to be happy. I just wanted to be left alone.

I closed my eyes, creating a mantra to calm my mind. *Calm down, you're fine. Calm down, you're fine.* When I opened my eyes, I saw something dark now standing in the hall. Startled, I gripped harder on the rail, my knuckles turning white. I was not scared, nor was I angry. I was just tense as I stood there, staring. My eyes were locked onto those of Edgar, his face like stone, his body tense.

His eyes were crashing like the storm outside, but it was not fear that I felt from them, but warmth. I felt my chest relax then, as though someone had poured me into a hot bath, warmth filling my heart as my body let go. My grip on the rail loosened and I allowed my hands to fall to my sides. He did not break the stare, or even breathe, but still, I could feel him. The breath in my lungs began to lighten, the blood in my veins slowing as my heart rate became even.

I moved then, still watching him as I made my way down the stairs. His eyes followed mine as I placed one foot in front of the other, as though in a trance, but I was still in control. I traced my hand down the railing, letting go as I reached the bottom. I walked up to him, stopping as our toes nearly met. I watched his eyes, feeling all my worries fade.

He did not move. "I'm sorry."

His breath fell across my face and I breathed deeply, wondering if giving into his control was what I really wanted, or if he had indeed enchanted me somehow.

"I'm sorry, for all of this. I don't want to fight, I don't want to look into our soul and see that kind of darkness. I can feel you, Elle, every emotion. But perhaps what I felt just now was the one I feared most: regret."

I took in his words, blinking only once. I was not ready to forgive him, but he put up a good fight, making me want to give in as his body invited me.

He remained still, his words the only thing that moved between us. "I can feel your hesitation, but please, I see now what my actions do to you. I am ready to help. I am ready to hand over the control."

A part of me wanted to retort in anger, but the invisible force between us did not allow my emotions to get in the way.

"You are the only thing that matters to me, and though it has taken me a long time to truly understand that, I finally see. It was my life's purpose to be here, to understand how to yield to the things I can't control. You are a part of that."

I still said nothing as something inside me began to shift and pull. I furrowed my brow, wondering why it was I felt that way, and recognizing the feeling. When I had first met Edgar, it was as though an invisible thread had connected us, always pulling me in and taking me in the direction I needed to go.

"Elle, I can feel it. I know where it is."

His eyes stopped storming and the warmth in my soul cooled. His power let go of me then, allowing my emotions to return. Though I wanted to feel love, I still held back, seeing that he had done it in the spirit of forgiveness, to help.

A smile spread across his face. "I know where it is, Elle. I can feel it pulling me now," he whispered again.

No longer able to hide, my mouth began to mimic his, and I smiled. "I feel it too. The string, it's back, guiding me in the right direction."

I jumped into his arms then, and he held me, our soul burning as we once again united as one, no longer denying what came so naturally. No longer thwarting the love we had been fighting to save. His lips were against my cheek, but he did not kiss me. He was cold, but in this moment it felt good.

"Come on." I pushed away from him and grabbed his hand, pulling him into the library where I leapt onto the ladder. He dropped my hand to help me up, then followed. At the top, I dashed around the upper level, diving into the small room as the singular candle burst to life. Breathing heavy, I could feel Edgar's presence behind me as I scanned the small space.

"*Of course*," Edgar whispered. "That's why this room was so small."

I came to the same conclusion he had. "It's because it isn't a room at all, but a *hallway*." I began to feel along the walls, but saw nothing. "How do you suppose we get through? How do we find it?"

Edgar was looking around as I was—our backs against each other. I secretly enjoyed his proximity, feeling that we were finally operating as a team, having finally put our egos aside.

"I'm not really sure." He ran his hand along the baseboard, moving the leather chair as much out of the way as possible. I kept looking, figuring it wasn't just going to appear out of nowhere. There had to be some sort of trick involved.

"Is this why they say prophecies are a myth, because they are close to impossible to find?" My arms were at my sides, my eyes squinting in the horrid light.

Edgar looked at me. "They do hide themselves, so I'm guessing you're right. It's said that everyone has one, it's just a matter of figuring out were that is."

"So do you have one?" I paused, awaiting his reply.

He snorted. "Probably, but if it's anything like me, no one would ever find it, no matter how hard they try." He laughed under his breath, still searching.

"Wait." My voice echoed off the side walls, but not from the back. "Do you hear that?" I had noticed it as Edgar was talking.

Edgar stopped what he was doing. "Hear what?"

I put my finger up to my mouth. "*Shh...* Now listen." I took a deep breath. "Hello!" I yelled.

Edgar jumped, bringing his hands to his ears in pain. "*Elle, what are you doing?*" he whispered in an angered tone.

I laughed. "Sorry. But did you hear that? Do you see now what I'm talking about?"

He looked at me, his eyes narrowed and annoyed. "*No.*"

A sharp breath of aggravation left my mouth, and I put my hands on my hips. "What I'm trying to get you to realize, is that this wall—" I pointed toward the back wall, "—does not echo back as these ones do." I pointed to the two side walls.

Edgar's narrowed eyes shot open. "Oh, yeah. Yes, I can hear that."

"Yeah, exactly." I shook my head, touching my hand to the wall. "It's as though it's open, but—" It was solid and cold, just as it should be. "How do you suppose we get in there?"

Edgar squeezed past me, also touching the wall. "There must be something we have to do. Let's think. This is your prophecy in there. There has to be something we say perhaps. Maybe give it something, like a gift?" He smirked and I jokingly hit him on the arm. "Well, *you* respond well to material things!"

"A spell perhaps?" I finished his thought.

He laughed. "We aren't really the spell making type, Elle. The term witch or *Wiccan* is a loosely used term. It doesn't automatically mean we have spells and powers."

I laughed. "I know that, but—" It was then that I remembered the book I had found while Margriete and I were searching for a reason why the world was dying. *"The book,"* I whispered.

Edgar looked at me, our noses close. "What book?"

I let one laugh pass my lips. "Our book! The book about us! Edgar, I need a light. The candlelight won't work. That's why I never saw it before!"

Edgar turned and walked out to the railing, looking below as he leapt over the rail, not bothering with the ladder. I also went to the rail to see where he had gone, watching as he left the room.

"Edgar?"

He didn't answer but I could hear his footsteps. The garage door opened and closed, so I waited. After a few moments, I again heard the door as he made his way back. He entered the room then, with something orange in his hand.

"Edgar, what is that?" He looked up at me, lifting his hand so I could see what it was. "Is that an—an *extension cord?*"

He then walked over to the one lamp in the entire house, the one he had gotten from Thomas Edison, with the very first light bulb. He ripped the cord from the wall, as though it was nothing.

I winced.

He plugged in one end of the extension cord, letting some of it out in a coil on the floor. Then he turned to me, tossing the rest of the loop up and over the rail. I caught it as I leaned over. He walked to the ladder, holding the lamp under his arm in order to climb with both hands.

Once back by my side, he took the coil from my hand and found the end, plugging the lamp back in and removing the shade.

"Are you ready?"

I took a deep breath. "Yes, I'm ready."

He lifted the lamp and the light fell upon the small space. My eyes lit up then, a bright shine reflecting back at us. We both winced and turned away.

"Whoa, a little bright," I remarked, shielding my eyes.

Edgar nodded in agreement. Bringing the lamp down and twisting the bulb slightly.

"What will that do? Won't it just turn—" I stopped talking then, amazed as the light dimmed rather than went out. I · was finding that there were a lot of things about this old light bulb that were much better than modern ones. For one: the bulb had never burned out, but I could also see why bulbs today did. If they never burned out, then you would never need a new one, hence, light bulb suppliers would go out of business. *Politics.* I shook my head.

Edgar winked at me. Then he lifted the light back toward the space. We both prepared ourselves for the blinding light, but this time, the light was perfect and we lowered our hands from our face.

"Edgar—" I was speechless.

There was a single line of text written across the wall, glimmering as the book had. It almost looked as though it were floating in air, written in a magical ink that left no mark that the human eye could see. I walked closer, laughing as I read it:

Password, please?

"Password? What do you suppose the password is?" I turned and looked at Edgar.

Edgar shrugged. "I'm not sure. Your prophecy sure has a strange personality, though."

I grunted. "You're a big help."

"What? I really don't know."

I took a deep breath, pressing my lips together. "Well, I guess I'll just start." I took a deep breath, shaking the energy from my hands as though preparing myself for a run. *"Abracadabra,"* I yelled. Nothing happened.

"Too typical, try something else." Edgar's gaze never left the wall and his stance like that of a football lineman, just waiting to pounce.

I laughed. "It was worth a shot, at least. Okay, how about—" I paused as I tried to come up with something new. "Open sesame?" Still nothing happened. *"Seattle, Scott, um... Edgar!"*

"Come on, Elle. It's not going to be *Edgar.* Besides, those are all new things, for the most part. You have to remember that this has been here for a really long time."

I nodded. "You're right. Okay, more creative." I paused, searching my head. "Oh I know! What about, *raven?"* The house shook then, and a yelp escaping my lips. There was a flash of light that grew from the corner of my eyes, spreading across them and blinding me. Thunder crashed outside simultaneously. I tried to look from the railing to the large window, but the bright light had blinded me. I shook my head, squeezing my eyes shut. As I opened them, color slowly filtered back, shapes once again forming.

Edgar placed one hand on my back, pulling my attention back to the wall. "Elle! look!"

I turned away from the window, seeing now that it was not the thunder alone that had shaken the house. Before our eyes, the wall began to dissipate into thin air, leaving the glowing letters floating.

The word lingered for a moment, and then I watched as the letters faded into smoke, leaving nothing but a black void where the light from the bulb could not reach. Edgar placed the lamp on the floor and I grabbed his hand, stepping forward with dilated pupils.

"Come on," I pulled. Edgar hesitated, but he still took the lead, afraid to let me go first.

As his foot crossed the threshold of the wall, light suddenly poured over him. Large torches burst to life, revealing a space that was about half the size of my bedroom. In the middle of the room, a light from above shown down on a cube that was floating in the air, turning over and over as though twisting on a string. Edgar's grip never left mine, my breathing shallow and his nonexistent.

I was in awe. *"Wow."*

Edgar looked back at me. "I haven't seen this in centuries."

I was surprised by his comment, "I didn't know you'd

seen it before." I felt a little jealous.

He let out a soft laugh. "You have, too," he whispered.

My eyes widened in surprise. "Really? I've seen it before?" I tried to remember it but there was nothing. It annoyed me that there was no memory of my life before. I still felt a certain disconnect over it, as though that girl was someone else. I was jealous of her, angry even. Hating that girl that had lived my life, a life I could not remember.

"Why didn't you tell me about it earlier?" We were advancing toward the cube at a very slow pace.

Edgar looked over his shoulder at me, bringing his finger to his mouth. He hunched down and I followed suit, not understanding what was going on. Edgar was moving very slowly now, bearing down on the cube as he very carefully let go of my hand, motioning for me to stop.

I was a little annoyed that I didn't understand more about what was happening, but I obeyed anyway, thinking that at a moment like this, jealousy should take a back seat. I watched him bear down on the cube as the cube changed directions very suddenly, as though sensing his presence. He stopped immediately, and so did the cube. They were both frozen, both seeming to stare each other down.

I exhaled, realizing I had forgotten to breathe. In a flash, the cube took off, dropping from the light and dodging away from Edgar. I gasped as I saw Edgar's body become a blur, dashing after it faster than I had ever seen him move before. I stepped back until I was flush with the wall, watching as they lapped around the room. The cube stopped, and so did

Edgar, again locked in staring and slowly pacing in a circle. Edgar had a smile on his face, enjoying this little game the prophecy was playing.

I was amazed. Never had I imagined that a prophecy had a personality of its own. But it did. It liked games, and I saw now how that was a bit like my own personality. I began to enjoy this, as though watching a sport.

The cube spun now, slow at first but getting faster, gaining speed as the cube blurred into an orb. Edgar stood tall, his hands at his sides as he watched it, the humor still glowing on his face. I was fixated on it now, as though it had put me in a trance. Edgar glanced at me, and without warning, he suddenly reached out with a lightning fast reflex and grabbed at it. There was a bright flash of light and I winced, looking away.

Edgar's deep laughter filled the room then. *"Gotcha."*

The light quickly dimmed, and I looked back at Edgar with hungry eyes. He rolled the cube in his grasp, his arm tight as the cube tried to move and get away. I walked up to Edgar, moving slowly though it didn't seem as though I was in any danger.

"Why did it do that?" The cube glowed in the reflection of Edgar's eyes.

His smile was wide. "It's just something it learns to do. A prophecy does not want to be caught."

I nodded. "Makes sense."

I blinked a few times, watching it as it glowed, the light from within the cube flickering as though trying to talk. I lowered my face closer, inspecting it and seeing that the outer shell was much like glass, though watery.

"What does it feel like?" I looked up at Edgar.

He turned his palm over as the cube tried to shift its weight and get away. "You can touch it, if you want."

I looked back at the cube, lifting my hand from my side and slowly advancing toward it. The cube's light calmed, pulsing as I got closer.

"It likes you," Edgar whispered.

I touched it then, feeling as the surface seemed to cool my skin, the pulsing feeling going through my hand and up my arm. The light began to dim as I felt the feeling continue to spread, filling my body with a wave of coolness. I looked at Edgar, but he was staring at the cube with a smirk on his face.

"What's happening?" I didn't want to let go, the feeling so euphoric that it left me wishing I felt this way all the time.

"It's opening for you, giving you the prophecy." Edgar's voice was soft and distant.

"But—" I felt my body erupt with goose bumps, and then I saw:

I saw myself, standing in a field, thunder crashing around me. I saw the wind howling, the trees uprooted. I saw Edgar leaving. I saw the griffins from before, angry and resistant, receding into the caves. I saw

everything die, the world a desert, my body lying dead.
I saw the whole thing crumbling, and then it went
black.

I yelped, letting go of the cube as the cool feeling was replaced with a burning one, the light in the cube returning as it shook in Edgar's hand. He was grunting as he tried to hold on, but his strength was beginning to wane. I was breathing fast, frightened by how real it had felt, as though I was there.

I still felt the wind on my skin, the smell of desolation stinging my nostrils. I still saw the outline of dead trees littering my vision and smelled the smoke in my lungs.

"Edgar."

He let go of the cube, watching it as it took off around the room, taking refuge in a corner where it seemed to shake with fear.

"I know, Elle." He looked at me. "I've seen it."

I shook my head. "It was horrible. Why? Why show me the future if I see that it will not work."

Edgar traced his hand down my arm, taking my hand. "It's not what will happen, it's what can happen. It is showing what will happen if nothing is done. It's showing you because it means there's something you can do about it. It's just a warning."

I swallowed, finding my throat was dry and swollen. "Just a warning? *It's horrible.* I will have nightmares the rest of my life." I shook my head. "There was so much death, bodies everywhere, just—"

"Decaying?" Edgar said, with a hint of delight.

I let out a sharp breath of disgust, narrowing my eyes and whipping my hand out of his. I turned away from him. "I can't believe you're finding pleasure in this."

"No. No, Elle," he denied, walking up to me and taking my hand back as he twisted me to face him. "I didn't mean it to come across that way. I mean, it's just my nature."

I thought about all the paintings in his room, trying to see his side of things. I exhaled. "I'm sorry. I understand. I just find it appalling because I see something opposite, something horrible."

He wrapped both his hands around mine, squeezing tight. "Elle, I think it's appalling as well. Don't get me wrong. It's just, I don't know. Something inside me surfaces that I can't control, that's all."

I nodded, squeezing his hand back. "I know. Just, let's change the subject, okay?"

I tried to push the image of death from my head but it was seared into my memories. I began to wonder why, if I had seen this prophecy before, I hadn't remembered it. Perhaps I just knew about it, but had never actually found it? Of all things, I would never forget something that horrible. *Never.*

I looked at the prophecy, seeing it had stopped shaking and was now staring at us, slowly twisting as though looking from Edgar to me, and then back at Edgar. I looked away.

"Elle?" I heard Margriete's voice echo from the library below.

Edgar put his arm around my shoulders. "Come on, let's go."

He pulled me away, leading me back out and into the library as I focused on my feet. It was then that I saw a dim light following us into the small hallway and I looked over my shoulder, seeing the prophecy floating just behind, looking sheepish. It darted around the corner, hiding, only to peek around a moment later. A smile began to grow on my face and I stopped walking. Edgar halted as well.

"What—" He looked down at me and then looked to where I was looking. He snorted. *"Great,"* he muttered, shaking his head.

I pulled Edgar's arm off my shoulder, turning around to face the prophecy. "Come on. It's okay." I patted my leg, calling it to me like a dog.

The prophecy was still peeking around the corner, acting timid now, a complete change from earlier.

"Come on," I urged again, in a soothing voice.

The prophecy popped out from behind the corner, seemingly excited, tilting back as though to puff its chest.

I laughed, waving it toward me. It floated up beside me then, floating just a breadth from my face. I felt its light warm my cheeks, glowing steadily.

"This is ridiculous." I heard Edgar turn and walk away behind me.

"Don't mind him," I whispered, giving it a wink.

The cube's light flickered as it bounced, as though to laugh.

I turned then, walking out to the rail. I looked down, and saw Margriete looking up at me. Edgar was across the opening on the other side, leaning against the upper rail, watching me with a humored face. I smiled, the cube floating up and hovering right next to my left ear.

"You found it!" Margriete's face lit up. "Wow." She paused as she took a moment to gawk. "I never thought I'd ever see one. It's so beautiful."

I could see the cube sway with delight from the corner of my eye.

Edgar threw himself over the rail then, and jumped down into the library below. I watched him as he walked past Sam, bumping him on the shoulder as he passed. Sam made an angry move to go after him but stopped himself, instead looking up at me from below. I shrugged.

Margriete pretended not to notice the tension. "Bring it down here." She smiled, summoning me with her hand.

I began to walk around the upper level and toward the ladder as I heard frantic footsteps rush across the foyer, entering the room. I halted at the top, looking toward the commotion.

"Elle!" Edgar Poe sang, throwing his hands in the air. "I think I found the—" His voice trailed off as he looked up and saw me, his face sinking. "Oh, you found it already." He had a sad look of disappointment on his face.

Sam walked up to Edgar and patted him on the back.

"That's okay, old chap."

For the first time Edgar gave Sam a sour glare. I laughed.

Margriete exhaled dramatically. "So, now what?" She looked at me. "Elle, how was your trip?"

I had almost completely forgotten about what had happened on my trip. An image of the tree lit across my memory then, and I saw the prophecy brighten as though full of hope. The prophecy was a part of me. This I understood from what I'd seen. I supposed, then, that it also felt me, and could see what I was thinking. I saw the tree against the walls of my mind, bright green with pink flowers, motionless as the world roared on around it. If it were true that I could heal all this and the world, it seemed then that I would become stronger and more beautiful than anyone could ever imagine.

"Oh, Margriete! I almost forgot!" I finally made my way down the ladder. "The most amazing thing happened." Everyone was watching me now, wondering what could be more amazing than finding a prophecy. "When I went to see Scott and Sarah, I had landed on this tree in their yard. You should have seen it, everything was a mess, and everything was dying. This tree, though, this tree asked me for help."

Edgar Poe looked as though he was about to burst, having been silent for too long. I quickly continued my story, hoping it would thwart him.

"I—I didn't know what I had done, but something happened. The tree just burst to life. Flowers, leaves, everything grew strong, and stayed that way. The next day, still, the tree was growing."

Margriete tilted her head. "But here, I mean, it's always been like that."

"No, Margriete." I took a step toward her. "This was different than that, much different."

Edgar Poe burst then. "*Show us, Elle.* Show us on a tree here. I would so like to see that. I've heard of your talents. Your Edgar has told me many stories!" He was shaking with excitement.

I rolled my eyes. "Alright, let's go now." I thought now was as good a time as any, and the sooner I practiced, the sooner I would be able to get this figured out. "Sam, do you want to come?" I began walking from the room as Edgar skipped after me. Margriete looked at Sam.

"Sam?" She asked.

Sam had a blank look on his face, showing nothing of what he was thinking. Perhaps he sensed my worries, listening into my thoughts as I wondered if the thing I had accidentally done to the tree in Seattle could be repeated.

"No, that's alright." He smirked. "Not feeling the outdoors today." He glanced outside, giving the field a once-over with his eyes. I also looked, seeing his point. The rain had now not only gotten heavier over the past hour, but had begun swirling into angry cones.

"Alright," I shrugged. The prophecy floated out into the hall, feeling brave and adventurous. I could hear Edgar Poe jumping around by the front door, so I grabbed Margriete's hand and dragged her out of the library as she waved to Sam. "See you later, then!" And with that we left, my nerves singing, but I knew it had to work.

FOR THE LAST TIME
Edgar

"Where are they going?" I sensed Sam enter as I stood looking out the window of my room. I watched as Edgar Poe ran across the field, Margriete and Elle walking after him.

"Out. To try and re-enact what Elle did while she was in Seattle." Sam made his way through the stacks of books, standing right next to me as we watched them outside.

Elle's prophecy followed like a pet, fighting with Isabelle as she tried to dive down on it, nipping with her beak.

"What did Elle do in Seattle?" I asked as though I didn't know, but I had my hunches.

"Do I even need to entertain that type of question?" Sam's hands were locked behind him.

I chuckled, knowing he was listening in. I knew what

she had done because her prophecy had shown me long ago. What I also suspected was that the reason why it had happened was because she was far away from me. She was growing strong at a rapid pace; growing back into the woman she was before. In our previous life, she was just as powerful, but being that she never left my side, she had never known just how much. It is my choking personality that holds her power at bay.

"When will you leave?" Sam broke the silence, finding a place in my thoughts to interject his opinion.

"Soon. She won't want me to leave, so don't tell her." I looked at Sam as he looked at me and lifted one brow.

"So you're going to cooperate then? I'm shocked, didn't know you had that sort of power in you. So far, it seems all you want is to foil everything."

I looked away from Sam, a little angered by his words. I was trying, wasn't I? *Give me a break.*

Sam snorted.

"When they come, then I'll go. But until then, I want to be here. I have to." I looked Sam in the eye once more. "I do love her, despite what you think. There will never be anyone like Elle. I want to spend all the time I can with her, before—" I felt my eyes begin to sting and I became angry at myself.

"You will do a noble thing by leaving her." Sam put one hand on my shoulder.

"But she will—" I stopped myself again, my voice cracking.

"I know what will happen to her, but there is nothing we can do about that. In the end, I believe she will understand. She will find some peace at last." Sam let go.

I nodded, finding I was at a loss for words. For the first time in my life I let myself be weak, allowing one tear to fall. It quickly dried against my cold skin. My eyes were locked on the field, now long vacant as they'd entered the woods and disappeared.

"She will fail today out there. It's going to crush her." Sam added.

I took a deep breath, hearing Henry enter the room as he fanned down and onto my shoulder. He leaned toward Sam as he gave him a discreet scratch on the head, afraid I'd get jealous, though I saw it anyway.

"What will you do?" I blinked as I said it.

I saw Sam shrug from the corner of my eye. "I suppose I'll leave. Go back to Heaven. There's not really much I can do here, especially if she fails."

"She won't *fail,*" my voice was low.

Sam laughed. "Well, either way, there won't be much for me to do. Especially if she does what she's planning."

I pressed my brows together. "What is she planning to do, other than save all this?"

Sam lifted his chin, gloating about the fact that he knew, and I didn't. I was aware of how out of the loop I had become due to my stubborn nature, but I had snapped out of it, finally seeing that there was nothing I could do to stop this. Ignoring it wouldn't make it go away. In the end I would still be without her, *again.*

"She's going to strike a bargain with the gods. She will forge a contract, agreeing to save the Earth, but only if all magic leaves, *forever.*" He made it seem so dramatic.

I had to leave anyway, so it didn't changed my plans, but still, it surprised me. "Why didn't I see that in the prophecy?"

Sam took a deep breath for effect. "Why would it show you that? It doesn't affect you. Either way you're leaving, and I suppose it knew that."

I agreed. "True."

It was hard to even think about. Leaving was not something I had planned for in the end. I watched the forest, the trees swaying. I looked at the ring in my hand, glowing white and then fading to black, repeating the motion as though breathing. I had lived a long life, and though it may not have been as glamorous as I had always wanted, it was still good enough. It was time for it to be over, and time for me to go home.

FAILURE
Estella

"Here," I trudged my way forward, the path now so washed out that it no longer made a distinct cut through the forest. Roots from the trees were exposed, and the ground packed firmly. "Let's try this one."

Edgar Poe set himself down beside me and retracted his wings, opting to fly in order to stay clean. His black hair was matted to his face with rain, his eyes beady as he watched me with intensity. He had calmed down since we'd gone outside and I was relieved, but also curious. It was as though the expanse of Earth was all that could calm him. A tree stood before us, bare and wet, its trunk swollen and rotting from all the water. I walked up to it, leaning in close.

"Hello," I whispered.

The tree creaked slightly. I smiled. Looking back at Margriete and Edgar I saw that they hadn't moved, too afraid they'd miss something. This was it, my chance to show them that I was *The One*—a chance to prove to myself that the tree in Seattle was not a fluke. I lifted my hand to the trunk, placing my soft skin against the rough wood. The shell of the tree seemed to squish like a sponge, water filling every cell of its existence.

The branches of the tree swayed and moaned, and as I stood there, I waited for something to change. After a moment, I grew frustrated. Nothing was happening, though the tree was thrashing about. I let go, looking up as it calmed down, almost as though I were hurting it instead.

"What's going on?" Margriete called from behind me, now standing a distance away, afraid the tree would hit her.

I licked the dripping rain from my lips, my brows twisted in to a frustrated mask. "I don't know. I did just as I always do, just as I did back in Seattle."

I turned back to the tree with determination, shutting my eyes and remembering what Edgar had taught me that day on the snowmobile, when we had visited our trees up the mountain. I tried to imagine what I wanted the tree to be, imagining the tree in Seattle and seeing it burn with beauty. I heard the tree before me thrashing again, branches whizzing by my face. I leaned forward, touching it as the image in my head thickened into reality.

I heard Margriete gasp and relief washed over me, but as I opened my eyes I was disappointed yet again. The tree had tried to do as I had wished for it, but it had failed, now only partially bloomed, the rest of it wilted and dying even more than before. I heard Margriete try to say something but I drowned it out, again focusing as I touched the tree. There was a sharp whoosh then and I felt a branch slice at my face. I yelped as I fell back, my cheek burning as I brought my hand up to touch it. The tree was angry with me.

I winced as the salt from my touch mixed with the blood from the wound. I then inspected my hand, watching as thick crimson dripped from the tips of my pale fingers, rain diluting the blood as it washed away. I cursed under my breath, standing with one hand on my cheek, the other propping me off the wet ground. Dead pine needles clung to my jeans, the wet fabric making my skin feel numb. A pained tear grew in my eye, forged from both the cut and the frustration. I watched as the agitated tree dropped whatever leaves I had given it, shaking like a wet dog before resuming its tired stand.

Edgar walked up to me, a handkerchief in his grasp as he pulled my hand from my cheek, now applying his own pressure. "It's okay, Elle. It will come to you."

I exhaled, my shoulders dropping. "Edgar, I don't know what's wrong."

Margriete walked up and rubbed my shoulders.

"Elle, darling. It's just not time yet." He smiled at me, a glimmer in his eye.

I saw something behind his stare. "What do you mean? It has to be time."

Edgar looked away from me, refolding the handkerchief

and looking for a clean side. "Well—it's nothing, my dear."

He was over compensating, and I knew there was something he wasn't telling me. "What is it, Edgar? You're a horrible liar."

A nervous look crossed his face and he stepped back, handing me the handkerchief. "Well, I—It's not my place to say, but I do know what it is." He chuckled, still stepping away from me as though to put a distance between us. "You know how fascinated I am with your kind. Well, I once read, in this very difficult to read book, I wish you could have seen it! It was white and shiny and—"

"Edgar," I stopped him, seeing that he was getting off track. His eyes had begun to glaze over and his movements had become poetic, clearly feeling a sort of passion for this book that only a literary genius like him could. I knew just what book he was speaking of, and I saw that Margriete knew, too, as her face lit up.

Edgar snapped out of it. "Sorry. Anyway, it said that as long as you are together, you can never be as strong as you would be apart. You see, when you are close, all your soul wants is to love. It is happy, and therefore it grows weak!" He walked toward me then, very excited. "Tell me, when you left for Seattle, were you angry with him?"

I did not want to admit that he was right, but he was. "Well, yeah."

Edgar jumped then, resuming his crazy behavior. "Yes! See! You cannot let him stay here for this. He must *leave*."

I thought about it for a moment. "Leave to where?"

Margriete stepped toward me, her face grave. "He probably means back. He needs to go to Heaven if you are to be at your strongest. There is no place else on this Earth he could go that is far enough, except there."

My heart sank. "But, I *need* him. I was hoping he'd be there to help."

Edgar laughed. "Help? My dear, he kills things. Of course he won't help!"

I sighed, seeing he was right. Why hadn't I thought of this, why hadn't I been able to see it earlier. I hadn't felt at all the way I had when I'd gone to Seattle, but I had figured it was the anger and hate I'd had toward Edgar, not the fact that his proximity was sucking the power from me. I felt stupid, again. I was so caught up in everything, that I didn't see the obvious things that were right in front of me. I pulled the handkerchief away from my face, the sting subsiding. I touched the cut. It was still tender but now healing over. By tomorrow, it would be gone as though nothing had happened.

"So, he has to leave." I let it sink in. "That's not so bad. I'll see him when it's over."

Edgar smiled. "Now that's the spirit, my girl!"

Margriete giggled.

"It's only temporary. I will take care of him, so will Sam. We will wait for you there."

I remembered my plan, and the idea that I was going to strike a bargain with the gods. The idea brought me comfort. I saw Edgar and me in Heaven then, our own house, no longer hiding from the world because we finally belonged. We would be happy there, in the end. It would be our happily ever after. All this was just temporary, and I knew I could handle that; I always did.

"Well, shall we go back?" I desperately wanted to speak with Edgar about this, find out what he knew.

Rain ran down Margriete's brow. "Let's go, dear." She looked up at the tree as though to tell it that I would be back. She put her arm around me as we both shook with chill. Edgar took to the air, and without hesitation, we hurried home.

BEGINNINGS

Estella

My Edgar wrapped a blanket around me as I sat on his bed, the fire in the corner now roaring as he had coaxed it to life with his hands.

"What's wrong, Elle?" His voice sounded shallow, as though he already knew.

I pressed my lips together, thinking for a moment. "I know that you know what has to happen. You have to leave, Edgar."

He said nothing at first, telling me that I was right to assume. "I know—yes." His voice was sad.

"I can understand why you didn't want to tell me that, either. This one secret is okay. I wish, in fact, that I still didn't know." My stomach twisted, the familiar anxiety that I had felt this entire life, returning with a vengeance.

"I'm sorry that you have to do all this on your own, but

it's true. Margriete has lost all her power. Otherwise, you would have had her to help, but—" I knew he was going to speak of Matthew but refrained.

"If you died, Edgar, then I would be very strong, wouldn't I?" The question sounded ominous but I was trying to understand. I looked him in the eyes as he brushed my hair away from my neck, his fingers grazing across my skin. I relished the feeling, now something that felt rare and fleeting.

"Yes, you would. I suppose that was why the god's wanted to keep me dead, but at the same time, I think they knew that if they did that, you would not want to cooperate." He leaned in slowly, pressing his lips against my neck.

I laughed. "I would hate them so much. *Let them die,* I'd think. They were smart." I brought my hand to his face, feeling as my touch grazed across the rough stubble on his chin.

"Exactly. But you will be alright without me."

"It's only temporary, after all," I added. I was justifying, trying to make myself less afraid.

His nose trailed up to my cheek. "I'm sorry for everything, I know that seems like the only thing I say anymore, but I am." His breath tickled my ear. "We're at the end of it now, and I promise there are no more secrets. I have shown it all to you, everything I've ever kept. I am completely exposed now."

I laid back and away from him then, my body wrapped in the blanket like a cocoon. "I can see why you did it now, and kept all those secrets from me. In truth, I think that was how it was supposed to happen. If I had never gotten angry with you, I would have never gone to Seattle. Without witnessing that tree first hand, I don't think I would understand how this is meant to happen. I can also understand your denial. If I had known that we had to be apart for all this, then I too would try to deny that it was even real, like you have."

"Exactly." He lay beside me, his head propped up on his hand. "I didn't want any of this."

The house rumbled then, causing both Isabelle and Henry to squawk and hop around on their perch.

I looked to the windows. "Things are getting really bad out there." Then I looked Edgar in the eye, hoping he could say something of comfort to me.

"Yes. It is. But just think, Elle. No matter what happens," his gaze dropped from mine, "just remember that we have lived long and beautiful lives, even in the bad times. What people don't understand is that you have to know the bad to appreciate the good." He sounded uncomfortable saying this, but still heartfelt, revealing a side of him we rarely saw, but I knew could exist. "Every moment is epic, even the smallest. And every moment is a new chance to change and live the life you want."

His romantic side was showing. "I know that, and I honor that idea everyday." His eyes began to filter to black as he leaned his body against mine. He kissed me, his hand tracing behind my ear, my blonde hair lacing between his fingers.

Our lips intertwined for a moment before I put my hand to his chest, wanting to say something more. I had been thinking of the possibilities and outcomes, the prophecy and the way it had shown me the end. I could die from this, and I knew that. But I did not want to dwell on that fact.

"If I die—" I licked my lips.

I heard Edgar grumble as he rolled away from me.

"Edgar—" I put my hand on his arm, making him listen. *"If I die,* I don't want you to worry about me. I don't want you to be unhappy, or suffer. Please, just live. Promise me?"

His eyes rolled back to meet mine. "Yes, Elle. I know."

I squeezed his arm even tighter. "Edgar, you have to promise me."

He laughed. "Elle—"

A smile grew on my face then as I used my strength to press his wrists away from me, rolling him on his back as I trapped him there beneath me. I leaned down, kissing his neck. *"Promise me,"* I whispered against his skin.

His laughed again. "Yes, Elle. *I promise."*

I laughed back, touching his nose to mine. "Find someone else."

He snorted then, overpowering me as he rolled us in the other direction. He loomed over me with blackened eyes. "There can never be someone else. I would never allow that." One side of his mouth curled into a sly grin. "You are my *wife,* but more than that, you are my only soul mate. Everyone else pales in comparison to you." I saw the prophecy hover over us then. I rolled my eyes as

Edgar became distracted by its presence, trying to swat it away. The cube hit his hand then, flying across the room and bumping into the wall where it fell to the ground with a thud.

I yelped. "Edgar! That wasn't very nice."

The cube lifted itself back off the ground before dimming its light, as though hurt, and then left the room. Edgar had a satisfied look on his face, bringing his attention back to me as he caressed my arms. "It had bad timing."

I giggled as his fingers tickled my skin, trailing to my neck where he leaned in and kissed my skin. I stopped breathing, the feeling of his mouth making me forget that anything else even existed. He kissed my chin, my bottom lip, kissing me with a passion I had learned to love and an edge of danger I craved. I let our bodies become one, willing myself to remember this, and us.

He stopped himself when he reached my neck, our hips pressed so close, that I knew we were nearing a dangerous point.

"Don't stop," I begged.

He laughed. "Too bad."

I felt his body pull away, his muscles tense and his spine steeled.

HEAD OUT
Estella

I was scratching Isabelle on the head in the morning when I woke, alone. Without fail, she slept at my feet every night, her graceful snoring something I had grown accustomed to in order to fall asleep with the roaring wind and rain. Hail had also started now, coming down in sheets of steeled ice, leaving everything white until it later melted.

I felt saddened as I felt Isabelle's feathers between my fingers, knowing that she too would have to leave me. Since the day I had gotten her, she'd changed, becoming immortal as I was. I felt bad that I never gave her the choice of being immortal or not, selfishly pressing it upon her instead. She had never complained, or rather, I doubt she even understood. She clicked her beak at me, feeling content as her feathers ruffled.

I slowly crawled from bed and made my way to the shelf that contained my journals. There were so many memories here, so many things I had found important to record, now left to be destroyed. I looked at the sheer mass of it all, amazed that it had all been me. They had served their purpose, though. They had brought me back to life.

Edgar entered the room then, holding a cup of what smelled like coffee as the steam awoke my senses. My tired head invited the aroma, my eyes still weary. I turned and walked up to him with a smile, my eyes fixed on the cup.

"Thanks." I took the cup in my hand.

"What were you doing?" His eyes looked at the shelf.

I took a sip of coffee, letting the bitter flavor wash across my tongue. "Just remembering is all. It's unfortunate that all this will likely be destroyed."

"How so?" Edgar tilted his head, his brows pressed together.

I took another sip of coffee before nestling the cup between my hands. "From what I saw from the prophecy, I think that everything man-made will be destroyed. It will all wash away, leaving nothing but the humans to start over."

Edgar laughed. "True, but I was actually planning to take the house with me."

Surprised, my eyes became wide. *"Really?* Oh. Well, I guess that changes things then, doesn't it?" I felt dumb for feeling so nostalgic all of a sudden. *"Really? You can do that?"*

He chuckled some more. "Of course I can! The house is

invisible already. It's not very hard to collapse when it's like this and take with me, though it is quite heavy."

I giggled then. "Are you serious, or are you just trying to make me laugh?"

"No. I'm serious. It collapses, but the weight remains. It was the heaviest marble ever, if you ask me."

"Really? Wow." I felt sad then, as though taking it made this meadow no more than a meadow again. It would be strange and empty, like it was meant to be.

"So, what are your plans for today?" Edgar asked, changing the subject to something new.

I cringed when he said it, hating the question as though it meant I'd had a plan, which I didn't. I had avoided thinking about what was coming in the hopes of relaxing, though that was hardly the case. I had tossed all night, which explains why Edgar had gotten up extra early, tired of my body thrashing about beside him.

"I hadn't really thought about it," I lied. I brought the mug back to my lips, hoping it would give me an excuse not to have to talk.

Edgar nodded slowly, suspecting my avoidance. "I see. Well—"

"How long do you think I have?" I looked at him over the rim of my mug.

He thought for a moment. "About a week, I suppose. The evergreens are no longer green. That's usually a bad sign."

I exhaled sharply with a smirk, looking out the window

of my room as Isabelle lay motionless on my bed. His remark was funny, but when put into perspective, it suddenly lost it's punch. *"Hmmm."* I was thinking dramatically. "It's probably a good idea to get the ground rules straightened out with the gods then." I still had not told Edgar about the plan. I was afraid he'd be angry. I knew that Sam knew. I only hoped that he hadn't told Edgar. Banishing us from this Earth was a major thing; we could never come back. "I suppose I should go get them. What do you think?"

Edgar nodded with enthusiasm. "Not a bad idea. If you ask the griffins, they should be able to relay the message."

Edgar confirmed what I was dreading: another journey to the entrance of the caves. It's not that I didn't find it fascinating—I did. I just didn't have my whole heart in this, a sense of dread floating above me like a dark cloud.

What if this didn't work? What if I said goodbye to Edgar, and it was finally for the last time? Even the gods still did not know my plan to banish them, but I did not doubt that they would agree to it. Things were desperate now. I could feel the fear all around us, even from below. They would agree because they had to.

I placed the mug on the nearby side table and walked to the closet where I dug for some clothes. I pulled a thick wool coat from within and knee-high socks. I grabbed my jeans from a pile on the floor where I also managed to rummage for a turtleneck. I was tired of being wet and cold—I was ready for the warmth. After fighting all of it on, I began to sweat, feeling even more anxious as the heat began to irritate me. *Relish it now,* I thought.

Edgar had been watching me. "Will you go with me?" I asked, looking at him with eyes that were begging.

He smiled, walking up to me and wrapping his arms around my shoulders. "Of course."

I felt better as he said it, and together we made our way downstairs to pack a few more things and gather Margriete and Sam. I wanted them to come. I needed as many witnesses as I could find.

SUMMONING

Estella

The prophecy was hovering around the library as I walked by it on my way to find Margriete, looking at books and minding its own business.

"Hey, where's Edgar Poe?" I saw her as I entered the kitchen. I hadn't heard Edgar skipping about like a mad man this morning, something no one could miss.

Margriete looked up from the fire where she was boiling a pot of water for tea. "I'm not sure. I haven't seen him."

Sam let out a sharp snort. "He left late last night. Said he had to get back to feed his chickens. He also said something about the food here being atrocious."

I gave him a strange look of skepticism, agreeing with him. "He sure is a strange little man, isn't he?"

Sam nodded with enthusiasm. "You could say that again."

Margriete poured the hot water into a mug and added a tea bag. "So what are you up to?" She looked me up and down. "What's your plan?"

I took a seat next to Sam on a stool. "We—Edgar and I—are going to the caves to summon the gods. Want to come?"

Margriete looked intrigued. "Yeah, of course I do. I love that place."

I snorted. "Well that makes one of us," I uttered under my breath. "Get ready, then. We'll leave in just a few moments. I want to get it over with."

Sam laughed to himself.

I looked at him. "What's your problem?"

He stopped laughing. "Just you, is all. I know what you're doing. It's good to know that this time you're doing it right."

I gave Sam a warning glare. I knew he knew my secrets, but still. "Five minutes, let's go."

Six minutes later, we all stood in the field, the wind threatening to whip us off balance. "We'll be going up the hill, so this should be easy," I yelled. "Just like last time."

We moved forward, working our way through fallen tree branches and wet mud. Hail began to fall about fifteen minutes into the hike and I heard Sam groan. I pulled the hood of my coat over my head, wishing we had used a vehicle, or some other form of transportation, though, with all the trees down, that would not have worked out too well.

Not before too long, things began to change and turn colder, the world around us slowing down. It was easy to find this time around, the path unchanged, or at least it seemed. In a way, I figured the god's were looking for me as much as I was looking for them at this point.

I looked back at the group. Sam's face was full of elation, looking forward to the moment when it all froze. I could see his mind swimming with mischievous things—things that were bound to anger Margriete. Edgar, too, looked excited. His black-opal eyes reflected the light, full of amazement. I stopped for a moment as he caught up, taking his hand as I startled him. He snapped out of his trance.

"Haven't you ever been here before?" I looked up at him, his skin glowing in the dim daylight, his body as striking as mine would be on a beautiful day. He always looked best in the light of a storm, but I could see why. His evil side thrived in this type of environment, giving him life and energy.

He looked down at me with black eyes, a smile on his face that played at the corners of his cheeks, creating deep wrinkles. "Believe it or not, I haven't. I've only been to Heaven one way: by force—never on my own free will."

I laughed. "Really?" Thinking about it, I saw he was probably right. I knew he had been to Heaven before me, while I was gone, but it was likely he had found a way to force himself in, or get dragged in by the gods.

"Yeah, I mean. I always tried to find the fastest way. But this is fascinating."

I looked up, seeing the trees above had now frozen, no longer blowing on the wind that was now also absent. "I think we're getting close."

Edgar nodded, as though waiting for me to say something.

I exhaled, rubbing my hands together with nervous energy. "You haven't asked me why I'm doing this, why I'm coming to talk to them. How come?"

I saw Edgar swallow. "I know what you're doing, Elle, and I'm okay with it. I can understand how you thought I'd be angry, but I'm not. I've done all I need to here. I told you that."

"So, Sam told you?" I guess keeping secrets was out of the question for him.

"Well, yes. But I had already figured it out on my own, just by the way you talked about it, as though it was the end of our time here—no matter what happened."

I clapped my hands together once. "Well, I guess that makes this easier on me."

Edgar's mouth curled into a smile. "Exactly. It's not worth being angry about anything anymore. We are doing a great thing here, a necessary thing. The two worlds should have never mixed to begin with."

He was right. There was nothing to worry about. For the first time, everything was finally getting straightened out.

I heard a twig snap behind me and I turned to look. Sam had two sticks in his hands, his eyes looking around for trouble. I saw Margriete swat the sticks from his hands with a frown, lacing her fingers in his and holding tight. I could see that she was hoping to keep him under control and avoid a repeat of what happened last time, but it wasn't going very well. Sam bickered at her under his breath and she glared back. Margriete was not ready to kill any wildlife, not when they were threatened enough as it was.

We crossed the same river we had before, the frozen water swelling to nearly five times what it previously was. I slipped my way across the first half before Edgar swept me off the ice and threw me over his shoulder. I giggled wildly. On the other side, he set me down as I continued to roar with laughter, my cheeks blushing.

Sam rolled his eyes at us, Margriete looking mildly jealous. I stopped laughing and righted myself, taking the lead. As expected, I saw steam begin rise from the forest, and as we drew close, I saw the gryphon's fires igniting through the tops of some of the trees.

Sam took the lead then, his wings extended, his drive to protect us taking over as he walked slow, creeping toward them as we came into the small clearing. They noticed us then, waking from a doze and rising to their feet. The head gryphon remained regal, while the young one shifted his weight from one foot to the next—clearly anxious.

I stepped in front of Sam as he tried to grab me, but I was quick to slink away. I walked right up to the gryphon, seeing him act appalled. "Gryphon, I need you to summon the gods for me."

The gryphon tilted his head, his chest puffed with pride. "You, again. Why should I help you?" His voice made me smile. On my last visit, the gryphon had managed to extract Edgar's voice out of me, but this time, it was Scott's voice he chose to use.

If anything, I found that hearing Scott made me feel at ease. "Because, by helping me, you help yourself to survive all this." I motioned to the world around us.

The gryphon looked around, hunger in his eyes. I knew for a fact that they came here to hunt, but since the storms had started, I was certain the hunting had been sparse. Flecks of molten iron fell from its body, sizzling as it hit the ground.

"I see." The rear gryphon turned and paced toward the cave, and then paced back, rearing in the air as he crashed down, shaking the earth.

"Do not help her," he uttered in the same voice. "She is a *traitor.*"

I laughed, mocking him. "I am no traitor. I am your *savior.* You should bow to me." It felt good to say it, and my heart fluttered with strength.

The gryphon laughed sharply. "I will never do such a thing! The gods are my creators. *Not you.*"

I laughed back. "Then you should know that I am in charge of the gods. They are at my mercy just as much as you are."

The gryphon remained stubbornly silent, giving me no reply.

I crossed my arms against my chest. "Fine. Then I'll leave."

I turned and began to walk away, hearing the gryphon move behind me. I waited for what I knew was coming, confidence streaming through me and giving me strength.

"Wait, human." The gryphon's movements lumbered to a halt.

A smile grew on my face as I looked into Edgar's eyes, seeing the flames of the gryphon's glitter within them. I could feel their heat close at my back, the sizzling sending a chilling noise throughout the dying forest. I slowly began to turn and face them, a smug mask pressed across my face.

"Yes?"

The gryphon puffed his chest, disliking the fact that he was forced to give up control. *Wait one moment.* He held his head high.

I stood with a relaxed pose, gloating as they had to me. "Why now? I gave you your chance and you failed. Just wait until the god's find out that their demise was your fault." Now I was just being arrogant, but they deserved to understand submission.

The gryphon exhaled hard, fire erupting from its nostrils. "Do not test me, human."

I laughed, but kept my mouth shut. The gryphon turned then and seemed to talk to the other gryphon without words. The second gryphon acted annoyed, pounding its claws against the ground. The head gryphon snapped at his friend, causing him to stop and turn, disappearing into the cave.

The head gryphon turned back to me. "One moment, please." He looked upward to the sky, trying all he could to avoid making eye contact with me. He flapped his wings, lifting one to clean underneath as sparks flew into the air, tainting it with the thick smell of sulfur. We all watched, and not before too long, the younger gryphon returned. The head gryphon turned to look at him briefly.

"It is done." He nodded slowly.

Confused, I took one step toward him as he turned to walk away. "Wait. When will they come?"

The gryphon laughed but did not bother to look at me. "Now."

I was shocked by his answer, figuring it would have taken longer for the gods to assemble. I had planned to go back, wait for them at my house where they could show up as before. I stepped back, walking to where Sam and Edgar stood, looking at them but not saying a word as I took a deep breath. It was as though my heart had gotten shocked back to life, the steady calm feeling threatening to leave as it thudded in my chest.

It was then that a small shiny crystal marble burst from the cave. It rolled and bounced its way across the rough dirt, causing both the gryphons to rear. They flapped their wings and backed up, making room. Our group backed up as well, seeing the marble landing on the open path before us. It then began to grow.

I watched in amazement as it took form, expanding at a rapid pace. I thought about what Edgar had told me about our house, and how he would collapse it down to take with him. I wondered if this thing before us was something similar. Edgar grabbed my hand, pulling me farther back as the object continued to grow. I gasped as two white towers erupted from within, the object finally assuming a solid form as it shot fifty feet into the air.

"Edgar, what—" I was in shock. A small stone castle stood before us, like a miniature version of the large one I'd seen in Heaven.

The gryphons rounded the structure, taking their places on either side of the archway that led into a center courtyard. We all looked at each other before moving forward, knowing there was no danger, or at least hoping so. We passed between the two gryphons as they sat motionless, like statues of burning marble.

In the courtyard, I saw that the two towers flanked a small white stone cottage. Also in the yard was a table, like one you'd find in a fancy garden. Around that table sat five gods. Nicholas was in the middle, and to his left was the beautiful god from before. Her hair was now a silky blonde and it sparkled in the sunlight that seemed to come from nowhere. I felt as though we had been trapped inside some sort of eternal rainbow. The small stout god was to Nicholas's right, smoking a cigar as Nicholas had been before. I did not recognize the other two gods, so I deduced that they had either been absent when I last visited, or were in fact just meant for intimidation.

We approached them, finding four empty seats at the table and taking our places. I sat with caution, keeping my back straight and my eyes steady. I quelled my shaking hands by folding them in my lap, leaning back ever so slightly so that I appeared at ease.

The beautiful blonde winked at Edgar. "Edgar. So nice to see you." She gave him a coy smile.

I growled under my breath, grinding my teeth.

Edgar nodded politely. "Ariana. Always a pleasure." I sensed hatred in Edgar's voice, and it put me at ease.

"Hello, Nicholas," I said in a dry voice.

"Estella. So lovely to see you so close to your—should we just say—*performance?*" He glared down on me from over his nose, tilting his head so far back, that I wondered if he could see me at all.

I nodded to him, leaning forward and placing my folded hands on the table before us. "I suppose you know why I've come?"

Nicholas smiled as the stout man beside him blew a cloud of smoke at Sam. Sam shifted in his seat and I saw Margriete grab his leg from the corner of my eye, trying to calm him.

"I suppose," he answered, rather annoyed.

"Then you already know what I will ask of you?" I lifted one brow, testing him.

He leaned back, showing his displeasure as well as

insecurity in the moment—I had control. His eyes were nervous, likely afraid of the things I could leverage at a time like this. "To some degree, I understand. Please elaborate."

I remained calm. "I am here to bargain with you. I want us both to benefit from this great opportunity that has been presented to us."

Nicholas leaned forward as Ariana snarled. "Yes. What a lovely opportunity. Go on."

I couldn't help rubbing my importance in their faces. "As *The One*, I believe I am entitled to some requests, and of course recognition. As such, I believe you have no choice but to honor my wishes. If you fail at your task, and refuse to uphold the contract that will be written here today, then I will let us all die, and you will never be trusted by Fate ever again. This Earth will be your last."

Nicholas shifted uncomfortably in his seat, and I knew I had said the right thing.

I continued. "It is my wish that, as payment for my deed, all magic is to leave the surface of Earth forever. Everyone, even Edgar and I, are included in this."

Nicholas nodded once. "That is a handsome reward you allow for yourself, especially considering that beings like you do not belong in Heaven."

I took a deep breath as though trying to show the fact that his ignorance had insulted me. "This is my wish, and I will not falter."

Ariana touched Nicholas's arm then, and he leaned

down so she could whisper something in his ear. I tried to read her emotions, looking to Sam for some assistance but saw that he too seemed to struggle, unable to read what she was thinking. Nicholas leaned back once more, his lips pressed in a thin line.

"We can do this, as long as you understand all that you must do, and take responsibility for every consequence of being *The One*." He seemed pleased somehow, but also troubled.

"This seems too easy." I read into his pleasure. "What is it you think you will trick me with this time?" I tried to read through his lies.

"Darling girl, if I were pleased, you would see me *smile*. I am content is all. I rarely visit the surface, so what harm does it do me?"

I smirked. "Like I said, though, everyone must leave, even the angels, unless sent to collect souls. You will have no part, or no way of knowing what is happening here in this world. You will be severed from it for all eternity."

I saw Ariana's expression turn sour. Clearly she wanted to find a way to work things in their favor. She tried to get Nicholas to look at her once more, but he refused. "Very well."

Ariana let one annoyed breath leave her perfect mouth.

"*Silence,* Ariana," Nicholas snapped, swinging his hand in an attempt to slap her—he missed. "You have your deal. Just fulfill the *prophecy*." He spit as he said 'prophecy', as though jealous of its very creation.

187

I saw Sam look at Edgar with frantic eyes, but Edgar did not respond. Sam looked at me instead. "Elle, are you sure about this?" His eyes seemed frantic, but I looked away.

"Sam, this is the deal and it's final. *Margriete*—" I barked. "Hand me your journal." I had seen her slip her gold journal into her belt before we left, and I remember thinking that it had been the perfect thing to use as a contract. The pages were strong.

Margriete was quick to slip it from her belt and hand it to me. I placed the book on the table, running hand slowly across the cover before hastily flipping it open and turning to the back. I found a blank page, and with a powerful snap, I ripped it from the spine. It took all my strength to do so, the paper laced with real gold. I then reached for one of Edgar's feathers, plucking it from his large protruded wings. I touched the feather to the paper as the page before me begun to write up a contract, filling it with words, faster than I could write.

On this day, the 11th of August, in the year two thousand and ten, the world of the gods has agreed to leave the surface of Earth for all of eternity, except when transporting souls to Heaven. Only then can a magical soul enter, and even so, only the angels are allowed. I will repeat, no god is to ever see this land again. Furthermore, under no circumstances, but the above mentioned, may they leave Heaven, and under no circumstances may magic return to the surface, or act to rule over the Human race. This is a binding contract, signed by the bloodlines of both the gods of Heaven and the human beings they have created. This contract is under the ownership of the humans alone, and will never be allowed to fall into magical hands, ever again. If the contract is broken, one or both parties may rebut their claim in a court of Heaven, and proper and fair punishment will follow.

Effective August 15th, 2010.
All Sales are Final.

I tilted my head in question of the last part, but figured it was okay in the end. Satisfied, I took Edgar's feather, touching the sharp tip to my finger and drawing a small bead of blood as I punched it through the skin. I let the blood fill the quill of the feather like a rich red ink. I placed the tip of the feather against the page and signed my name, the blood seeping into the gold and creating a deep ridge. I plucked another feather from Edgar as he winced with an angered face. I handed the contract and the fresh feather to Nicholas, instructing him to do the same.

Nicholas took the page with a wary hand, looking it over and then looking at me. I sat still, my jaw clenched and my head spinning. He followed my lead, punching the feather into his finger. As I watched, I saw that the blood was black, indicating the true color of his heart. He showed me the bleeding finger as proof, and then signed the page. He set the feather down when he was finished, shoving it back toward me with a frown.

"It is done," he added.

I took the page in my hands, rolling the thick foil in my grasp. "Thank you." Satisfied, I stood.

He reached over and grabbed the cigar from the stout man's mouth, putting it in his own and inhaling deeply. He held the smoke in his lungs for a moment before slowly exhaling. "Edgar, Sam, Margriete—*Elle*—we'll see you soon." He nodded once more and I took it as our cue to leave.

Sam and Margriete stood, turning without a second look

and walking beside me through the archway and back into the forest. As our feet crossed the threshold, the small castle began to implode. Folding in and on itself until nothing but a marble remained. I watched as it rolled vigorously back to the cave where it disappeared. The gryphons resumed their stance beside the cave, no longer concerned by us. I smiled, looking at Edgar. He smiled as well, though there was something about it that seemed off, something that was missing. Perhaps it was the fact that he would miss it here.

WALK HOME
Edgar

"Hey," Sam barked, walking up beside me as Elle and Margriete walked on in front of us. They were laughing and talking amongst themselves, the air filled with their happiness. "Are you alright with this?"

I nodded.

Sam exhaled and looked to the ground. "I know the risk here. I know Elle doesn't quite understand what can happen. I know she thinks about it, though. I hear her mind whisper in her sleep."

I nodded again, feeling my heart sink. "I just hope that doesn't happen. I hope things go seamlessly."

"The gods are also aware of the same risks we are. That's why they pressed that particular point." He was being vague in case anyone overheard. I could see he was trying to keep this conversation amongst us, for once.

I glared at Sam anyway. It wasn't a subject I really wanted to address, either.

"Oh, chill. I bet everything will be fine." Sam rolled his eyes away from mine.

Elle was so worried about what happened to us, that she barely cared about what happened to her. I knew that either way she would be safe, either way she would have someone there. This was the part I had dreaded, though, and the root of the reason behind my faltering mood and lies.

I nodded once more as Elle turned. "Hey, hurry up. I want to get back so that we can have a few more night of fun before you all have to leave. I want to enjoy this!" She bounced in the air, happiness seeping from her as though nothing were wrong. She made it seem like a vacation, a mere week or two away. I didn't blame her for thinking that way at all. How else do you cope with such a burden?

I smiled. I was glad that she had struck her bargain, and happy that she would at last find her peace. There was nothing I could do but love her, and hope that it was enough to guide her back to me in the end.

THE BLACKOUT
Estella

"Edgar?" The room was dark, the wind roaring outside. "Edgar?" I whispered louder, shaking him awake.

"Hmm." He moved, rolling over.

"Edgar, I'm scared."

He took a deep breath. I saw his eyes blink open in the dark, glimmering with whatever light filtered into the room. "Elle, don't worry."

I let a sharp breath leave my lips. I was wide awake, finding it annoying that he could sleep at a time like this.

I felt his hand grasp my wrist then, his fingers cold as they felt the bones that were beneath. My heart rate slowed and his energy entered my body like a drug, making every fear dissipate. "Is that better?"

I nuzzled against his body. "Yes, but still, I'm frightened. I'm afraid of what will happen. What if it kills me?"

Edgar's palm traced up my arm. "You will be fine,

darling. I promise."

His words brought me comfort, and as I lay against his body, I felt as he relaxed and his breathing became shallow. He fell back to sleep, leaving me once again in silence. I watched the shadows as though something was there. I pulled my arm out from under Edgar's grasp, looking at it, wondering where the power was.

It was then that a light flashed across the floor of my room, leaking in from under the door. I carefully lifted my head to look, sliding away from Edgar and to the side of the bed. I watched the light, as the dust from the room rose through the single ray. The light moved then, fading as though to leave. I looked back at Edgar as he let out a heavy sigh of dreaming. Content that he was still asleep, I slid my feet from the bed, gently placing them on the chilly floor. I let my nightgown fall around me as I stood, walking away from Edgar on tiptoes.

Reaching the door, I saw the light almost completely fade. My anxiety to follow grew. As slowly as I could, I placed my hand on the handle, opening the door and poking my head out to inspect. My eyes met the source of the light then, and a smile grew on my face. The prophecy was floating at the top of the stairs, its light a welcoming glow.

I stepped out, turning to shut the door of my room behind me. I waited for the gentle click of the latch, then let go. I turned back to the prophecy and it floated toward me.

"Hi," I whispered, reaching up and tapping the top of the cube with my fingers. The prophecy twisted from side to side with apparent happiness. I let out a gentle chuckle, wiggling my toes against the floor. The prophecy turned then, and floated away from me. I watched, wondering where it was going when it turned back, as though to urge me to follow.

Curious, I did as it wanted, walking down the stairs as the prophecy made its way to library. I rounded into the room, watching as the prophecy continued forward and out into the greenhouse that I had all but abandoned. The prophecy's light reflected of the glass wall, beautiful as it filled the room with a blue green glow. I watched as the prophecy moved over a few of the tables, swaying down toward the dirt in waves.

"What?" I asked, wondering what it was trying to say. "Do you want me to grow you something?"

The prophecy shot upward with a sharp swing, as though to show excitement. Then it bobbed up and down and I smiled, enjoying this more than I was enjoying my attempts to fall asleep. I walked up to the table, running my hand through the barren dirt as a trail of small poppies grew behind my touch.

The prophecy's light grew bright and cheerful, shaking with joy. I chuckled as the sound echoed off the glass and back to me. The prophecy moved to the next table, making the same side to side swaying movement. I followed its lead, moving to the next table where I buried my hand deep inside the dirt. I rubbed my pointer finger and thumb together. A seed grew between them and I left it behind, pulling my hand from the soil, a vine following fast behind it. I smiled wide as the seed grew into a large sunflower that grazed the ceiling, the head of the flower at least a foot across. The sunflower's seeds began to shed from it, sprouting in the nearby dirt and creating a whole grove of yellow. The prophecy glowed even brighter then, picking up excitement as it circled the room and ceiling, finally resting near a pot in the corner.

"Oh, I see what you're saying," I sang.

I tiptoed over to the pot beneath the prophecy, the pads of my feet gathering up the dirt that was on the ground. I knelt down beside the pot as the prophecy watched over my shoulder. I dug both hands deep inside, the dirt reaching my elbows. I pinched my fingers together once more, leaving two bulbs behind. I quickly pulled my hand out as the plants shot skyward, bright purple clematis blooming across the ceiling and latching onto the grids of the glass.

The prophecy spun then, following the vines as they continued to spread, outlining the frame of the door and causing the echo in the room to fade. I had forgotten the beauty in this world. Forgotten what a flower even looked like. All summer it had rained, the plants dying. But here, looking at all this, you would think all that was nothing more than a bad dream. I pulled myself off the ground, wiping my sodden hands on my nightgown and leaving it covered in dirt.

I approached another table that was full of small pots in every size and color. I touched the tip of my finger to each as a different type of perennial bloomed behind me, in every color imaginable.

The fun began to snowball, and I moved on to the next table. Here, I grew my favorite plant, the purple clover. I waved my hand, allowing it to spread across the whole table as the small lavender flower and deep purple leaves grew larger than ever. The prophecy continued to dance about, growing brighter and brighter by the second. I was dancing now, too, imaginary music playing in my mind. It was then that I saw the prophecy begin to shake. I watched the light inside it grow brighter and brighter, like a burning sun.

I stopped dancing, the flowers continuing to spread around me, filling the room with fragrance and color. The prophecy was shaking faster now, and I felt my heart begin to race, my eyes growing wide as I watched it. I didn't understand what was happening. What had I done? My feet were flat against the moist greenhouse floor, the feeling of grit and gravel between my toes. My hands were stiff at my sides, my nails blackened. The smell of earth filled my nostrils as I puffed hard.

The prophecy froze.

I took a deep breath, feeling it fill my lungs in slow motion, oxygen seeping into my blood. I exhaled hard, and it was then that the prophecy flashed, a red light beaming out toward me and filling my mind with thoughts and images.

I saw myself by the lake, holding a red cube in one hand, my other reaching toward the sky. I heard myself utter something low, something I could not repeat but knew like my own name. My face was fixed, there was not a soul in sight.

I screamed.

Everything went dark as I felt my body go limp. My body fell limp to the floor.

LITTLE HELPER
Edgar

I woke alone in Elle's room, something that felt foreign to me.

"Elle?" My voice was still hoarse from sleep. *"Elle?"* I asked again. I had grown so used to waking with Elle at my side that it alarmed me. I sat up, throwing the covers off the bed, burying Isabelle inside them. She protested with one sharp *'caw.'*

I stood, walking to the door with heavy steps. Something was wrong. I felt it. Throwing the door open, I stormed out into the hall and bounded down the stairs. Sam opened the door to my room, having heard the commotion.

"Edgar, what's wrong?" He knew, but probably felt he should say something to get my attention.

I turned to face him, halfway down the stairs. "Sam,

where is she? Do you hear her?"

Sam drew a shirt over his head. I had given him and Margriete my room, tired of seeing them passing out on my couch. "Yeah, I hear her. Take a deep breath, Edgar. She's just sleeping."

I looked around the hall with frantic eyes. *"Where?"*

"Well, not in the hall, obviously." Sam smiled, running his hand down his chest and smoothing his shirt. He made his way down the stairs, passing me. I followed, annoyed that he wouldn't just say it and tell me where she was.

His gait was superior as I followed him into the library. We both slowed our pace as we saw vines of clematis growing up the stacks of books and leading us in through the door to the greenhouse. With caution, we entered the room, seeing that every inch was layered in thick foliage and flowers.

"What the—" I stopped just inside the door, looking around as Sam walked down one of the aisles. He reached out and touched a flower. The flower seemed to nip at him. It was then that I saw a dirty foot peeking out from behind a table, just inside the door and to the right. I lunged toward it, dropping to the ground and crawling up to her. She was laying on her side, curled in a fetal position.

"Elle," I gasped, shaking her. I stood up. "Sam, over here!"

I heard him round the tables, rushing to where we were and kneeling to the ground.

"Elle?" I shook her gently. She moved, dropping

something that was held tightly against her chest. The object made a clanking crystal sound as it hit the dirty cement. Her eyes fluttered open at the sound, dirt covering her face and in her hair.

"Elle, are you alright?" Sam brushed the hair from her face.

She smiled as she looked up at me. "Hi, Edgar." Relief washed over me—she was fine.

"Elle, what happened?" I motioned toward the room.

She rolled over, revealing the object that had made the sound. She saw it the same time I did, her brow furrowed as she reached toward it, taking it in her grasp. She sat up, bringing the object to her face. I watched her, also inspecting the object. It was a ruby cube, clear, solid, and void of any imperfections.

"What is that?" I asked. Her sleepy eyes met mine.

"I—" She began to talk but stopped herself as though trying to remember.

Sam spoke, probing her mind. "It's the prophecy, or rather, what's left of it."

My eyes grew wide. "That is the prophecy? What happened to it?"

Elle was dumbfounded, so Sam continued to fill me in. "It has fulfilled itself. I mean, not the future, obviously. But it has fulfilled its task here. It has changed into its final stage."

"What do you mean its *final stage?*" I was lost, why hadn't I known about this?

"From what I can gather from Elle's thoughts, and what the prophecy revealed to her, it seems that this cube is the key to it all. This cube will be able to spread her power across the entire Earth. She came down here last night, and they did this." He motioned to the plants in the room. "And by dong so, the prophecy learned how to spread her powers. It is now the tool she needs to make it all happen."

I was shocked as he said it. I hadn't known any of this, but I was relieved to hear it. I had worried about how she was going to accomplish such a huge feat in such a short amount of time. I knew she would grow powerful, but just how much I was uncertain. With this, though, she would be able to channel her talents, spread her power like a lighthouse in a storm.

Elle hugged the cube to her chest, her dirty hands smearing fingerprints all across it. I hooked my arm under Elle's legs and behind her back, hoisting her off the ground and holding her against my chest. She began to hum, as though lulling a small child.

"Is she alright?" I asked Sam.

Sam lifted one brow. "Yes, I think she's just tired. That, and she's likely loosing it. She has a lot on her shoulders. I don't blame her. Some rest should do the trick."

I walked her from the room. "I'll take her to bed." Elle seemed to wake from her trance.

"Wait! *No.* I'm not tired." She wiggled from my arms, to stand on her own two feet. She held the cube between her hands. "I have a lot to do—*we do.* I don't want to sleep anymore.

I nodded with concern. "If you say so."

She smiled, reaching up and placing her hand on the nape of my neck. She stood on her toes and kissed me on the cheek.

Her lips were warm, and I could smell the dirt on her skin. "How about a shower?" I felt the dirt on her hands fall and roll under my shirt, tickling down my back. She giggled.

"Yeah, that's a good idea."

She looked at herself, realizing how much of a mess she was. She tried to rub he dirt from her knees but it only made it worse. I watched as the floor of the library absorbed the dirt that had fallen from her, disappearing to leave it once again clean.

"I'll be right back." She turned with the cube still in her hand, skipping from the room and making her way up the stairs, the trail of dirt slowly disappearing behind her.

"Sam, did you know about this?" I turned away from the door to the hall.

Sam shook his head. "Nope, not even me."

"Do you think this could change things? Reduce the risks?" I folded my hands across my chest.

"Maybe."

Hearing him agree with me made my body loosen up. "Well, that's good. Takes a load off *my* mind."

Sam chuckled. "Mine too." He lifted one brow, looking at my head. He was referring to the fact that he wouldn't have to hear me worry about it anymore.

I laughed in return, allowing myself the rare pleasure of relaxing. I looked down at the clothes I had been sleeping in, suddenly embarrassed.

Sam laughed again, glancing at my boxers before looking away.

An awkward feeling filled the room. I turned to leave. Sam laughed louder behind me, angering me slightly. I kept my arms crossed against my chest, squandering my desire to attack. I exhaled as I reached the stairs, climbing with an added energy. Things were going to be fine—things had to be.

DEPARTURE
Estella

I walked up behind Edgar, running my hands up his back as he stood, packing a few of my things into a bag. I didn't want to pack, but I didn't even have to ask—Edgar did it for me anyway. The red cube sat on the bedside table, still as a stone. I felt Edgar's muscles flex, his attention still on the satchel before him. I had changed into an outfit fit for winter, with tall laced hiking boots and a warm v-neck sweater.

"Edgar?" I asked.

He stopped, no longer able to avoid talking to me. "Yes?" I heard his voice waver.

I gripped his shoulders, firmly turning him around.

He turned with reluctance, his eyes avoiding mine. As he moved out of the way of the bag, I saw for the first time what he was packing. I stared for a moment, trying to make sense of it all. There were a few journals shoved deep inside, their dates too hard to read but I was certain they were journals that were important to him as well as me. On top of the journals was a change of clothes, likely the things he figured I couldn't live without for the next few days.

"Thanks for doing that, Edgar." I tried to get him to look at me but his eyes continued to avoid mine.

"I'm sorry I have to take all this." He motioned to the house around us.

I laughed. "Edgar, it doesn't matter. Why are you so scared? It's only a few days. Then I'll be back."

He frowned, fidgeting with his hands. "I know."

I tried to be the strong one as I touched my hands to his arms. I felt his energy seep into my skin, and it knocked the wind from my lungs. He was so frightened that it chilled my whole body, making me more afraid than before. I shut my eyes, trying to calm myself.

"I saw the future, Edgar. Have faith in that." He looked at me as I opened my eyes.

"Faith? That hardly makes me feel better."

I slid my hands under his shirt, splaying my fingers across his back. I smiled. "Well, you have to believe in something. You are an angel, after all."

I saw his mouth begin to curl, though I know he was trying as hard as he could to remain sullen. "I believe in you," he reassured me, knowing that I was just as scared. He wrapped me in his arm, pulling me against his chest.

I breathed in his scent: lilac. I exhaled. There was

nothing that could replace the way his body felt, though the absence of the heat I once loved was gone. The physical pressure of his touch made me want to stay here forever, forget everything and just live. There were things to be done, though, or it was all for nothing.

He kissed the top of my head. "Elle, I don't know what I'm supposed to say." His voice wavered.

I looked up at his face, resting my chin on his chest. "About what?"

He backed up and sat on the bed, his hands resting on either side of my hips as I stood before him. He thought for a moment, his eyes dark and black. "I've always left you under sudden circumstances, never like this. A long goodbye does not suit me." He leaned his head against my stomach.

I placed my hands on his head, running my fingers through his hair. "It's better this way, Edgar. This way we can say our good-byes in a proper way."

He looked up at me with an angered face—not anger toward me, but something else. "It's not goodbye," he protested. "I refuse to say that to you. I've been so afraid of losing you, and I am ashamed of the way I've been acting. I fear I've wasted the time we had together."

I laughed. "I know that. I realize now why you were acting so stubborn." I bent down, putting my face close to his. As always, I felt our soul stitch us together and pull me in. His breathing stopped.

"Elle, do you know how much I love you?" His words

found their way into my heart, touching it gently.

I nuzzled my nose against his. "I know." His eyes were a deep black as he tried to pull away from me.

"Elle, don't." I saw the struggle in his face.

I took one step back, letting go. Since the day he came home, there had been a distance between us. I still longed for the intensity we once had.

He sat up straight, his eyes looking away from me and to the ground. He looked nervous and bothered. The wings on his back extended across my bed. I watched as they rose and then fell in gentle waves, as though he were breathing, though he wasn't.

I turned away from him, walking to the wall across the room where my paintings hung. My jaw was tight, as it had been for the past few weeks. I looked at the one painting of myself.

I used to see this girl as someone that was happy and carefree, but now that I knew better, I saw something far darker. What I saw was someone that struggled with her confidence day by day. She was someone that was tormented in the same way Edgar had been. I over-drove my emotions in the hopes of achieving my idea of true happiness, but was that even possible? What would have happened if I had let go of all my responsibilities and just lived? Would we even be here?

I turned away from the wall, annoyed with myself. My eyes locked with Edgar's and I realized he was still here. I needed to stop pretending he was gone. His face was impassive, as though he were no more than a statue. I licked my lips, watching him as he watched me walk back toward him. When I reached him, I saw in his eyes something I'd missed. I thought back to the first day we met, back to the day when I didn't know who he was, and the way his eyes had both frightened and amazed me.

My fingers touched his collar bone, tracing back and around his neck. I was remembering his outline, and the way I worshiped every inch of it. He put one hand on my waist, the ring on his finger burning through my shirt and stinging my skin. It was the only part of him that still glowed with life. I lowered my face until our eyes were level with each other, my breath passing my parted lips. He leaned toward me but I mirrored his movements, leaning away from him. I was too drawn by his gaze to lose it just yet. I saw calm and unity locked inside those eyes, something the world held little of these days.

He did not smile or find my resistance at all amusing. His hand on my waist tightened, pulling me toward him. Still, I resisted. The look on his face grew frustrated and angry as he tried ever harder to lean in and kiss me, but as I stared at the voids of his eyes, I could not give in. There was still a part of me that wanted to punish him for the way he'd acted toward me, but I found it was hard to resist falling in love all over again. My mind began to fog.

He stood, putting his other hand on my waist and gripping tighter. I dropped my hands to my sides as we stepped backwards across the room in a dance. My back met the wall. I was trapped, and though I could not take another step back, he took one step further, closing any gap that was left between us. His hands left my waist, trailing up the wall to my neck where his thumbs grazed my collar bones, his fingers wrapping my shoulders.

His touch was light, but I knew if I tried to move, he wouldn't let me. I lifted my hands from my sides, and put them on his waist, feeling his belt below his shirt. He was breathing now, falling into the old habit easily in his distraction.

His fingers slipped into my hair as he pushed my long locks back from my face, twisting it into a pony tail and then letting it drop. He was stalling, fighting with himself and the things he could, or could not control. I leaned toward him, our noses grazing. I touched my lips to his upper lip, kissing it as he stayed frozen.

His lips were cold but soft, almost foreign to me. It felt as though I was kissing him for the first time. My lips were hot as I leaned back, allowing our eyes to focus on each other. A tight but warm feeling filled my chest. It was a feeling I had missed, a feeling that tingled through my every limb.

He pressed me against the wall with more force. His mouth parted, and I saw that his teeth were clenched, trying his best to hold onto his sanity. He exhaled hard, pressing his cold cheek against mine. My face was flushed, his lips kissing down my jaw with an electric chill. He kissed my neck, and as much as I knew we should stop, I also knew that he was not going to be the one to initiate it this time. I tilted my head back, allowing his mouth to become the only thing I felt.

His hands left my neck and pressed against the wall on either side of my head, his breathing erratic. I pressed my palms against his chest as though to playfully push him away, but he resisted, pressing back. I felt his teeth bite the skin on my shoulder with a gentle pressure, annoyed that I had tried to drive him away.

He continued to kiss my skin, so I pressed harder on his chest. His hands curled against the wall, pushing back with an even greater force than before. It was becoming clear that I would not win this fight. My heart was racing, my body heat causing the sweater I wore to grow warm. With all the strength I could muster, I pushed once more. At last, I was able to break him away from me. He stumbled back in shock, as though a spell had been broken between us.

His expressionless face never turned away from me, and his black eyes were fixed. I had a look of anger on my face, the feeling of my weakness toward him teeming in my blood. The tight feeling in my chest was one I had begun to forget, one I hadn't felt in what seemed months. I did not want it to go away, and I certainly did not want to forget it ever again.

I stared at him for another moment, his eyes showing that his control had been regained. I gave up thinking, instead stepping forward with haste. I pressed my lips against his. His arms wrapped around me like a snare, our lips intertwined. I pushed him backward but he lifted me off the ground instead, taking control.

The world around me whirled as his drug finally engulfed my last ounce of sanity. I could not shake the feeling that it felt like the end, the real end, but I had to believe that I would succeed. I would never rest, always fighting. This was the way I was made. No matter the cost, I had to find my way back to this feeling. It was my only hope.

Edgar grasped the hem of my sweater, pulling it over my head. Our hips pressed together, and my hand found the buckle of his jeans. This was it, he wasn't going to stop me this time. His hand trailed up my bare back, his kissing controlled, and his mind made up.

I opened my eyes, seeing him watching me. His lips curled against mine before he shut his eyes once more, twisting my body onto the bed and under him as all control was lost.

FALL OF DARKNESS
Estella

It was dark when I slid from the bed, dressing quietly as Edgar slept. I couldn't bare another long goodbye. I had to get started, now. Carefully I slid the red cube off the night-stand, stashing into the leather satchel as I tied the flap shut. I tiptoed to the door, slipping out and shutting it behind me as the candles in the hallway came to life. I brought my finger to my mouth, hushing the light and it dimmed. I threw the satchel over my back and began to descend the stairs.

I heard a small creak behind me, twisting as I looked back. A part of me expected it to be Edgar, but as my eyes met those of my follower, I saw it was Sam. He had one hand on the rail, his mouth drawn into a gentle smile. He said nothing, just stood there, watching me in a relaxed pose.

I was afraid he would stop me, but then again, that wasn't his nature. He nodded slowly, and I nodded back. *Goodbye,* I thought. He smiled, letting me go for the first time since we met.

I turned then, making my way down the rest of the stairs and walking to the door, opening it without a second thought. I took a deep breath as the wind fell across my face. The smell of death lingered within it, the scent of ash and mold. I glanced over my shoulder once more as I stepped out and shut the door behind me.

The whole house slowly disappeared, the handle gone from my grasp. I shivered, knowing that was the last time I would ever see it as it is now: in the meadow of my past. Now alone, with the familiar black feeling of my youth returning to my soul, I disappeared into the night before I could allow myself to second guess my actions.

ALONE

Estella

I watched as the sun rose above the lake, now a river since damn had given, leaving nothing but rubble and rushing water. The beach was wide, more like a long sandy beach where the water had once pooled. The university lay behind me up the bank, abandoned. I let the deafening sounds of waves and water drown the thoughts in my head. I picked at the gravel on the ground, rain falling around me as I huddled under my hood. Overhead, the cry of flocking birds cut through the noise. Looking up, I saw ravens fighting through the wind, headed toward the cave.

Since the age of Matthew, I hadn't seen many of his magic ravens. I had figured that they'd all died when he did, but since the contract had been forged, I had begun to see them everyday. Any bird that Matthew had cursed was forced away from here, forced back to their own magical world, though their power had little effect on human life.

Regardless, they had been touched by Matthew's evil, and evil was contagious.

The trees around me were all browned, their dead needles lying in piles at their trunks. The school itself had taken quite a beating. The cafeteria that once seemed so solid had collapsed. Shards of glass were strewn across what once was the path I had taken to the hatchery, the door to the nurse's office off its hinges and shattered on the nearby rocks. The water of the lake had washed a ways onshore before the dam had broken, leaving everything waterlogged and gathered into piles. It was as though a bomb had gone off—the sticks of bare trees a chilling sight, like skeletons on a battlefield. The decimation spanned as far as I could see.

I pulled the satchel that was next to me into my lap, reaching inside and grabbing the red cube. I rolled it in my hands as I exposed it to the daylight, bringing it to my face as shards of luminosity streamed inside it. I peered through it, the world doused in red. I blinked a few times, surprised at what I saw, looking over the cube to be sure it was real, but it wasn't. I looked through the cube again, seeing the world perfect and alive, the trees lush and the skies open. I looked above and over the cube once more, comparing the two worlds.

I pressed my lips together thoughtfully, wondering exactly how this worked. I unfolded my legs and pushed myself off the ground, holding the cube in a ray of light that tried to shine through the clouds. It was then that the sun burst from the cube in a bright beam, lighting the spot beside me as the sand there began to move.

I watched in amazement as some groundcover rose from the spot, spreading rapidly as it wrapped around my ankles and continued on across the entire beach. It spread to a nearby tree trunk, climbing slightly before giving over all control as the tree began to grow back. I stopped breathing as pine needles sprouted from bare dead branches, the growth finally stopping as the clouds closed in and the ray of sun was lost. I expected the plants to die then, but they didn't. I dropped the cube to my side, breathing once again.

Sunlight, that's what I needed. I looked to the sky, inspecting the thick cloud cover and the mist that rose from the water. I would need to get above this to make it work, but not yet. It wasn't time. I sat back down on the beach, rain continuing to fall as the groundcover around me created a bed. The dawn was now turning to morning, the last morning this sad world would see before the new beginning.

I wondered what it would be like in this new world. Hopefully, it would be more beautiful than I had ever seen it before. I thought about the cities we had seen crumble, wondering what would come of it. I thought about all the souls we had already lost. It should never have happened this way, and I felt ashamed that the decision was left to me. Edgar hadn't understood, but it was his nature to kill, after all. Perhaps he knew, perhaps those that we lost were meant to *be* lost. I could only hope that there was a reason for all this, and a plan that was bigger than me. Perhaps I am only one small part.

By mid afternoon, I found myself flipping through the pages of the *Book of Us*, idly reading but finding myself far too anxious to allow me to pay attention. I kept looking up at every little sound, watching as one creature after another made its way into the forest and toward the caves, each somehow touched by magic. I exhaled in amazement as a large eagle flew overhead, letting out a heavy cry that echoed over the roaring wind. As daylight began to fade, I put my head in my hands, feeling my cold, numb skin and trying to warm it. I tightened the strap around my head, hoping the hood could shelter me, but it didn't. I allowed my whole body to shake for a moment as the groundcover around me also tried to help keep me warm, growing up my back.

Twilight came and the wind began to calm. I allowed my body to relax, my muscles sore from shaking so much. It was then that I saw a bright light flicker on a wave and it distracted me from the chill. I focused on the spot, hoping to see it again, but as I waited, I saw nothing. I tucked my satchel under the bend of my knees, sheltering it as I stuffed it away from the rain.

Another flash of light lit up my vision and I looked up, squinting as I watched the water with increased intensity. I dropped every thought that racked my mind as a glow began to form under the waves. It was hard to see at first, but as the murky green water, rich with debris, glowed with an ever lighter shade of turquoise, I recognized what it was. I watched as the light approached, my spine steeled. A slow breath released from my lungs as the source of the light threatened to break the surface of the water. I grew anxious, wondering if I should stand or stay still. It was then that the source of the light emerged from the water. Its shrieks broke the surface as the large Pegasus fought through the waves. Water washed over its crystal body, quickly channeling down its flawless surface. It hoisted itself up the bank as its wings emerged from its flanks, flapping off the excess water and glittering like glass in the moonlight.

It walked right up to me, as though I were nothing more than a rock. I heard it snort, sniffing the ground, its long neck reaching toward the lush groundcover. It grabbed a mouthful and yanked it from the earth, sand flying from the roots as they curled in agony. I winced, watching as it continued up the hill, its feet smashing through the glass shards that were left on the path. It swished its tail once, sending a spray of glittery water floating to the ground. As it entered the copse of barren trees, I inhaled deeply, realizing I had stopped breathing as my lungs began to sting. I watched it for a while longer, the bare trees allowing me to observe as it climbed at least a half mile up the hill. As it finally disappeared, I turned back to the lake, impressed that I had never seen it here before and wondering how long it had been living there.

At last, the final glow of daylight disappeared and I

moved toward a nearby log and began to gather wet wood. My eyes enjoyed the darkness, preferring it to the dismal of the recent days. I tilted the larger spare pieces of wood against the main log, creating a sort of shelter that I then covered with loose bits of bark. Sounds began to rumble from deep in the woods behind me, and I knew it was nearing the time for the caves to close. I heard an owl hoot, echoing the noise. I shivered. The sounds were eerie, cries of defiance and sadness. I felt sorry for all those that had been touched by the magic the gods had brought upon the Earth, but it was the way it had to be. Humans and magic did not mix. Together, we could never survive.

At last, night fell and I crawled inside my shelter, listening as the rain ran down the man-made roof. Everything was quiet now, the pulse of the Earth faint as it drew in its last few breaths. In the morning sun, I would change it all. I would bring back to this planet what it deserved, and then I, too, would leave it.

I put my hand against the dead log that lay beside me, feeling nothing but sadness. I would miss it here, but as I had seen in Heaven, it was obvious that I belonged there. In Heaven, nothing needed me—it only wanted me. In Heaven, I could finally breathe. My life was better served in a place where I could blend in, just another being with some magical talent, as all the others there.

When I was a little girl, in my human life, I used to think that magic was what I read in fairy tales. I imagined goblets of fire and wands, flying beams of light and *hocus pocus*.

Now, though, I saw that magic was much more tangible, something much more organic. It was not like that of the magic in books. It was something that was individual to most, something like a notion. It was the kind of magic no one saw coming, the kind that if they did witness, they wouldn't believe. I knew that tomorrow, though, my magic would leave behind believers. I would spawn a world of grateful humans—humans that will either loathe, or love me.

My thoughts next fell to Edgar, wondering how he was, wondering *where* he was. I didn't expect that when I left, he would come after me. He knew as well as I that saying goodbye would only feel like another end, which it wasn't. This time I knew he was safe, I knew he was alive, and I knew my way back to him. But something inside me still could not shake the feeling. I was so conditioned to lose him, that there was no way I could make the ache in my chest stop. I had ignored it a good portion of the day, but now it was boredom that was calling in the doubt. That was all, and I needed to understand that. This would work.

I balled up my satchel and pushed it under my head. The damp leather smelled like dark coffee as it entered my nostrils. Unable to handle the scent, I breathed through my mouth instead. I forced my eyes shut, hoping that sleep would make time go faster. I heard my heart beat in rhythm with the drops of rain and it lulled me, the steam from my breath began to fill my small enclosure, finally warming my frozen skin. In the morning, everything would be better.

THE NEW WORLD
Estella

I woke to a dull silence, light filtering through the woods. It had stopped raining, and the wind was silent. I furrowed my brow as I slid from my enclosure, looking toward the sky as an indicator of what was happening. The clouds there were thick but still, lurking down on me as they engulfed the mountains. I cursed under my breath, wondering how high the clouds reached and hoping I could still get above them. At least the wind had stopped, which was a good thing, making my flight there easier. For the first time in a while, I could hear my footsteps while outside, reminding me of my presence, but also loneliness. My feet sank into the drying sand, the groundcover around me still thriving despite the fact that the sun did not shine.

I examined the landscape around me, seeing it was completely dead now, all but my little area. I let out a slow breath, my ears filled with sound of lapping waves from the lake. I walked back to my small shelter and grabbed my satchel. I walked to a clear spot in the groundcover and sat in the sand, pulling the satchel into my lap. I dug inside, pulling out a new journal, a pen, and the red cube. I set the red cube in the sand before me, snuggling it down as it formed a bed around it.

I then brought the journal into my lap and opened to the first page. This journal was to be the first to denote a new time in my life, a new era. I was nervous, there was no denying that, but writing would calm me. I pressed the pen to the page and ink flooded into the paper.

Here I am, on the cusp of it all, wondering what will happen and how it will be from here on out. I want to say goodbye to so many things, but I will not get the chance. I think of Scott and Sarah, and my foster mother, Heidi. I think about the day I came here, the way it felt to finally break free. I have come a long way, far further than most ever will in their lives. When I think about it, I see that it was all for love, the love of happiness and the love of Edgar. I still wish I could remember before, but I am at peace knowing that I never will.

I put the pen down and grabbed the cube, taking a deep breath as I looked through it, seeing the beautiful lake as it once had been. I tried to remember every detail, every wave and every line. I balanced it in one hand, digging the other hand into the sand beside me and scooping up a handful, letting it filter back to the ground through my fingers. It felt dry, gritty and tired.

I stood then, finding that waiting was not making this any easier. I dropped the cube onto the ground, watching as it sank with a dull thud. I shook the jitters from my hands and held them at my sides, shifting into my changeling as I flew across the lake in a circle, diving back for the cube on the shore, grabbing it with my talons.

I flapped my wings a few times as I took off skyward, ducking into the dense clouds and working my way up. I couldn't see anything, the dense cover like cotton. The sight of the cloud brought me back to my time in Heaven, when we had descended into the thick mists over the lake. It had taken us a long time to get through it, and I only hoped it wasn't the same now.

I kept moving upward, beginning to doubt myself as I pressed the thoughts away. For as much as I wanted to believe I was failing, that I would never reach the top, I knew that I would. I had seen it, as though it had already happened. The prophecy showed me many views of how it would happen, so I knew it would because no matter what, I made it at least this far every time. I felt my wings begin to tire, the cube beginning to slip in my grasp. I let go with one foot before grasping again, my claw trying to find traction but the cube was too strong to allow it.

I was sweating now, my mouth dry. I closed my eyes, thinking of everything that was happening below and building the strength to go on. When I opened them, I saw sunlight was beginning to shine through the thick clouds, glittering off the misty dew that now coated my feathers. I breathed harder now, knowing I was almost there.

With what little energy I had left, I burst up and through the cloud layer, flying above it as the sun blinded me and I was forced to look away. I blinked a few times, feeling the cube in my grasp begin to burn. I looked down at it, squinting through aching eyes. Red light was pouring from the cube now, glowing onto the clouds as they began to burn off, forming a funnel that shot downward like the eye of a hurricane. I saw the Earth below, the color of it slowly changing from brown to green.

I gasped as I blinked a few times, my eyes watering in pain. The clouds continued to dissipate, my view on the world opening up as the blanket that wrapped it began to unfold. Tears were running down my white feathers, my feet burning. The pain was unbearable but I held on, flapping my wings as a way to distract myself. It was then that I felt the cube begin to shake, overloaded with sunlight as I came to the end of what I could handle. The cube began to expand and I could no longer hold on. I suddenly felt faint as my heart filled with fear. I could not pass out. I could not let go.

I looked down at the cube with frantic eyes, my feet trying to hold on but I could no longer make my feet move. I felt myself falling now, my wings too stiff to fly any longer. The air around me was warm, and I let myself go, my mind telling my body that this was it—it was time to give up. My heart sank as I fell, leaving all I had loved behind, all the beauty, and all the life.

Edgar...

NIGHTMARE

Edgar

In my dreams, I saw Elle falling. I felt her heart stop, a ripping sensation burning inside my cold chest. *No!* I thought.

"No!" I woke with a jolt, the foreign room in Edgar Poe's house dark and forboding. My chest throbbed, my heart breaking as my forehead beaded with sweat. I sat up, my wings surrounding me as I lay in a pile of black feathers on the floor.

"Elle!" I yelled. I hoisted my body off the floor, my muscles aching. I stumbled to a nearby table, grasping it as it threatened to snap under my weight.

My body was numb, my feet responding in a way that was no longer controlled by my own mind. There was a sharp feeling in my soul—a feeling of loss and darkness. I heard a commotion outside the door as Sam stormed into the room.

"Edgar, what is it?" Sam looked at me, horrified, his face suggesting that he already knew.

I gasped for air, bringing my hand to my throat. Sam dove under me as I began to tumble to the ground, catching me and pulling me up. Edgar Poe rushed into the room, his face hallowed and frightened.

"Sam, what's going on?" he asked, touching his arm.

I saw Sam give Edgar Poe a grave look as his eyes sank to the floor.

"She's gone," Sam replied. His voice was plain, but his grasp on me was firm.

PART II
RENOVATIO
Rebirth

JUST MOVE...

Shallow breaths were all I could manage, my limbs still feeling apart from my body, as though I had been ripped apart. I kept my eyes shut because it was the only thing I could control, but also because I was too afraid to see what had happened. My ears slowly stopped ringing and I could hear the sound of a gentle breeze working its way toward me. At last it fell across my skin. I felt my body stitch itself back together with each hair that rose, reminding me of limbs I still had. I slowly spread my fingers, feeling the ground where I lay, feeling the waxy texture of vegetation and the rough sandy dirt. I swallowed, and then slowly filled my lungs with a large gulp of air.

I opened my eyes, blinking a few times as everything came into focus. Blue sky slowly filled my vision, so rich and dark that I hardly recognized it.

The sound of rustling leaves rapidly flooded my ears, ringing less and less with each passing minute. I let my eyes roll around in their sockets, looking from one side to the other, noting that not a single cloud marked the sky. There was a sharp pain in my chest, like an acute burning sensation. I slowly lifted my hand. It felt weightless as I brought it to my chest and I rested it just below my collar bone. I felt my heart beating, slow and steady, envisioning the blood as it rushed through my body. I tried to locate the exact point of the burning, but it was like an itch I couldn't scratch. I tried to move then, but stopped. Every muscle in my back ached like it never had before. I winced, allowing the ground to hold me a minute longer.

My hand slowly fell from my chest and back to my side. I was unable to force my muscles to work much longer. I felt along the ground, feeling sand and foliage. The waxy vegetation tickled my fingers, but it did not try to wrap itself around me as it normally would. It no longer gave me comfort as it had for so long. I grabbed a bit of it and tugged, pulling it from the Earth. I brought it to my face, seeing that it was thicker than I had ever seen it before, the roots well grown and deep. I dropped the handful to the ground and tried again to sit up. My back cried out in pain and I let a whimper pass my lips. Painful sharp breaths escaped my lungs, my eyes watering so I shut them. Once up, I pulled my knees into my chest, hoping the pain would stop but it was relentless. My mind began to remember all that had happened as the previous events rushed back to me.

I opened my eyes then, feeling something warm drip down my leg, suddenly feeling cold as the wind blew across it. I touched it with my hand, wincing as it stung. I pulled my hand back, seeing it was now stained with blood. I gasped and craned my neck to inspect my leg, watching with horror as blood dripped into the Earth. There was a deep crimson stain in the sand, suggesting that I had been bleeding for quite some time. I wiped my hand across the vegetation and once again touched the gash with my finger, frightened by the fact that it wasn't clotting. I swallowed, grabbing at my shirt and ripping a strip of fabric from the hem. I pressed the fabric against the wound, applying a painful amount of pressure to try and stop the bleeding.

I looked up as the pain shot through my bones, seeing I was back on the beach by the lake. I forgot about the pain completely as I saw that the lake was transformed, shocked by its sudden beauty. A blue heron flew just inches from the water, its image reflecting on the calm surface. Sunlight glittered off a forest of green trees, the gentle breeze taking every leaf, and every pine needle, for a ride. I watched the trees, seeing them sway as though waving at me. I heard a hefty grunt from nearby, and I shifted my gaze to the left and up the hill, seeing a bear climb from the woods and walk to the water's edge for a drink.

I froze, watching it and hoping it wouldn't see me. When he had had his fill, he backed away from the water's edge and walked to a nearby tree where he reached up and grabbed a fat pinecone, bringing it to his mouth for a nibble before lumbering on down the bank and out of view. A splash of water pulled my attention away from the bear and back to the lake, just in time to see the water ripple away from what I suspected had been a fish.

I rubbed my forehead, trying to center myself and put things back together. It was obvious that the cube had worked. The world had returned, more amazing than ever, just as I had suspected.

I tried to stand on weak legs, wobbling precariously as I turned in a complete circle, positioning myself. I spotted my shelter from the night before and walked up to it, seeing my satchel lying in the sand beside it. I lifted it from the ground and threw it onto my back with great effort. My thoughts were fogged so I did the only thing that seemed to make sense and began to head up the hill toward the woods, toward the cave and back home. I walked on the path where the college once stood, seeing that it now was almost completely swallowed by the earth, leaving only the faintest sign that humans had ever been here.

I hobbled along, moving slowly but determinedly. As I reached the forest, I found that it had grown thick, making it hard to find my way. As I continued, the bit of cloth on my leg soaked through with blood, dripping down my leg and into my tall boots. I stopped for a moment, sitting on a fallen log and untying the bandage. I revealed the wound, seeing it hadn't changed, and in fact, had even gotten worse. I frowned, wondering why it wouldn't hurry up and heal.

I twisted the rag in my hand, wringing blood and sweat

from it. The cut was too deep to leave alone. Something needed to be done.

I rummaged through my pack, finding my pen and then unraveling a bit of cloth to make some string. I disassembled the pen with a shaky hand, carefully placing each piece on the log beside me so that I could put it back together when I was done. I took the spring from inside, figuring the pen could still work without it. I carefully unraveled it, creating a sort of needle. I wrapped the string inside the loop of wire, pinching the end and hoping this wouldn't hurt as much as it looked like it would.

I closed my eyes and took a deep breath, exhaling as I then opened them and looked at the gash. I pinched the skin together as my stomach lurched, blood oozing. I swallowed, placing the end of the wire against my skin as I applied pressure, testing the level of pain I was about to endure. I licked my lips, and plunged the wire into my skin, letting out a low cry, my eyes filling with tears of pain. I clenched my jaw as I threaded the string through my skin and back again, my leg numbing as I went along. At the end, I finished with a brave tug, leaving the string to hang loose down the face of my boot. I sat up, proud of myself for accomplishing something so rugged.

I looked at the surrounding forest, trying to remember what it was that Scott had told me about survival in the woods. I stood, throwing my satchel onto my back and walking on up the hill. After a while, I saw a willow tree up ahead and I walked up to it, grabbing a hunk of the bark and putting it in my mouth. I heard Scott's voice in my head, reminding me that by chewing on the bark, it would help sooth the pain. I had ignored him at the time because I had never really felt pain like this before, and I usually had something more modern to swallow in its place. The gash concerned me, but I kept the thought buried, unwilling to allow it to create too much worry. I swallowed the last of the bark. The pain lifted slightly, but the swelling did not tire.

As I limped on, I became unsure of exactly where I was going. Nothing looked familiar anymore. Everything was so dense now, that it was hard too look beyond ten feet. After about an hour, I stopped to rest. Never had I felt so tired and winded.

I tilted my neck from side to side, stretching the muscles. I hunched on another fallen log, touching it and wondering why it did not respond. I felt the moss, my fingertips pressing it down but nothing happened. I slowly lowered my body against the log, laying my head on the soft moss and resting my eyes.

Not certain how much time had passed, I woke to the sound of something rustling through the forest. Suddenly alert, I sat up, moss falling from my cheek where it had stuck to my skin. I was not used to being so attached to nature—nature usually was the one attached to me. Magic was gone, though, I needed to remember that. I sighed as I heard another rustle of leaves. I was not in the mood to wrestle a bear, especially when I could barely walk. I moved slowly as I reached to grab my satchel and leave, but I froze as the bushes in front of me began to shake. My heart erupted to life, pounding like a hammer in my chest. I held my breath as the bushes parted and the creature in question let out a sharp snort.

I yelped, falling backwards off the log. I was quick to right myself as I sat on the ground, my hands holding me up. I looked up in alarm, the face of a horse staring at me from the bushes just ahead, chewing on a bunch of vegetation that hung from its mouth. It glanced at me but didn't seem interested, grabbing another bunch of vegetation and yanking it from the ground.

I slowly stood, brushing myself off as I checked the wound on my leg, seeing it was growing swollen and caked with dirt. I stepped forward and winced. The weight of my body on the leg ached throughout its every muscle, the red veins of poison creeping across my skin. My blood was infected now. I knew this from the extensive study I had done in the medical field, thinking that it was perhaps a career option. I laugh now, knowing it was foolish thinking. *Why wasn't I healing?* I thought.

The horse snorted once more. I watched it for a moment as I waited for the pain in my leg to subside. It was light gold with a blonde mane and tail. Its coat was glossy and clean, and it stood about sixteen hands tall, or what I guessed would be about that. One of the foster kids that had lived with us in Seattle had been adopted by a family that owned many horses. I was invited to visit once. When I went, of course, the horses had clamored to me as though I were a bale of fresh alfalfa. This horse, however, didn't seem to care.

I bit my lip and furrowed my brow. "What is wrong with me?" I said out loud, hoping someone would answer, but no one did. I felt the same twang in my chest and the acute burn. I thought of Edgar then, wondering how he was, and that's when I felt it; I felt nothing.

My heart stopped, the horse still chomping away beside me. *What did this mean?* Surely they hadn't tricked me again. I knelt down and grabbed my bag with haste, no longer caring that the horse was there. I stuck my hand inside the bag and felt for the contract, pulling it out as I tried to unroll the metallic paper. I struggled with the page, finding it was difficult, like trying to bend heavy metal. Once open, I squinted at the words, seeing that they were now hard to read. *Why couldn't I see?* I dropped the contract to the ground, hastily grabbing the *Book of Us* and flipping it open. I was also unable to read the words there, seeing nothing but blank pages. I discarded it next to the contract.

"No," I whispered. *"No!"*

I looked back at my leg, feeling it pulse. I was human, I had to be. For the first time in my life I could feel everything. Breathing hard, I looked around. I felt alone. The equine did not count. There was nothing but my own pain, my own thoughts. I did not feel the darkness that I should and the same heavy heart I had when I was young. I did not feel the electricity of Edgar, or the light of my soul, either. I felt so apart from everything, the Earth no longer talking to me.

239

Nothing was talking to me. Edgar's heart was his own now, as was mine. Our soul had at last split.

I looked to the sky as my mouth fell open and I let a scream escape my lips. The horse jolted as it stood in the bush, but did not run. When all the breath was exhausted from my lungs, I breathed deeply and collapsed to the ground, crying. The horse began to chew again, gnawing on a thick branch and rolling it in its mouth as the foam dripped onto a nearby fern. A whiff of wet wood and vegetation wafted toward me, and I felt myself gag. I brought my hand to my throat, feeling as it swelled with anger and fear.

"How do I get back?" I looked at the ground and then at the horse, feeling the need to talk to something that was alive.

The horse blinked and chewed. I let a sharp breath pass my trembling lips, almost like a laugh. I was at the end of my rope, bordering on crazy. After a few last quick breaths, I shut my eyes and calmed myself. Moments later, I was asleep once more.

In my dreams I saw everything as it once was. I saw Edgar and Margriete, Sam and everyone I had known. I dreamt that I could still feel that connection but then slowly, it all faded away, and I was locked in darkness. The darkness felt comforting somehow, and warm. I fell into a trance as I stared into nothing, swirls of blacks and grays like water on a river. I felt myself smiling, wanting to dance with it but unable to move.

There was a distant voice then, and I heard my own in

reply. *"Hello?"* I said to the voice. The voice called back, louder this time, but still muffled. *"Yes, I can hear you. What was that?"*

"Elle!" The voice was suddenly clear as day.

I felt my heart stop, the call coming from right beside me now, in my dark room.

"Sam?" I asked, looking through the swirls but seeing nothing. *"I'm dreaming,"* I told myself.

"No, Elle. You're not." The reply was rather blunt, and certainly not something I would have thought to dream.

I tried to look around again, hearing him as though he were right there, inches away.

"Sam, I can't see you."

I tried to reach out but I couldn't make my arm move. It was then that a sharp pain pulsed from my injured leg to my head. I let out a cry.

"Sam? *What was that?"* My voice was frantic now, as though I were stuck in a paper bag with no way out. I was being eaten by wild animals. That had to be it.

"Elle," his voice was calm.

"How are you here? You can't be here." I felt delirious as the stinging sent chills all across my body. Sweat dripped across my face.

I heard him laugh and it brought me a sense of comfort. *This had to be real.* I could not dream in such vivid detail.

"Elle, I am trying to *help* you, so stop twitching. You are nearing death. This is why you can hear me."

I breathed in fast. "You're an angel. *Of course!"* I thought about Edgar. "But where—"

He sighed, cutting me off. "He's not *your* angel. He cannot come."

I felt frustrated. "But I want him here. I want to see him, Sam." I felt tears began to grow but I could not wipe my eyes.

"I'm sorry, Elle. I hoped it wouldn't be this way, but—"

"You hoped? *You knew this could happen?*"

Sam sighed again. "It was a possibility, but there were many possibilities."

I was silent for a long while as the stinging began to fade and the darkness began to lighten ever so slightly. I was getting better.

"Elle, you need to stay alive. The gods request that you live a full *human* life."

I whimpered, *"A full human life?* And then what?"

Sam was quiet for a moment. "And then—I don't know."

I was speechless, staring into the grey nothingness, hopelessly paralyzed. I thought about all the time I had in front of me, by myself. I did not want that.

"You'll have a lot to do, Elle."

His words were true. There would be a lot here to accomplish. I could lead them all. I could show them how to live a better life. I had taken a lot of my life for granted, but now I was given this gift, this chance to stand on equal ground with them. I loved Edgar more than anything else, but I owed it to all the others I loved as well. I was finally getting what I always wanted growing up: *a real life*.

"Sam? Are you still there?" I felt my fingers begin to twitch as the feeling returned to them.

"Bye, Elle." His voice was already distant.

The darkness was creeping toward light now, like watching the sun dawn over the horizon.

"Sam?" I asked once more, but there was no reply this time. I was alone, again.

I woke as sounds returned around me, blinking away the bright light that filtered through the canopy above. I heard a rustle at my side.

"Sam?" I turned my head, seeing the horse still grazing nearby.

I rolled my eyes and tried to sit up, my leg no longer pulsing with such pain. I looked down at it, wrinkling my nose as a sharp pungent smell wafted into them.

"Garlic?" I asked myself, touching my finger to the wound where I saw something had been rubbed into it. The swelling was down, and the red veins of blood poisoning fading.

I furrowed my brow, unsure why garlic had been rubbed on my leg, although it did seem to work. Infection had been what brought me to the brink of death, but I really didn't believe that all it took was garlic to fix it. It had been Sam. Knowing him, he likely spiked it with something far more effective. I touched my brow, finding it coated in a dried film of sweat, but at least I was no longer burning up.

I still felt the comforting warmth I had while I was

sleeping, almost like a coming to terms with the fact of what had happened to me, and the fate I was now faced with. I was at ease. It was always better to know your fate than to have to wonder.

I saw a stick jutting from the ground a few paces ahead, with a white piece of paper stabbed through it. I grunted as I tried to stand, the horse noticing me and letting out a low whinny. I put weight on my injured leg, taking one step forward and then another, until I reached the stick and pulled the paper from it. As I saw the writing, my heart leapt…

Elle,

Dearest, I am sorry I could not come and be there for you. I truly did not know. At the worst, I feared you would simply die, but not this. I already miss the way I could always feel you. Look what you have done, though. Be proud. You are magic. Never forget that. And though you may not see it around you, it will forever be in your heart and in your memories. Maybe one day, somewhere free, we can be together again.

I love you,
Edgar

I pulled the letter to my chest and hugged it, knowing that now this was all I had of him. One tear fell but I was quick to wipe it away. I carefully rolled the page and hobbled back to my satchel where I carefully placed it inside and set it back down by the log. I ran my hand through my hair, feeling it tangle like it never had, frizzy and clumped into a matted mess. For the first time since Before, I was finally relieved that no one was here to see how awful I looked.

There was a rubber band around my wrist and I pulled it off, trying my best to flatten the nest of hair into a pony tail. *"It is what it is,"* I whispered, meaning it in so many ways other than my hair. *"What could I do?"* I had agonized over losing Edgar so many times that it no longer felt like the thing to do. I had played this role time and time again. The best I could do was hope and try to heal.

Exhaling away the worries that I could not control, I looked back at the horse. I focused on what I could do, and the things I could control right now. I hobbled to a nearby tree and braced myself against the trunk for a rest before stepping gingerly toward the horse once more.

"Hey there, pony," I sang. I slowly lifted my hand as I got closer, my feet shuffling through the lush green ferns. The horse's chewing slowed, then stopped as I inched closer. It was blinking now, swishing its tail ever so slightly. Its eyes stared keenly into mine, watching me. I paused, staring at it as it stared at me. After a moment, it began to chew once more and I relaxed. I balanced myself on one foot, thinking about the horse as I bent down to determine its gender.

I felt a bit invasive doing it, but I was tired of thinking of the horse as an *It*. I giggled and straightened—a gelding. I rolled that fact over in my head, deducing two things: he had once been domesticated because he was not a stallion, and he was also from *Before*. He had survived, and with any luck, he had some training as well.

He must have made his way here when the storms began, searching for food where the lowlands provided none. I took one more step as he watched me, clucking my tongue. His ears perked at the sound, and his chewing stopped. I clucked again and again as I drew closer. He watched me but did not move, lowering his head slightly as though to show submission. I was right next to him now as I reached out to touch his mane. He murmured slightly, chewing his jaw as though he'd liked my touch.

I ran my hand down his neck as he bobbed his head. I let go and dropped my hand to my side. He looked at me as though disappointed that I'd stopped. I stepped back and he stepped forward, following me, wanting more. A smile spread across my face. For the first time in my life, this animal liked me not for my scent or my power, but for me.

"Hey there, boy. Do you like me?" I stepped back again, and he stepped forward twice, his nose resting against my arm.

I ran my hand down the length of his forehead, straightening his forelock into a little twist. I turned and walked toward the log where my satchel sat and the horse followed. I stopped, turning as I ran my hand down the length of his back from his withers to his rump. He swished his tail.

"What should we name you?" My stomach growled as though to answer, and the horse blinked a few times. I hadn't eaten in a long while and I was not used to the hunger I felt now, making my limbs shake and my head feel loopy.

"Should we name you, *Jack?*" The horse bobbed its head and I laughed, finding it too perfect. "Alright, Jack. It seems you found some food, but how about me? Do you know where some *human* food is?"

This time Jack did not reply. I tilted my head, patting him again as I gained his trust. He was just as alone as I was, but together, we could be great friends. I turned back to the log to grab the bag from the ground and threw it on my back. I then hoisted myself up as my feet struggled to find traction on the moss, placing one hand on Jack's withers for support. He sidestepped closer to the log as though he had done this before. I, on the other hand, had little experience as an equestrian and feared how I would handle this. My friend from the foster home had made it look easy, but then they'd also had a saddle and reins for help. I brushed the dust from his back and tried lifting my leg as Jack shuffled his feet.

"Stand still, Jack." I had my injured leg in the air, ready to throw it over his back.

I finally managed to get my heel high enough to slide it over, but Jack refused to make things easier on me as he stepped forward. *"Whoa!"* I screeched, throwing my weight onto him and wrapping my arms around his neck. My head was resting on his mane, my hands locked at the knuckles. Jack walked forward, his head bobbing, dodging around trees as leaves brushed along my body. I continued to hug his neck, afraid that if I let go, I'd simply slide off.

Jack headed downhill as the warmth of his large body began to make me sweat. I breathed in rhythm with his heavy steps, slow and soft. When I could not bear it any longer, I relaxed my grip and adjusted myself until I was balanced on his back. My seat was learning his motions, the rhythm repetitive and predictable. We followed the same path I had taken on my way up which had left a sort of opening for us to walk through. As the trees thinned and the sparkling lake began to shine through the trees, I gathered enough strength to sit up taller, my fingers lacing into Jack's mane, my knuckles turning white from my strong grip.

I felt the cool air blow off the lake and toward us, Jack's feet crunching across what used to be the gravel path at the college. I tried to loosen my body in the hopes that I could relax into the same rhythm as Jack, the whole world being jostled about as I rocked back and forth. Jack's feet left the path now, sinking into the sand of the beach as he walked toward the water. I felt myself slipping forward as he walked downhill and I tried my best to push off his neck and back. At the water's edge he stopped, lowering his head as I yelped and slid forward. Though I tried to prevent it from happening, I toppled down and off his neck, landing on my butt in the shallow water.

Water splashed into my face, and I drew in a sharp breath of shock, the glacial chill of it leaving me breathless. Jack's eyes watched me before focusing back on the water, his lips touching the surface as it guzzled down his throat. He made small sucking noises as he drank. I tried to stand, feeling instantly warmer as the humid air of late summer began to work to dry me.

It hadn't been this warm in months, and for what the weather had been, it was as though I was in a different place entirely. That other place I had been was just a nightmare. I looked to where the dam used to be, seeing that what had been left was now covered in vines as though nature wanted to hide it, as though it was ashamed of that era. I felt like I had been launched into the future, like a time traveler, seeing the world after humanity had long left it.

Jack finished drinking as he shuffled his feet backward, turning on his rear hooves as they twisted into the sand. He took a few steps up the hill and stopped, looking back at me. I had no way to keep him, no restraints or ropes. He continued to stand, as though waiting for me. I stepped toward him, reaching his side as he took a few more steps forward and up the bank to what used to be the shore.

What to do now? That was the question that was haunting the back of my mind. How long would I have to wait? Jack let out a whinny as his whole stomach tightened. I walked up to his side once more, tracing my hand down his neck, the soft fur like silk under the pads of my fingers.

"Jack, do you know the way back?" I asked, looking

into his large eyes. He blinked. "Do you think you can take me?"

I looked down the hill between the two mountains where the river ran. I pointed west. Jack rolled his tongue around in his mouth.

"I'll take that as a yes?"

I grabbed his mane, and gently tugged him toward the log where my small shelter had been. The satchel on my back was still dripping with water and I feared checking the contents, afraid all the papers were ruined. I once again performed the same awkward dance as I had before, wrestling my way onto Jack's back.

Once up, I let out a loud whoop of accomplishment, figuring there was no one around to hear me. The trip down the mountain was going to take much longer than the few minutes it took to fly, or the hour it took to drive. I settled on a few days, maybe a week, depending on how the horseback riding panned out. I looked up at the sun in the sky, seeing it was already low, just inches from the top of the nearby mountain. I wanted to make progress by nightfall so I urged Jack forward, swinging my legs like a buffoon.

My grip on Jack's mane tightened as his body lurched and he made his way across the tall grasses of the bank and to the edge where the dam once was. He gingerly made his way down the steep cliff side, the water pouring over what was left of the dam below.

I held tight, looking down and praying I would survive this, though dying was not necessarily a bad thing, either.

We inched down, weaving back and forth until we at last met the river. The bank of this side was tight, and as I looked across to the other side where the road used to be, I saw the land there was far more desirable.

I pulled on Jack's mane and he stopped. For a moment I was amazed it had worked at all, laughing to myself. "Okay, Jack. Let's cross."

Jack seemed to know exactly what I wanted him to do as he stamped his feet.

"Come on, boy. This is easy." I scanned the river, seeing a shallow portion up ahead. "See, up there." I gave him a gentle nudge with my heels and he stepped forward with a hesitant shoulder.

We weaved our way through the trees that lined the bank. I ducked low, knowing that Jack was not paying attention to the branches that were now slapping me in the face. We reached the spot on the river and I pulled on his mane once more, this time yanking it slightly to the left. He turned his head toward the river.

"Come on," I urged, digging my heels in his sides.

He shuffled one foot into the water, followed by the other as he struggled to find footing. I kicked him again, this time with forceful persuasion. Jack reared his head, disliking my form of influence. He stopped and I grew frustrated as he went no further. The water rushed around all four of his ankles. I took a moment to regroup, adjusting my position on his back before pulling my legs away from his sides and then letting them go as they kicked him forward once more.

Jack grunted, flicking his tail once before lunging forward suddenly, digging his back hooves into the river rock and leaping into the water. I screamed as I toppled off his back, hitting the water as the cold took my breath away for a second time. I flailed my arms as I fought to get back to the surface, gasping for air as I came up. I cleared the water from my eyes and looked for Jack, seeing he was now swimming across a deep pool toward the other shore.

I cursed myself and slapped the water as the river carried me. The water had looked far shallower from the bank, certainly not deep enough that I could not touch the bottom. I began to swim, seeing Jack floating away from me as I bobbed in the fast end of the river. Water threatened to choke down my throat as I plunged one arm in front of the other, making progress as I swam into the slow side of the river where I finally felt rocks under my feet. I tread water for a moment before I was finally able to grab onto the rocks enough to remain stationary. I walked out of the river and onto the bank. Jack walked over the rocks and toward me, stumbling as he went. His head hung low as though sorry.

I was breathing hard, dripping from head to toe. "Jack!" I yelled angrily.

Jack reached me, nudging his nose against my wet sleeve. I shook my head, blowing air at his face and teasing him. He shook his head and sneezed. I grabbed my hair and rung it out, twisting it into a knot. At least I no longer needed a shower.

I looked up at the hillside we had just descended, seeing now how steep it really was. I exhaled hard. "Well, that was about enough for today. What do you think?" I looked at Jack but he turned away from me and hobbled off the rocky bank and to a nearby patch of grass where he began to eat. I followed, sitting down beside him as I felt even weaker than I had before, my stomach still hungry, but now to the point where it had begun to hurt.

I pulled my wet bag from my back, opened the latch, and reached inside. I pulled out my journal and the seemingly blank *Book of Us*, laying them on a patch of grass to dry. I looked up to where the sun had been, now gone behind the mountain as the cool ravine air surrounded me. I grumbled, knowing that now, I would probably remain wet all night unless I got a fire started. I stood on shaky legs, leaving my bag as I made my way further in toward the trees, searching for fallen pieces of wood.

There was a bush of berries near the edge of the tree line. When I saw it, I dropped my task and ran toward it, ravaging the vines as I stuffed my face with blackberries. They were ripe and juicy, likely staining my face a deep purple. After about two cups I stopped myself, knowing that eating berries alone would not make my stomach stop aching.

I focused back on the task of collecting wood, searching the edge of the forest. Filling my arms, I made my way back, dropping them on the ground as I cleared the vegetation and dug a shallow hole in the sand. Then I took each piece of wood and balanced them into a cone shape. I was proud that I knew so much about surviving in the outdoors, especially considering the fact that I had never even been camping. I know now that it wasn't the wilderness aspect that had attracted me to the college. Obviously it had been the fact that Edgar had been here.

I collected some dried leaves and placed them inside the cone in a tidy pile. I sat, taking a deep breath as my hands shook. The berries began to work their sugars into my blood, and after a moment, some of my energy returned. I grabbed two small twigs that sat nearby, rubbing them together in the hopes of creating a spark.

After about fifteen minutes, sweat coated my brow and still I had no fire. Jack was standing nearby, his back foot relaxing as he dozed, fat and happy. I was jealous of him, angry that he could survive the night because his coat had dried rather fast. I let a shiver consume my body as I shook. Cursing under my breath, I decided to change my technique, grabbing a bit of the dry leaves and placing them beside the sticks. I then rubbed them together once more, this time faster, summoning strength I no longer thought I had.

I saw a small wisp of smoke rise then, and adrenaline took over my body as I kept at it. It was then that a spark flashed across my eyes and the smell of burning vegetation wafted into my nostrils. I yelped, quickly tossing the bunch of smoking leaves in with the rest and lunging forward onto my hands and knees. I blew on the leaves, coaxing the fire to life.

I looked at Jack. "Jack, look! *Fire!*"

I leapt to my feet as the leaves ignited, dancing around. I wished Edgar could see me now, even Sam. They would not believe this new me, a human, making fire. I stopped dancing then, huddling close to the flames as I continued to assist them, watching the sticks smolder, then burn.

Jack, too, walked closer, seeing now what it was I had been trying to do and sharing in the wealth of the warmth the fire now created. I sat, reaching for my journal and placing my hand on the page to measure how damp it was. It was still cold, but the fibers of the paper were dry enough to write so I reached into my bag and rummaged for the pen. Pulling it out, I saw it was streaked with blood from the surgery earlier and I wiped in on my shirt. I drew the pen into my hand and began to write.

Though it had not been long since *Before,* I could not escape the feeling that I was living some other life completely. It wasn't even a new chapter of my life so much as it was a whole new book. I felt so alive, though. I felt *real*—bound to myself like never before. For the first time, I could look at the world through the same eyes. I *had* done it.

I placed the pen in the journal and shut it. This was to be the second entry of this new life, this new world. I put the journal back on the patch of vegetation and looked at my leg in the firelight. I was not used to watching something heal so slowly, still a deep gash as the thread held it together. The garlic had been washed out of it now, and I'd tried my best to keep it clean this time, hoping that it would be fine on its own.

I leaned back onto the sand, propping my hands behind my head. I sighed, telling myself that this was it. This was my life now. Closing my eyes as the sound of the fire lulled me to sleep, and though I tried to convince myself no to, all I could think about was Edgar.

HUMANITY

"Jack!" This was the third morning that I had managed to lose him. "Jack!" I trudged through the trees as they whipped back at me, slashing my face. I was frustrated at this point, my progress continually thwarted by a stupid horse. Over the past six days we hadn't gotten very far. I could still see the mountain where we had come from behind us, and that was not a very encouraging sign. It was not only that, though. The berries I had been living off of were making my stomach twist and knot, forcing me to rest more often than I'd liked. At least I had an abundant supply of fresh water, but I needed something real to eat, and soon.

"Jack! Where are you?" I called, bringing my hands to my mouth. Though Jack had wandered off before, he had always come back when I called for him—at least eventually. I stopped to listen, hearing nothing but the wind in the trees and the sound of the river behind me. I didn't want to lose that sound, it was my beacon and my way back.

I walked on a little further, grabbing a branch and breaking it from the tree. I picked off the small twigs that sprung from it, creating a walking stick that I used to break down some of the soft low-lying nettles, a nasty little plant I had discovered for the first time. Never did I think plants could actually attack, leaving an array of throbbing red bumps around my ankle.

"Jack!" I continued to call, hoping he would hear me. I needed him, not just for transportation, but for social connection. Talking to plants, which no longer talked to me, felt insane. I grumbled. "Jack!" I had thought we were inseparable, but apparently not.

I began to sweat, so I pulled the pack from my back. I yanked my sweater over my head, straightening my tattered tank top. I balled the sweater up and shoved it into the bag, pushing down the journals. I let the bag rest on the ground for a moment as I enjoyed the way the breeze cooled the sweat on my skin, making it prickle with goose bumps.

It was then that I heard a rustling behind me and I spun around to see what it was. "Jack?" I whispered. It sounded smaller than Jack, perhaps a skunk or small deer. Just in case it was the skunk, I lifted my walking stick into my hands like a sword. I heard the rustle again, this time closer. I took a step away from the sound, hunching down into a readied pose.

The bush before me shook violently, followed by a high

pitched scream. My heart leapt into my throat, the sound seemingly foreign. I stood frozen for a moment, hearing whomever it was struggle, and recognizing it to be a female voice.

"Hello?" I took one step forward as I tightened my grip on the stick, my palms sweating. The voice continued to swear and I took another step toward it. "Um—*Hello?"* I asked again, this time louder.

"Hello?" The voice finally answered, sounding a bit flustered and annoyed.

Another rustling came from my left and my gaze shot to the source of this new noise, seeing Jack emerge from the trees with a mouthful of grass.

I exhaled hard, relieved that this wasn't some sort of ambush. *"Jack,"* I whispered. I felt better now that he was here, more confident when it was two against one. I heard the voice again, and looked back to the bush.

"I don't know who you are, but, would it be a bother if I asked you for help?" The voice sounded scared and desperate.

"Uh—" I paused, putting my hand up in Jack's direction, telling him to stay put. *"Uh—Yeah,* sure." I craned my head from side to side, trying to look through the thick bush to find the woman. I saw a hand reach out toward me, scuffed with dirt and speckled with scratches. I took the hand and pulled as hard as I could, a struggle as my weak muscles were rivaled by her weight.

She flew out of the bush then, toppling over me as we

fell back onto the moist forest floor. Jack jumped, throwing his head in the air. I was quick to shove myself away and stand. I guarded myself, unsure exactly what kind of person I was dealing with. The girl lay on the ground with her arm across her eyes, exposing a cluster of scratches that spread from her wrist to her elbow. *"Nettles—"* she muttered. I lowered my walking stick as she moaned. Jack walked up behind me, sniffing the air.

After standing there for another moment, I decided to talk. "Are you alright?" I asked, still standing about five feet from her. She looked about the same age as I, or at least the age I appeared, about eighteen. She had long brown hair that was about as mangled as mine, too, her roots in need of a touch up they would likely never receive.

She moved her arm from her eyes then, staring at me. "That really hurt," she half laughed as she said it, clearly not as concerned about me as I was about her.

"I bet."

She blinked, her brown eyes looking at Jack. She looked to her side, grabbing a bunch of ferns and proceeding to rub the yellow pollen side against the red bumps from the nettle.

So that's *how you ease the pain,* I thought.

"Nice horse." She spoke, wincing as she continued to rub the fern vigorously against her skin.

I nodded. "Oh, thanks." It was strange to hear a human voice. It had felt like forever, though it had only been six days.

The girl stood. "You scared me to death." She brushed the dirt from her pants, inspecting her wounds.

"You should probably put something on that," I pointed to one scratch that was dripping blood.

She wiped the blood from her arm and then wiped it on her pants. "It'll stop eventually." But I saw her reach for a nearby bush, grabbing a new handful of leaves and tossing them in her mouth. She chewed on them for a moment as I stared, curious about what she was doing now. She had a tart expression on her face, shaking as though the leaves in her mouth were almost too bitter to handle. After a sufficient number of chomps, she spit the green substance in her hand, and then spread it across the scratches.

"There, I think I finally got it all covered," she exclaimed satisfactorily. She then wiped her tongue on her shirt, as though trying to rid her mouth of as much of the taste as possible.

I nodded. I still was not used to a human body, still unsure just what would kill me and what wouldn't. Clearly, those particular leaves had some sort of medicinal quality.

"How did you know to do all that?" I finally ask, finding I was still gawking at her.

She shrugs. "Trial and error really." She snorted. "Some of those plants can really give you a good ache in the stomach, though. I tend to stay away from the really colorful ones, just out of general safety."

I find myself shocked. "Aren't you afraid they'll *kill* you?"

Her following laugh was cool. "I try just a bit at first, and if I don't feel ill within the hour, I figure it's alright. Then I start to experiment."

I nod. "I wish I had your bravery," I muttered. She didn't hear me.

"So, what's your name? Where are you from?" She stood casually, asking the questions as though she had asked them many times before.

I stabbed my stick at the ground, finding I was nervous to talk with her, intimidated even.

She laughed. "Don't be so nervous. I'm not going to hurt you. I think at this point we all need to stick together." She rolled her eyes. "And I can tell by the gaunt look on your face that you could use a little help and guidance."

I let a small polite smile pass my lips. "Well, my name is Elle. And I'm from—" I paused, not knowing what to say.

The girl waited for me to continue with eager eyes, but when I didn't, she didn't pry. "Well, I'm Heather. I'm from Seattle." She put her hand out toward me and I took it, assuming it was for a shake.

"You're from Seattle? How is it there?" I tried to carry the conversation further in my attempt to redeem myself.

Her eyes got grave. "Not good. That's why I'm here. There's a group of us, about a days hike from here. We've already organized a town of sorts. We were actually here before all this," she motioned toward the trees. "We were told it would be safer here."

I nodded again. "By who?"

"Our leader," she replied frankly, which told me nothing.

"So why are you way out here and away from this town?" I pressed.

She narrowed her eyes in a strange way. "My friend and I are looking for people, like you, and hunting as well. You would not believe the abundance of wild game! Tastier than anything I've ever had, too!"

I nod. "Ah." She was acting as though she were hiding something, so I brought up the friend. "There's someone with you?" I looked to the woods behind her.

She blinked, "Yeah, just a prophet of sorts. She's back near the river. We saw your fire and figured we'd search the woods for the source."

"I see." Perhaps she was protecting this prophet of hers.

"You should come with me. I'll take you there." Her face was happy again.

I nodded with reluctance, patting Jack.

"They have to approve you, though. Our town is rather strict. We've had a lot of groups trying to invade us. People are desperate." We began to walk back toward the river. I walked ahead a bit, trying to keep up with Jack as Heather kept her eyes on the ground, as though looking for something. "The prophet will be able to decide if you're worthy by the time we arrive. If not, you can travel on down river. There are many towns popping up along the way. I'm sure it won't be hard to find shelter."

I made a sort of snorting noise in reply. "Strange, isn't it?" I looked back at her, watching as she looked up at the trees. My long blonde hair swung off my back and over my shoulder then. Her gaze dropped to my back and she froze. Her mouth fell open, the blood draining from her face. Alarmed, I stopped as well, my brows pressing together as I watched her face.

"Heather, what is it?" My heart began to pound, thinking there was something there, like a giant spider.

She smiled then, rather suddenly. *"Elle—"* she kept her gaze on my back. Laughing with disbelief, she covered her mouth with her hand. I watched as she muttered something, then stomped the ground with excitement.

"What?" I began to spin in place, trying to see what it was.

She dropped her hand, "It's true!" She walked up to me, covering the ground between us in two large steps. *"It's true!"* She jumped up and down, touching her hand to my back as though it were made of delicate paper. "Oh, I'm so sorry. I didn't realize." Her attitude toward me suddenly changed, and I sensed she no longer felt superior. "She's going to be so happy to see you!"

I clenched my jaw. "Who is *she?*"

She stopped jumping around, her demeanor calming and her eyes fixed.

"What is it?" I tried to look at my back again, but I could not see.

"I thought it was a lie, something I had imagined. But,

it's *you*. Look, clear as day." She was pointing now.

I rolled my eyes, grabbing her shoulders as I shook her from the trance she seemed to be in. *"Heather—"* I said her name in a sharp tone.

She looked deep in my eyes. "You did this. That's what she said."

"Heather, what's there? What is on my back?" I was focused on one thing only, freaked out by whatever it was she seemed to find so enamoring.

Heather finally replied, as though my words were a command. "The marks on your back—" She faltered for a moment. "You have to be *The One*. You have to." It was as though she was convincing herself.

The title brought pain to my heart. A part of me was hoping it was behind me.

"We all saw it, back in Seattle. It was the tree and the raven. The mark on your back, it's—it's the *raven*."

I tried once more to look, grabbing at my skin with my hand, unable to see.

"Here," Heather grabbed me and began to trace my back with her finger. I followed the sensation, feeling as she traced the outline of a small raven that seemed similar to the ones I'd seen before—on the tree where Edgar had died, on the trees I used to make into a swing.

"What?" I felt a bit violated, wondering how it was I could receive such a mark unnoticed. "What does it look like?"

Heather sighed impatiently. *"Like a raven."*

I turned to face her. "I know that. But, like a burn? A

tattoo?"

She nodded, finally understanding, "Like a tattoo. Only it's white, and barely visible. But it's there!" She tilted her head with a baffled expression. "You didn't have that before? It looks old."

I snorted. "No. At least, not that I know of." There were many things I never knew about myself, but I figured that this was likely something I would have known. Someone would have said something.

She looked star struck. "I am so honored!" She began to jump up and down. "Come, I need to show it to *her.*" She grabbed my arm and began to drag me forward.

I still did not know who *her* was. I felt awkward all of a sudden, pulling away from her and refusing to go any farther. "How do you even know what this tattoo thing means?"

She laughed. "The tree also bears the very same mark, the same exact carving. I wouldn't mistake that for the world!"

I stood frozen, my hand on Jack. What was happening? Was I really this important? I wanted to blend in here, not this. I did not wish to *lead.* At least, not like this.

"This is a miracle. *I found you.* She will be so happy!" Heather bowed then.

I was annoyed now. *"Who,* Heather? Who are these people? Who is *she?"*

Heather was eager to divulge her secrets, "Well, the mayor of our new town, his name is Scott. And well—"

My eyes flew open. "Scott?" I interrupted. It was too

266

much of a coincidence to ignore the fact that it could in fact be *my* Scott.

She smiled big, "Yes, Scott! It was his tree, the sacred tree! We brought it with us. It's in the village! Do you know him?"

I laughed to myself, seeing now what I had created. When I had instructed Scott to lead the world to safety I hadn't really expected for him to do it, no matter how hard he'd tried. I thought back to the day in Seattle, and the tree. The neighbors had watched me leave, seen what I was and what I could do. I had left myself exposed. It had only been three days since the end, three days and these people were already worshipping me as though I were a god.

"Well. Don't get too excited, Heather. I'm not what I was."

Heather's eyes were beaming now. She walked back toward me and took my hand. "Come, *please?*" She was begging now.

I nodded my head, giving in. "Fine."

We trudged the rest of the way out of the forest. As we walked out and onto the beach, I saw an older woman standing by the water. It was not what I had expected. A part of me wanted her to be Sarah. She was gazing at the river, her back to me.

"This is *amazing,*" Heather kept muttering, dragging me across the rocks and toward the woman.

The old woman heard us and turned, her aged face like a ghost as my eyes fell across it. I halted, my heels digging into the sand, which gathered around my feet. Heather stopped muttering and looked back at me with a confused expression. Then she looked to the old lady, seeing that we were now staring at each other.

"Uh—" Heather began to talk but the old woman lifted her hand and silenced her. Heather pouted.

I breathed slowly, tears welling in my eyes. The old woman smiled, wind catching in her grey hair. There was a horse nearby, digging in the rocks. Jack made his way toward it.

"I—" I tried to speak but couldn't.

"My dear." The old lady tilted her head.

"How are you here?" Never had I expected her.

"I wish I could have told you sooner, Elle. But, you see, I couldn't."

"Heidi, I—"

She continued to speak. "All my life I have been watching over all of you, each as different as the next. I tried to hide you from them. But, you were different. I knew you had a greater path ahead, so I had to let you go."

I shook my head. "Heidi, I don't understand." A tear ran down my cheek.

"There were more of you, my dear. Many more. All your siblings, all my children, each of you had magic inside you. I had to protect you."

My breathing was sporadic. *"You knew?"*

Heidi nodded slowly. "I always knew. I kept you for him. I nurtured you."

"For *him?*" I gasped.

"Yes, Edgar. I was the human end of this whole plan. I knew all along what would happen. Scott found me in Seattle and I told him, but, he already knew." She chuckled. "You have brave friends."

I shook my head, still frozen in the sand. "He knew this would happen?" I motioned to myself.

Heidi shook her head with a grave face. "No. He really thought that it was over, that you would find your way home. I didn't expect to see you ever again."

I believed her words because I always had. "And my brothers and sisters?"

A look of happiness and loss crossed her face. "They went home at last. You made sure of that. They were lost children, just as saddened as you were, but they had tried to forget it. I tried to help them forget."

I thought of all the kids we had in the house. I remember how they watched me, watched everyone, as though frightened. Now I saw that aside from fright, they were also hiding. I then thought about all the foster families Heidi had placed me with, each trying to make me forget, each trying to make me smile. It was all connected, it was always the plan. "And—" I paused, faltering over my words. "And the money?"

Heidi laughed, her wrinkles collecting around her eyes. "It was yours all along. Though, I did love the painting you sent. Don't see many of those."

I couldn't help but smile. There was something

comforting about all this, as though I was never alone, always guarded.

"I will take care of you, though. Just like always." Heidi took a step toward me, a slight limp in her step.

"Oh, Heidi." I closed the gap between us, wrapping my arms around her. "Why didn't you just tell me? I loved you so much. You were a mother to me."

She rubbed my back with her hand. "I couldn't, my dear. I couldn't."

I let go of her.

"Let's get you home, shall we?" She patted me on the arm.

I nodded.

Heather whistled and her horse lifted its head. Jack also looked. Her horse was grey and tall, much taller than Jack. To their advantage, the horse was also tacked up with a bridle. The horse made its way toward us and Heather helped Heidi onto her back. Jack whinnied, clearly in love with this new mare.

"This is Sugar," Heather whispered.

Jacks ears were perked. "I think I'll walk," I added. Jack was prancing around like an idiot, making controlling him close to impossible.

Heidi laughed and we began forward.

"Will you tell me about it? About what happened, about magic and dreaming?" Heather whispered as she walked beside me, holding onto Sugar's reins. It was as though she was afraid Heidi would hear.

I rolled my eyes. "Magic doesn't exist." At least, not anymore it doesn't.

She frowned, sensing my cold demeanor toward the subject. "Oh."

I turned back to the river and walked on. After all that had transpired, I was in no mood to be worshiped and I certainly was in no mood to feel as though I were important. All I cared about was trying to understand, my head filled with the memories of my foster brothers and sisters. I tried hard to remember each, trying to pick their talents but seeing none. For the last three days I had been formulating a plan to blend into society, live a simple life and learn to grow a garden for real. Now, though, it seemed I was a legend.

After a few moments of walking, I heard Heather take another deep breath. "What about dreaming?" she whispered, keeping her eye on Heidi as she dozed on the back of Sugar.

I rolled my eyes again. "What *about* dreaming?"

I heard her hesitate, afraid to ask but clearly too eager to care about repercussions. "Well, it stopped." Her voice shook as she said it, as though I'd find the news to be disagreeable, which I did.

My pace slowed as I rolled her words over and over in my head. *It stopped?* How does it just stop? I thought about the changes that forging the contract had made. I hadn't thought about dreams, and that they would just stop, but it made sense. Dreaming was a magical thing, a place we were never meant to go. Falling asleep and waking up in their

Heaven was a gift, a treat, but I had taken it from mankind forever.

"It just stopped?" I asked, hoping she could solve this problem for me.

"Yeah, about three days ago. A lot of things happened to us then. That was one, but now we all feel empty, disconnected somehow. It's hard to explain. It was as though we were unplugged from a socket of sorts. We all seemed to black out. I remember being in the woods when it happened, and everything went dark, but when I woke, I had traveled about a mile up the mountain. By then, everything was like this, alive and thriving. I don't know how long I was like that. It could have been hours, or even days. There is no way of knowing time anymore, so the best we can do is acknowledge that it happened, and try to move on."

She was like a spout of information.

I stopped to look at her as Heidi snorted in her sleep. "You blacked out?"

She nodded gravely. "Every single one of us did. Luckily, no one in our group was hurt. It seems that though we weren't there mentally, at least something was working. It was like we all were put on autopilot."

I was shocked. I had created a worldwide reset of everything, launching my once fantasy life into a science fiction horror classic. "And now you say you feel disconnected?"

"Yes." She thumped her hand to her chest. "As though

272

I'm all alone. I feel none of the echoes that I used to. Do you know what I mean by echoes?"

I remembered the way I used to be able to feel Edgar. "Yes, I know what you mean."

"It's just weird. I used to be so intuitive, so in tune with things, like others' feelings. But now, I just feel my own feelings. It's very strange."

"Do you feel sad?" I asked, wondering if her feeling was similar to what I once felt, before Edgar. Perhaps she was a lost child that had been forgotten like I had, saved by Heidi.

She smiled. "No," she replied simply. "No. Actually it's nice, like there's no need to worry. It's as though I actually have to take care of myself for once, and that's all that matters: living."

"Oh." I was relieved. I don't think I could have ever lived with myself knowing I had caused billions to feel the same pain I had felt. I knew exactly what she meant.

I, too, felt the disconnection from everyone else and the absolute unity of my inner being. It was as though someone had enhanced the hearing in my soul, forcing it to listen to what I wanted, and what I needed. I hadn't thought about Edgar too much over the past few days, far less than I would have thought. It was as though I wouldn't allow myself to feel sorry about it, to feel sad or helpless. I could only listen to what was happening here and now. I missed him, of course, there was no denying that. We had shared the truest of loves and I wanted it back, but in due time.

We began to walk again, Jack straying on ahead as though the appointed leader.

"How do you get him to stick around like that?" Heather spoke in a normal tone now. I could tell that talking of the dreaming and magic was a *'hush, hush,'* thing.

I shrugged. "I guess he's just like that. I used to be able to attract them to me with a sort of scent, but that's gone now. I'm just like you."

It seemed as though Heather could not understand what I was saying. "But you're *not* like us. You're something much more." Her eyes were wide. "You are *The One.*"

There was that title again.

She pointed all around us. "Obviously you were touched by something none of us can ever understand. Even if now you are a physical equal," she pointed to my head, "up there knows you are something much different."

I laughed, feeling awkward still, but not quite as much as before. Heather was growing on me, and though she still seemed amazed, she wasn't as crazy about it as I had originally deduced.

Heidi began to snore and Heather looked happy about the fact. "So, now will you tell me about the magic?" She smiled widely with eager eyes.

I looked down at my feet as I walked through the sand and dirt along the bank. "Sure."

MORNING

The smell of last night's campfire wafted into my nostrils as I sat up, my back stiff. I saw Heidi rolling a stick in the fire, smoke rising and blowing toward me. I brought my hand to my mouth as I leaned over and instantly threw up on the sand beside me, revealing last night's dinner of more berries. Heather promised that in the morning light she would catch us a fish.

Heidi chuckled, "Still getting used to this, aren't you?"

I was too ill to answer.

The morning light was grey as it lit the trees and river. The sun had not yet breached into the valley, but I felt the warmth of it coming. I wiped my mouth and buried my vomit with sand, standing and walking to the river where I washed my hands and splashed water on my face. I hadn't thrown up in what felt like decades, and I had forgotten what it even felt like to be sick. My head whirled as I watched the river, so I shut my eyes. I leaned back onto my hands, trying to will the stomach ache away.

"Awake already?"

I heard Heather's voice then, and I looked back, seeing her face through a few wisps of smoldering wood. I nodded.

"Are you alright?" She began to stand, glancing at Heidi as she continued to burn the end of the stick.

Heidi was old, and I was amazed that she was even out here. Perhaps she knew, though. Perhaps something told her to find me.

I exhaled. "Yeah. I'm just a little sick from all the berries. I need something real to eat." A flash of macaroni and cheese crossed my mind, causing my stomach to rumble, the sick feeling forgotten.

She smacked her lips. "Yeah, I feel weak as though I were up all night drinking. Clearly *that* was not the case."

I laughed.

"Here, let me teach you to fish." She walked away from the fire and to the river's edge beside me. She grabbed my hand and yanked me up as my head rebelled, whirling once more as I leaned away from her and threw up again.

"Whoa there. I think sick was an understatement." She rubbed my back, slowly lowering me back to the ground.

I leaned forward, once again washing in the river.

"Well, maybe you just sit and watch today."

She grabbed something from her pocket and began to unwind it. I watched as she knelt at the water's edge and began to dig in the mud, finding something to use as bait and shoving it onto the little hook on the end of whatever it was she'd unraveled. She then tossed a small wad of it in the air as she began to swirl her arm above her head, causing the line to go taut before she released it forward, leaning her body into the river. As the hook and bait hit the water she leaned back, wrapping the end of the line around her hand and giving it a few soft tugs.

I began to doze as I watched her hand, but after a second she yelped and yanked back hard. *"Not very hard to catch anything these days,"* she struggled to speak as she wrapped the twine around and around her hand, reeling it in as the line thrashed about.

"Wow," I said under my breath.

She gave me a proud smile as the fish began to jump above the water, revealing the fact that it was huge. With one last tug she flipped the fish onto the bank, grabbing a nearby rock and smashing its head before I had time to look away. The nausea rose in my stomach once more, but this time there was nothing to throw up, so I just dry heaved instead. The bones in my chest felt as though they had been crushed together, my stomach muscles flexing uncomfortably.

Heather looked at me with alarm. "Oh, I'm so sorry."

I heard Heidi laugh again, like she did when I was little and the older foster kids teased me.

I grimaced and looked away from Heidi and back at Heather. I had my hand on my chest. "No, it's alright."

My mouth was pursed and stung, the acid eating away

and leaving a bad taste. I walked to the river and dug a hole that was about a foot from the water, allowing it to fill. I cupped my hands inside it and brought water to my mouth. The sand would filter it; at least enough that I hoped it didn't trigger another kind of sickness.

I watched Heather take her prize and walk back to the fire where she stoked the coals and added leaves. I was afraid to walk back and sit, afraid that the scent would be too much to handle. Heather combed the beach for a long stick, finally finding one. She brought it to Heidi, handing her both the fish and the stick. Heidi shoved the stick through the center of the fish and then held it over the fire.

I looked away, trying to find something more appetizing to watch. Jack was grazing nearby. Living like this was hard. I was used to the pampered lifestyle of the house in the meadow. My whole body ached and I saw now why it was so many people always seemed so grumpy. The human body was soft and I was amazed that they had lasted so long. It was as though I'd downgraded, finding that what I thought was pain before was nothing in comparison. I took a deep breath and slowly stood, feeling a little bit better as the fresh air by the river cleared my lungs. Willing to try again, I walked to the fire and sat between Heather and Heidi.

"So how long does this take?" I asked, pointing at the slowly charring carcass.

Heidi shrugged. "A bit longer." She turned the stick, cooking the other side as the fins curled.

"Tell me about Edgar." Heather was fidgeting with her

hands.

"*Heather,*" Heidi scowled at her, as though asking me about Edgar was a dumb thing to do.

Heather scrunched her nose at Heidi.

"No, it's okay." I added, defusing the situation.

Heather smirked. "You mentioned him yesterday, quite a bit, actually. I was just curious who he was to you?"

I watched Heidi's face from the corner of my eye, seeing it stretch into a smile. I felt my heart tighten in my chest. The first real feeling of anguish I'd felt toward the subject.

"Edgar was my husband," I said plainly.

Heather looked a little shocked. "You had a husband? But you're so young!"

I laughed. "Not really." I watched Heidi, judging her reactions and hoping it was acceptable to divulge myself to Heather. I was *The One* after all. I suppose I could do what I wished. "I know that I look eighteen," I continued. "But I used to be immortal. I have been alive for over a millennium. Edgar and I have been married for a long, *long* time."

"*Millennium?*" she gasped. "Wait a second. I don't believe you." Her eyes narrowed, her fox like features sharp with doubt.

"I'm serious. Given all that's happened, can't you believe that?" My face held no hint of a smile.

"Then why didn't you tell me that yesterday?" she challenged.

I laughed again. "I was telling you about magic, not immortality."

Heidi scowled at Heather again, now learning about the conversations we'd had while she was sleeping. "Heather, your manners?" she threatened.

Heather ignored her. "But now you're no longer immortal, right? Clearly I can see because of the gash on your leg, and the obvious fact that you are quite ill, and famished."

I tilted my head in thought. "I suppose not anymore." I pinched the skin on my arm. "I'm not used to feeling so soft and vulnerable. When I was a little girl—"

"Little girl?" Heather interrupted. "I thought you were immortal?"

Heidi chimed in then. "She was re-born, into my care."

Heather nodded slowly. "Oh, I get it now. So that's how you two know each other. I didn't quite understand before. You keep everything so *secret.*" She was mocking Heidi.

I let out a slow breath, trying to think of a way to explain it more clearly. "I am immortal, or rather *was.* There was a time when I was badly injured and I sort of died, but really I was being held by the gods."

I saw Heather was trying to follow as she mindlessly watched the fish.

"They eventually let me go, and I was re-born. I grew just like any child, and I had no memory of my life before. I was always different and I knew it, but I never understood how." Heidi was nodding. "I was sad and alone. Nothing brought me any joy. I couldn't smile or laugh, and because of that, I was never adopted. Nor did I want to be. I hid my talents from everyone," I paused. "Well, I guess you knew, Heidi. And well, it was that emptiness that brought me up here. I thought that by getting away, I could remain inconspicuous, but then I met Edgar."

Heather's face lit up. "Tell me more. Did you recognize him right away?"

I shook my head. "It wasn't that I recognized him as much as I felt something pulling me toward him. Now that I know, it was our soul that had brought us back together. By then, I was back to being who I was before. Back to the same age, and I think fate knew that. It was my time to return to what I was meant to be. Together, Edgar and I shared the same soul, and the heart of the raven that you saw on the tree." I smiled. "You cannot understand how it felt for me to feel that way again. It was beautiful."

"Are you sad now because he's gone? I mean, of course you're sad, but are you sad like you were before?"

I shook my head, touching my cheek and remembering the feeling of his touch. "I still have a piece of our soul, enough to be human. But, he has the rest of it."

"So you seek to feel that again, with him?"

I wanted to scream that of course I did, but I did not want to be rude. My body erupted with chills, remembering his touch like a drug. "Yes. Whatever it takes, I will feel it again, even if that means waiting."

"I wish I could love like that," she added under her breath. Heidi took the fish from the fire.

"You can. You are no different than me. You have a soul

mate out there, just as I did. It's harder for you because all the feelings you have are so numb, it's hard for you to find each other. But you will. It could take many lifetimes, but I do believe that when you do find him, that lifetime will be your last because you are finally together."

Her eyes looked into mine with hope. "Like the stories you hear of the old couples dying together in their old age. They're true soul mates, aren't they?"

I blinked a few times. "Yes, they are. Love is the one thing we all truly crave in the world, but we are faced with so many challenges, that we forget that. Money, power, and greed have no place here. But, they are put in our path to make our journey to love more fulfilling. The gods never wanted us to be happy. They wanted to use us for their entertainment. Now, though, I believe we can get back on track. This new world will be free."

Heidi poked the fish and then began to pull it apart. "Here." She handed me a chunk from near the tail.

I took the chunk greedily, the white meat now appetizing. I ate like a pig, the protein bringing me back to life. When I was done, I could only hope that the food would remain in my stomach this time.

"Thanks for that." I announced to both of them. I felt helpless for relying on them, but I could not survive alone. That much was obvious.

Heather swallowed her last bit of fish. "Shall we get going? If we leave now, we can make it there by sundown."

I stood, holding my stomach with my hand. "Yes, I think

walking would be good for me." I whistled to Jack as his head shot up out of a patch of grass and he walked toward me. Sugar also came, following behind Jack.

By evening, we had made it far enough that I no longer recognized the peaks I had grown so used to seeing everyday. The valley was wider now, and I knew we were getting closer to the foothills. Heather was pulling me and Heidi as we both sat on the horses's backs. I had grown used to Jack's lulling motion as he stepped with his large hooves, rocking me to sleep. Unfortunately, the fish had not stayed in my stomach as I had hoped, leaving me even weaker than I was before.

The sun's rays sliced through the branches of the trees, a deep orange as it began to sink below the mountains. My eye lids were heavy and tired, longing for a good night's sleep someplace warm and comfortable. It was then that I saw a long straight log jut from behind a tree up ahead. I felt Jack's pace pick up in time with Sugar's, Heather tugging at both their manes.

Heather said nothing as I watched the log, now growing into more logs, lined in rows near the river. My excitement grew, now seeing smoke and hearing the echo of voices off the hillside.

"Are we here?" I asked, rather shakily.

Heidi nodded beside me, looking at me with a grave expression. "We are. You can rest now."

Heather looked up at me then. "Yes, time to get you something real to eat. Introduce you to the *world!*"

Heidi hushed her, seeing that I was too weak and tired to handle the excitement.

I blinked a few times, finding my eyes had a hard time staying focused. My stomach ached with starvation and I had already lost weight, my arms thin and frail and my ribs showing.

I heard a cry of happiness echo from a distance away. I squinted as I saw a small figure burst through an opening in the log wall. Its miniature legs beat the earth with such fervor, that I knew this small being must have thought Heather was rather important.

"Aunt Heather!" The being got closer now and I saw it was a boy of about four. I couldn't help but smile as he ran into Heather's arms with the trust of a mother.

Another figure emerged from the opening in the log surrounding, walking toward us slowly at first, then very fast. He was stumbling over the ground as he came, his red hair bouncing on his head. He grew close enough for our eyes to meet, and I saw him nearly topple over in shock and happiness.

"Elle! *Elle!*" He yelled, now running, his arms flailing at his sides for balance. "I never thought—" his voice trailed off as he reached us, reaching up to hoist me from the horse and into his arms.

"Scott," I murmured. He seemed stronger now.

"What's wrong with her? I've never seen her in such a

grim state." I heard him ask Heidi and Heather.

"She's weak. She can't seem to keep any food down. I just hope she didn't eat anything before I found her that was poisonous."

I felt Scott's arms wrap around me even tighter, inspecting my face closely. "We need to get her inside. We'll see what we can do. Heather, take the horses to the barn."

I had never heard Scott respond with such direction, and I knew he had found his calling.

"Elle, darling, you'll be alright." I felt him begin to walk, jostling me as he went. Though I was too sick to talk, I prayed he wouldn't trip.

SAM

I felt warm wool against my cheek as my eyelids fluttered open. My body felt relaxed, the warm light of a fire flickering across my vision. I moved slightly in my attempt to see if anyone was nearby to notice. I heard nothing. Slowly, I sat up, feeling as my greasy hair stuck to my brow, coated with a thin layer of sweat.

I looked down at my clothes, seeing that someone had changed me into something that resembled a potato bag and I cringed. I swallowed some spit down my swollen throat, mucus slicing its way down my esophagus like knives.

"Hel—" I tried to say something but the words came out like a croak. I cleared my throat and tried again. "Hello?"

No one answered. I was alone.

The fire crackled as I pushed the blanket that covered me to the side. I twisted and sat up, pulling my legs around and placing them on the floor. I felt the soft dirt under my feet, and the warmth of the earth. I inspected the space, seeing it was a built into a perfect square. It had respectable construction, each beam placed perfectly atop the other. The fire was set into a crude pile of stone that stacked up and out the top of the cabin, guiding the smoke out and away from the room. The space was no more than a couple hundred square feet. It was windowless, the doorway covered by an old green door that didn't quite seal the entire opening.

The bed on which I had been laying was set up on large chunks of wood and then covered with dead grasses and a blanket. I slowly stood, wavering for a moment before catching my balance. I shuffled to a basin that sat on a coil of rusted steel cable in the corner. I looked down into it, bracing my body on it. The water there looked fresh and cold. I cupped my hands inside it, splashing it on my face as I let it drip down my neck and into my potato sack gown.

I wiped away the water as my vision began to clear. Next to the basin sat a broken brush, a razor, and a gritty looking toothbrush. I felt nauseated at the sight, looking away and back to the fire as I breathed through my mouth. Why did I feel so weak? Why wasn't I like Scott? I looked down at my injured leg, seeing it was just beginning to heal, a salve of some kind sparkling in the light of the fire.

I looked back at the basin, grabbing the razor with a shaky hand and making my way back to the bed where I sat down. A bowl of boiled grains and oats sat on a small table beside the bed that I hadn't noticed before. I did not feel like eating it. I looked at my bare knees as they protruded before me, thinner now than I had ever seen before. I swallowed and continued to breathe through my mouth, hoping to avoid smelling anything that could make me nauseous.

I lifted the razor in my hand, looking at it and allowing the thought on my mind to manifest. I lifted my other hand, turning it and exposing the veins on my wrist. I held my two hands before me, a few inches apart, looking from my wrist to the razor and then back again.

Slowly, I brought my hand with the razor to my other, pressing the sharp tip against the soft skin and pressing lightly. I held my breath, judging the sensation and finding it didn't hurt as much as I had expected. Pressing harder, I then felt as the razor broke the skin, a small bead of warm blood oozing from the cut and staining the razor's tip.

I took a deep breath and dragged the razor back, blood oozing faster now as it trailed from the cut down and over my skin. I felt it pool on the underside of my wrist where it released from my skin and dripped to the dirt. I watched it, seeing as the brown dirt coated the small pool of crimson. I licked my lips, pulling back once more as the dripping became more frequent, and then a steady stream. I dropped the razor to the ground, watching as the warm crimson stained my pale wrist. I blinked slowly, the blood dripping into my palm and through my fingers. It was warm and thick, like the way I would imagine honey would feel.

I began to feel weak as my eyes fluttered. I lay back against the straw bedding, closing my eyes to wait. My breath dragged in and out of my mouth, becoming more laborious with each drip of blood. I listened to the sound, like a ticking clock.

I felt myself slipping away. *Where are you?* I grew frightened then, wondering if he would ever come, wondering if—

"You think a little cut is going kill you? If you know anything about medicine, than you know that eventually the blood will clot."

I wanted to smile but I couldn't. My body felt paralyzed by weakness.

"What are you doing, Elle? No wait, don't answer that. I get it. *You missed me.*"

That time I managed a laugh. Opening my eyes ever so slowly, I saw the whole cabin spin around one central figure. Sam's wings were at his sides, yellowed from the light of the fire.

"You'll get better, Elle. And I'm not referring to the cut. You, the way you feel, it will pass. Unfortunate side effect, I'm afraid."

I tried to understand what he was saying. For the first time since I'd known him, I was glad he could read my mind. This way, I didn't have to talk.

"I remember that first day in the meadow, do you remember that? You were so rebellious then—naive." He chuckled. "Yeah, you remember. I remember that you thought I was a cute. *Ha!* Good thing I never told Edgar." He paused as though hoping I'd fear his warning, but I didn't. "I won't tell him about this, either. I promise," he added, still hoping to bug me.

The stream of blood was slowing now, reminding me that I had little time left to be with him before the blood would clot the wound.

"You really want to know what's wrong with you? Are you sure?"

My breathing shook, my lips trembling.

He laughed. "You've got a bun in the oven, Elle. You're pregnant. So, I guess what I'm saying is, you're *not* dying." He snorted as though embarrassed. "It seems as though Edgar was good for something after all. He *finally* got the guts to take the dive and now you're knocked up."

I felt my body weaken as the blood drained. My mind was not clear, but I was certain of the words he had said. *I'm pregnant?*

Sam laughed at my thought response. "Buck up, girl. You finally got what you wanted."

It was hardly what I *wanted*. How could I do this here? How could I do this *alone?* I felt the warmth of blood begin to return to my toes.

"It seems it's time for me to go." I felt a cold hand on my cheek. "This time, Elle, it's goodbye for real. Till death." I felt him kiss me on the forehead, leaving me chilled. I blinked a few times but he was already gone when my focus finally returned. The door to the cabin creaked open and I heard a woman gasp.

"Oh, Elle." It was Sarah's voice.

I heard her feet shuffle across the dirt and to my side where her hand grabbed my wrist, squeezing it to stop the bleeding, though it already had. I heard her rip a piece of wool from the blanket at my feet and take it to the basin where she dipped it in the water and came back to me.

"Why did you do this, Elle?" She pressed the cold rag against the wound, cleaning the blood from my hand.

"Sam," I murmured, watching her. "Sam was here."

I saw her shocked eyes relax at the utter of his name, seeing why I had done what I did. "You are one crazy girl. You know that?"

I tried to smile. "Sarah," I whispered. I waited while she continued to tend to my arm. "Sarah."

She finally looked at me, seeing I was smiling.

I smiled back. *"I'm pregnant."*

Part III
EVER AFTER

August, 2091

Many years have passed since then, and our small village grew. I gave birth to my little girl in the afternoon the following spring. I named her Margriete, unable to completely forget the days I spent with my dear friend.

I reluctantly brought her into a world of change, afraid of what it would do to her. Soon, people flocked to our small village, brought by the passing tale of the tree and the white raven.

Over the years, we managed to rebuild, moving back into the cities and rebuilding civilization. But things were different. The departure of dreaming had left us hollow. Though our independence was great, it came at a steep price.

Eventually the world grew used to things, and only the elders that were there could still recall what dreaming was even like. Legends were born in their place, and stories like dreams themselves.

Smarter forms of conservation were finally put into use and everything changed. The world was now self sustaining. Seeing us now, you would never have believed that anything had happened at all, except for the few telltale signs.

I aged and my life prospered, but I never could forget the way Edgar's blue eyes would watch me as I fell asleep.

At times I tried to dream of him, but it was useless. I was no longer welcome in that world.

When we migrated back to the cities and the lush shores of the Puget Sound, we left the tree behind in the forest. There, it lived as it should in the place where it truly belonged. I was no longer stitched to nature as I once was, and though it fought with me, I learned to eventually cooperate with it.

In my older years, I finally saw the beauty in humanity. I had never understood it growing up, the feeling void from my life. Emotion was a powerful thing: to cry, to laugh, even hate. But above all that, it was love that truly mattered. All I wanted was the love of a man and the love of family. In the end, it was the most powerful weapon we could ever possess against evil.

Now in my true eighties, I had found the gift of living. I've learned that it's one thing to fear life, but another thing to allow it to happen and be happy along the way. When I was so lost and empty, I did not see things outside of my own world. In that darkness, I only saw the hurt. But now, I understood. Now, I could finally go.

WAKING

"Hello."

I was playing with my doll on the stoop of our house when the voice interrupted me. I looked up, my eyes meeting that of a man I did not know. His hands were clasped behind him, his leather coat dangling from his broad shoulders. I looked away and back at my doll.

"Well, aren't you going to say hello in return?" the man asked.

I began to hum, ignoring him.

"Samantha?" The man said my name.

I stopped humming, looking back up at him. I frowned at the strange man. "I'm not supposed to talk to strangers," I said frankly, tucking my black hair behind my ears. I heard the front door open behind me.

"Sam?" My mother's voice echoed in my ears as she called my name. I turned to look at her. She took one step down the stoop before noticing the man as he stood half hidden behind the brick wall and mailbox. She froze as her eyes met his. My mother held the door in one hand and I watched as her grip on it tightened. She swallowed.

"Yes?" the man replied.

I turned and gave him a nasty glare. "She was talking to me, *mister.*"

The man laughed. "Maybe, but I think that now you're mommy is thinking that it was meant for *me.*"

"I—" My mom could not speak.

The man rocked onto his toes. "Margriete, it's great to see you again." He addressed my mother in a way that seemed old fashioned, giving her a small bow.

I looked back at the strange man, seeing his face was twisted into a smile, like a clown. He did not look at me, so I continued to observe.

"Sam—" my mother's voice cracked.

I turned back to face her, but the man was right. This time she was not referring to me. Their eyes were locked in a stare, neither one blinking.

The man let his hands fall to his sides. "Margriete, you were, well, not much the last time I visited. You're mother was just a few weeks along at the time. But, I heard you in there."

My neck was getting sore as I kept looking between my mother and the man.

The man tapped his head with one finger. *"I heard you,"* he repeated.

My mother laughed as her face suddenly became

bashful. I did not understand what was happening, now completely forgetting the game I was playing with my doll. I watched my mother's grip on the door relax, her hair catching in a bit of fall wind.

Since I was very young, I had begged my grandmother to tell me the stories of her youth. For ten years now, she had filled my head with fairy tales of angels and living forests, magical birds and dreaming. I never believed her, but something about this strange man made me want to, something about it made me believe.

"So, then it's really time. It's really *real.*" My mother's voice sounded sad.

"Did you ever doubt it?" The man replied. "No—no, you always believed." He nodded

"Is he—" my mother began.

I watched as the man smiled and took a step forward. "May I see Elle?" He distracted her from what she was going to say.

My mother did not move for a long while, as though rolling the man's question over and over in her head. At ten, it was still hard for me to understand adults, but I knew enough about my mother to know that she seemed nervous and scared. Being that I was the granddaughter of to the most important person of recent history, I had been raised to be proper and educated. But, I also knew that it came with its consequences.

My mother swallowed. "Yes. You may see her."

I watched as the man made his way up the step, touching

my mother on the arm and leaning in to give her a kiss on the cheek. He brushed past her and went inside as my mother's eyes dropped to me.

"Samantha, come along."

I hated it when she called me Samantha, but since there seemed to be some sort of name confusion, I went along with it. My mother had a stern look on her face and I was in no mood to be defiant. I followed her into the house and down the hall after the man. We entered my grandmother's bedroom on our tiptoes, afraid to wake her too suddenly. I watched, now far too curious to even blink.

My grandmother was asleep in her bed with the TV on. My mother was quick to rush in and shut it off, crossing her arms against her chest as I watched her eyes begin to well with tears. She was shifting her weight from one foot to the next. I licked my lips, not knowing what else to do as I walked up to her and put my arms around her waist. She sniffled, placing one hand on my back and rubbing it.

"Mamma, what's happening?" I whispered, looking up at her, now building on her energy as my heart began to race.

The man named Sam looked at me. "Samantha, there is no need to be frightened."

It was then that something began to protrude from his spine, unfolding like a fan. My mother gasped and I looked up at her, watching as her hand covered her mouth. A tear fell down her cheek. I looked back at the man, not believing what I saw. Memories of my grandmother's stories flooded my mind and I recalled why his name felt familiar. *"Sam,"* I uttered.

His eyes glanced at me with a glimmer.

My grandmother woke then, her eyes fluttering open as we all froze. She stared at the ceiling for a moment, the look on her face indicating that she knew he was there, even before she saw him. She slowly dropped her gaze to meet Sam's, her eyes glimmering with a tear. Her lids closed as a smile grew across her wrinkled face, her long white hair twisting about her ears.

Grandmother let out a soft chuckle, opening her eyes. *"Old friend,"* her voice was low and melodic.

The man snorted. "Look at you! You look like a grape left out in the sun."

My mother laughed through soft sobs.

Grandmother laughed as well, lifting her weak arm and giving the man a soft nudge on the arm. "You *arse.*"

Sam looked at her with fond eyes. "It's been a long time, Elle."

Grandmother nodded slowly. "Too long, my dear, too long."

Sam lifted his hand and touched my grandmother's face, causing her to gasp. *"So cold,"* she shuddered.

He looked at my mother and then me, causing my mom's body to tense. He turned away and back to grandmother, slowly bringing his hands to her sides as he lifted her gently from the bed. He cradled her in his grasp, as though she were nothing but a child. I had never seen my grandmother smile so widely, chuckling ever so lightly as she watched Sam's face.

He looked at us again, his golden eyes telling us to follow as he turned and left the room. We followed him back down the hall to the door, but as I rounded the entry into the living room, another figure caught my eye.

I froze, my mother catching up to me as she again gasped, grabbing my shoulder with a hard hand. The figure in the living room was staring at my grandmother, his eyes as blue as the sea. I turned to ask my mother who he was but she refused to let me move. I looked at my grandmother instead, seeing her stare back at the man. Her face was no longer smiling, but showing some other expression I had never seen from her before. I tried to place the look on her face, finally realizing that it was the same look I'd seen from my mother when she'd looked at Father.

Sam walked up to the other man as he placed my grandmother into his arms. I saw them shake with fright as the man took her from Sam. I kept my gaze on my grandmother, watching as she watched the man, her face unchanged.

The man also cradled her with one arm, as though she were as light as air. Something black began to fan from his back then, just as they had with Sam. This time, it was me that gasped. The black wings spread the length of our living room, like black curtains. The man touched her face with the tips of his fingers, smoothing them across her skin. I watched in disbelief as he seemed to wash away her age, her face growing taught and her hair beginning to glow.

The woman I saw moments later was not the woman I grew up knowing. My mother's sobbing grew worse as we watched, grandmother's hair now cascading in luscious locks of blonde, her skin like porcelain. My grandmother giggled then, her voice like music to my ears.

The man's mouth curled into a smile as he leaned close, kissing her softly as he set my grandmother down on her feet. I hadn't seen my grandmother stand in quite a few years, but the way she stood now was unlike anything I'd seen. She was tall and thin, her shoulders back and her chin up. A glow surrounded her.

Grandmother gazed at the man for another moment, and then slowly turned to face me. Her bright blue eyes blinked a few times, her smile full of happiness and youth. I looked at my mother, seeing her hand shake as it rested on her heart, attempting to hold back tears. Grandmother stood still while the man finally moved, his large black wings retracting behind him. He walked up to me, his gaze fluttering between my mother and me.

I felt my mother's hand drop from her mouth. *"Father,"* she whispered, almost too low to even hear.

I was shocked by my mother's words and what she had called him. I had heard my mother talk about my grandfather many times, always wanting to know more from grandmother, and I did too.

He was a mystery to us, someone my grandmother spoke of in a voice I could not explain. I knew he was a powerful man, but not a man to fear. I was gawking at him. I knew it was rude to stare, but I couldn't help it. The man smiled.

My mother let her grip on my shoulder relax as she stepped around me, the man walking into her and giving her a hug. They remained in that embrace for a long while as I watched my grandmother, gazing upon her as though she were art. She was still and calm like a ghost, somehow at peace. Her eyes were so bright they were hard to look at, her skin glistening as though dipped in pearl paint.

My mother finally let go and stepped behind me, placing a hand on the center of my back. She cleared her throat. "This is your granddaughter—Samantha."

The man's gaze broke from my mother's and fell to me. His mouth sank into a solemn line. He slowly knelt until our faces met. Feeling frightened, I watched his black eyes, moving like storm clouds and glittering like an opal. He leaned in then, kissing me on the forehead as I shut my eyes.

His lips were like ice as they touched my skin, and I felt a cold sensation sink in. The sensation spread across my head, flooding my entire body as it rushed through my veins. Something inside me burst open then, blooming like a flower in my heart, warm like a smoldering flame. I shuddered as he stood tall once more, saying nothing as he turned and made his way back to my grandmother's side.

Sam cleared his throat. "I love a good family moment, don't you?" He stole the energy from the room, causing my mother to relax as she laughed. "Time to go, Edgar." Sam was watching us.

I had nothing to say. I was too speechless by the whole thing to even believe it was really happening. *Edgar,* I repeated his name over and over in my head, holding on to the sound and cherishing it.

"Goodbye, mother. Goodbye—*father*." My mother was barely able to whisper her valediction.

Grandmother smiled as Sam came to her side, taking her hand in his. Grandmother raised her other as though to wave, but as I watched it—it slowly disappeared like dissipating smoke.

She was gone.

My mother knelt down beside me, wrapping her arms around me as her black hair curtained my face. She sobbed hard as I rubbed her back. Magic was real, I thought. It all was *real.*

ESTELLA

I felt his hand in mine, so cold, but so sweet. I saw the world I had known for the past eighty years disappear around me. In the bright light that followed, my skin glistened with a youth I had all but forgotten. I heard myself giggle, as though it was not my own.

A hand touched my chin, coaxing me to turn my gaze. My eyes met his, eyes I had seen in the darkness of every dream, burned there by a love so deep, I could never forget.

The corners of his mouth curled. "Welcome home, Estella."

As soon as the words left his mouth, familiar sounds and smells invaded my senses. I took notice of the new surroundings, seeing the meadow, seeing *home*. The sun was shining, but it was the sun I recognized seeing long ago, deep down through the caves. I smelled the lush grass below my feet, and the flowers on the wind.

Edgar's finger traced the length of my arm, causing it to shiver. His face was as striking as I remembered, every feature just the same as it always was. He lifted his hand and brushed the back of his fingers along my jaw line and past my ear. His other hand was laced behind my back. He pulled me against him, holding me in the arms I had longed for. He leaned close, his eyes so real and so sharp, that I could not deny the fact that this was really happening.

He leaned in, whispering as his nose nuzzled mine, "You're all mine now."

I smiled, feeling the chill of his lips hovering so close to mine. "No, Edgar." I denied. I saw his eye glimmer. *"You're all mine."*

He pulled me into a kiss, his cold sugary lips the drug I had been craving. A warm feeling filled my chest, the same warm feeling I swore to fight for, to find at any cost.

I had finally found my way home.

I was in Heaven.

SAMANTHA

I never understood exactly what happened that day or why, but that was the day I began to understand what the world was like *Before*. All that I know is that when my grandmother left, a part of her was left behind, in me. She was once a great leader, once a great sorceress. I still hold on to her stories as though they were my own, her journals and belongings the tools I now need.

My grandfather's kiss awakened something inside me, something that wants out.

That day he came, I fear he opened a doorway to my soul, a door that was never meant to be opened. Since, nothing has been the same. My horrid luck and the death of my parents was no accident. They were murdered. The images of blood never leave me, their last breath a chilling echo that whispers through my soul. I know what I saw that day, and I know that something is coming back…

My name is Sam, and I am *Gifted*…

Still want more?

Be sure to check out Abra Ebner's blog at:
www.featherbookseries.wordpress.com

or tweet with her at:
www.abraebner/twitter.com

and of course, become her fan on Facebook!
Just search for *Abra Ebner…*

Also check out her other book:

Parallel: The Life of Patient 32185

Coming Soon

Knight Angels Series

with Book One

Book of Love

www.AbraEbner.Blogspot.com

Sample on Following Page

Knight Angels Series
Book of Love

~

When seventeen-year-old Jane Taylor witnessed her father's death, something happened to her. Ever since, her thoughts have been consumed by death, going so far as to foresee the ever-changing deaths of those around her.

Sixteen-year-old Emily Taylor resented her sister's closeness with their father, who died when she was six. With the strange ability to read minds, she drowns the voices out with drugs, sending Jane over the edge.

When seventeen-year-old Wes Green was adopted, he moved in next door to Jane, finding in her a childhood friend turned high-school crush. All summer, the pain in his bones seemed unwarranted. He was done growing long ago. When senior year starts, however, the pain only gets worse. The foreseen changes are not expected, and far to *animal* for his taste.

When Max Gordon found himself standing above her dying body, he saw in her eyes something he hadn't seen in the century he'd spent roaming Earth. Her father was already dead, but there was hope to save her. Jane was her name, and already she was all he ever wanted. It was his job to bring her back – the biggest mistake of his life.

When these four teens enter Glenwood High senior year, no one but Max could understand the future ahead of them. Drawn together by blood and friendship, they each hide a dark secret that will soon bind them together.

When the face Max hoped to never see again shows up at school – his twin brother, Greg – he knows that coming back was the wrong thing to do.

Max has to protect Jane, Jane wants to be normal, Wes wants Jane to love him, and Emily just wants the voices to stop…

And Greg… he just wants everyone *dead.*

Diary of Max

I was too young to die, and I was not ready to leave… above all else, I was not prepared to be murdered. Because of my fight to live, I was cursed to roam somewhere in the in-between, somewhere that's cold and lonely—a choice I've regretfully made.

It wasn't long after my decision to stay behind that I started to hear the cries of the dying souls. I wanted to help them, but I knew I couldn't save everyone. No matter how hard I tried, it was never enough. The guilt drove me to insanity, and I was forced from the place I called home in order to escape the grief.

That was—until I saw *her*.

She made the world silent again, and the guilt retreated. She was my angel—my everything.

The day I found her, I knew she was beyond the sanctioned point of saving, but she was so small, so innocent, that already I loved her. In that moment I had to change, and in that moment, I broke the rules. I couldn't let her go, knowing that if I did, my fight to remain here would be over. I couldn't let her slip away from me. I had to help her to live.

Now, I fear that it was the wrong thing to do. I should have let her go. I should have gone with her. It was a selfish mistake to bring her back. Because of my actions, she suffers as I do.

Diary of Jane

When I think of death, I don't see what everyone else does. There's a soft whisper when you find it, and a voice telling us that everything will be okay.

We never die alone, because they are always there watching over us, protecting us, and guiding us. They are silent, like a simple gust of wind, but it is in that wind that our world can change.

Mine did.

When the accident happened, and my father died, I was there. I saw them. I can't remember their faces, but I know they weren't human.

There were two - one was the murderer, and one was my knight. I was spared. Ever since, the nightmares of death haunt me.

Somewhere deep inside, I know that I should have died.

Coming Spring 2010

Follow the blog for more info...

www.AbraEbner.Blogspot.com

ABOUT THE AUTHOR

*A*bra Ebner was born in Seattle where she still lives. Growing up in the city, as well as the mountains of the North Cascades at her family cabin, has granted her the experience of a life full of creativity and magic. Her craving for adventure has taken her into the many reaches of the forest, instilling in her the beauty of a world not our own, in a place where anything can happen and will. Her studies in Australia, as well as travels to England, Scotland, Germany, and Switzerland, have also played as a colorful backdrop to her characters, experiences, and knowledge. Come visit the untouched world of Feather, a place where eternal love, magic, beauty, and adventure are just the beginning.

Special Thanks To...

My Mom and Dad

My Mother and Father-in-law

My brother for the amazing cover images

My late grandfather for his name,
Edgar

My editor for teaching me a few
things about grammar, and wine.

My friends that were there all along,
you know who you are...

and of course *my* Edgar,
my husband, Erik.

Edgar A. Poe
1809 - 1849

Over a century of your joy...

Made in the USA
Lexington, KY
01 April 2010